SONS OF THUNDER

SONS OF THUNDER

The King Family Legacy

Alveda King

Library of Congress Number: 2003093407
ISBN : Hardcover 1-4134-1127-4
Softcover 1-4134-1126-6

This book was printed in the United States of America.

To order additional copies of this book, contact:
Xlibris Corporation
1-888-795-4274
www.Xlibris.com
Orders@Xlibris.com

19156

This book is dedicated to God, my heavenly father, the
author and creator of all families. I thank God for my family,
our past, present and future. I extend a special thank you to my
mother, Naomi King, for her love, strength, support and faith.
Also, I extend a special thank you to Jeff Prugh, who believed from
the beginning. I thank God for all of our friends and pray his
blessings for all of our family, friends and foes. To God be the glory,
praise and honor for the shed blood of His Son, Jesus Christ
my Lord, and for God's precious Holy Spirit. Amen.

Mark 3:14 & 17

And Jesus ordained twelve,
that they should be with him,
and that he might send them forth to preach.
James, the son of Zebedee,
and John the brother of James;
he surnamed them Boanerges, which is
The Sons of Thunder.

Other King Family Books

The entire collection of Dr. Martin Luther King, Jr.
Daddy King by Martin Luther King, Sr.
My Brother Martin by Christine King Farris
Martin Luther King Curriculum by Christine King Farris
Growing Up King by Dexter Scott King
Hard Questions, Heart Answers by Bernice King
Dr. Martin Luther King, Jr. and the Bible by Alveda King
The Spirit Of A Dream by Alveda C. King
My Life With Martin Luther King, Jr. by Coretta Scott King

Other Books and Songs by Alveda King

Books:

The Family of God (Formerly God's Plan for the Black Man)
For Generations to Come (A Collection of Poetry)
Images
The Arab Heart
Ketura's Song
Missed Fortunes

Songs:

Let Freedom Ring
For the Lord is Here
Love Will Live
Little Girl
Let Me Explain
I Ought to Tell
Sons of Thunder

A Partial Family Legend/Including Bloodlines and Descendants Of Martin Luther King, Sr. and Alberta Williams King as of June 2003

James Albert King and Delia Linsey (daughter of Jim Long and Jane Linsey) became the parents of Martin (Michael) Luther King, Sr., Henry, Joel, James, Lenora, Woodie and Cleo (Henry and Woodie had no heirs)

Adam Daniel Williams (son of Willis Williams and Lucrecia Creecy) and Jennie Celeste Parks Williams (daughter of William and Fannie Parks), parents of Alberta

Martin and Alberta King, parents of Christine, Martin and Alfred

Christine King Farris and Isaac Farris, parents of Isaac, Jr. and Angela

Angela Farris Watkins and Willie Watkins, parents of Farris Watkins

Martin and Coretta King, parents of Martin III, Yolanda, Dexter and Bernice

Alfred King I and Naomi Barber King, parents of Alveda, Alfred, Derek, Darlene and Vernon

Alveda is the mother of Jarrett Ellis (father is Jerry Ellis), Eddie Beal, Celeste Beal, Jennifer Beal, Joshua Beal and John Beal (father is E. Clifford Beal)

Jarrett Ellis and Annetta Ellis are the parents of Uriah, Gabriel, Daniel, Aaron and Jaden

Derek King and Janice Withers are the parents of Derek and Kyle

Vernon King and Robin Scott King are the parents of two deceased sons and two daughters, Venus and Victoria

FOREWORD BY NAOMI RUTH BARBER KING

The fabric of any family is woven with many threads. There is laughter, there is pain, there is romance, and there is tragedy. Such is the story of the life of the King family. To many people, the King family is only Martin, his widow and four children. This is because history and the public eye ever seek celebrities. In reality, the King family is so much more than Martin's branch.

For many years, the vibrant, creative members of our family have lived in Martin's shadow. Yet, each of us, in our own way, has shared and experienced the pain and the triumphs of the legacy for which Martin is remembered. So often, we are asked, "How did you do it? Did the same things happen to you as happened to Dr. King and his family?" The answer is unequivocally yes! We were threatened and harassed. We lived in the center of the storm. How did we do it? We had faith in God! When others would have fainted, we prayed. Like the song "We Shall Overcome" says, "God is on our side, we are not afraid, the Lord will see us through." And truly, God has always been with us. We are a family of faith. The manifesto of the Civil Rights Movement was centered around the Lordship of Jesus Christ. History sometimes fails to emphasize the importance of our faith during our times.

The magical, mystical "King Legacy" of our times started with the bloodlines of Martin Sr. and his wife, Alberta. They had three living children. I have known and loved them as my family and Alfred as my husband.

Theirs was a loving, colorful childhood. In her book *My Brother Martin,* Christine shares stories about their exploits. Two of my great grandsons, Uriah and Gabriel, are models for Martin and A.

D. in the beautifully illustrated book. We all still laugh today at how the three siblings used a stick to poke their grandmother's fox stole through the hedges in their front yard, to startle unsuspecting passers by. Then there's the time when they sawed the legs off of the piano stool to disrupt a piano lesson with a strict taskmaster. They also played a game called *Score*, where they challenged each other with vocabulary words. Martin usually won hands down.

Early in life, the three siblings encountered the effects of racism, when traveling with their parents through segregated stores and establishments to do business. Daddy King was an activist in his own right, and Alberta's father had been an activist. Their children learned first hand that they didn't have to accept treatment as second-class citizens.

Christine was the first black woman to enroll in Columbia University's School of Business. There, she experienced the subtleties of an oppressive, racist, male-dominated setting, and when she did not receive necessary support and instruction from the administration and students, she was forced to change her major to education.

Christine and her brother Alfred had sharp minds for organization, and from their youth, were interested in business. Alfred was in pursuit of business strategies even as a youth when his natural charm and cheerful personality endeared him to potential clients. Some even smile and tease about how, at church, Alfred, or A. D. as his daddy called him, would open the doors for the ladies, and they were so impressed with his gentlemanly conduct, that they would give him quarters, and pat his back or pull his ear. Yet, God had other plans for A. D. It would become Martin's and Alfred's destinies to preach and march in the crosshairs of danger and hate, under death threats and police surveillance.

I came into the King family when I married my late husband, Reverend Alfred Daniel Williams King, I. Because he lived in the shadow of his very famous brother, Dr. Martin Luther King, Jr., many people don't know that my husband was a hero in his own right. A. D.'s life mirrored Martin's in many ways. Firebombs devastated the Birmingham, Alabama house where we lived with our five children. Later, during our ministry in Louisville, where A. D. spearheaded demonstrations for open housing, the chapel at our church, Zion, was bombed. A. D. was a major strategist and organizer for the Movement, and he is often called a giant of a man.

People often ask me if my husband participated in the marches and demonstrations with his brother. When I tell him that A. D. was at almost every march and demonstration led by his brother, the next question is invariably, "Why don't we ever see him? There are not many pictures and historical accounts. Many people don't even know there was an A.D. King."

Perhaps the answer lies in the very character and nature of my husband. A. D. and Martin were always very close, even from their earliest childhood days. Martin was always more staid, studious and philosophical. A. D. was more outgoing, charismatic, and bold. Yet the two always stood up for each other. Because Martin was the firstborn male, his father was grooming him as the heir apparent. As the second son, A.D. was never afforded the same kind of attention and support that Martin received from their father. As a result, A. D. was rebellious. Yet, the two brothers remained close and fierce in their love and loyalty to each other. In the movement, Martin relied heavily on A. D. for unconditional support, advice and his organizational skills. Used to being in the background, with his brother as the focal point, A. D. had no jealousy. He was resigned to his role as second, and remained unwavering in his love and support of his brother. Martin remained a "protector" for his younger brother.

I often noticed that while most of those in Martin's inner circle often pushed to have the most prominent seats and positions next to Martin, A. D. was often pushed into the background by those more aggressive in seeking positions. A. D. was so secure in his relationship with his brother, and with his calling from God, that he often worked unceasingly and effectively from the shadows of the dream.

I met A.D. when he was a young man. We were in our early teens. My mother and I attended Ebenezer Baptist Church, where

A. D.'s father, Martin Luther King, Sr. was pastor. In those days, Daddy King was the famous "King." Having followed in the footsteps of his late father-in-law, Reverend Adam Daniel Williams, Daddy King was a fiery preacher and civil rights advocate in his own right.

I was born in Dothan, Alabama. My mother and I moved to Atlanta to live with her brother in the mid-1930s. In Atlanta, we moved across the tracks to Mechanicsville. The Kings were an affluent, middle-class family. My mother, Bessie Barber, married Mr. Bailey. I never knew my father.

God, in his infinite mercy, sent us to Ebenezer, where Daddy King was the "father" of his congregation. What has always been remarkable to me was that in his church, Daddy King treated everyone as equals. We found a home and a family in the congregation of the saints.

As young people, A.D. and I courted pretty much according to the customs of the day. There was no "dating" as it is called today. He was always very attentive and considerate of me, even to the point of showering me with gifts when his family would allow it. Having a sister of his own, and his own "mother dear," A.D. knew how to treat women.

When I was sixteen years old, A.D. sponsored my first major social event. He gave me a "sweet sixteen party" at their family home. The elegant environment and the sense of family prepared me for the years to come. A.D. was my knight in shining armor. I was his "virgin princess." Today, chastity is almost unheard of. In those days, it was regarded as something special, to hold yourself pure for that one special person with whom you would spend the rest of your life. A.D. would be that special man for me.

We married while we were young. Our first home was the family birth home where Christine, Martin, and Alfred had been born years before. Daddy and Mama Alberta King had moved on to another home, and their first home was available for us to live in. We lived upstairs, and another family lived below.

At the King birth home, as it is known today, there were joys and challenges. Our son Derek broke his leg in the tree out back.

Our precious Darlene suffered severe burns in an accident caused by a gaslight stove. Alveda cut her teeth there, and she cut her knee on the towering steel steps out back. She still has the scar today.

Yes, we had trials and joys. God was blessing us, and our family increased, and all five of our children—Alveda, Alfred, Derek, Darlene and Vernon—were born while we lived in that home.

Of course, children of African-American descent were born in the black hospitals of that day. Years before, A.D. and his siblings had been born at the house, with Daddy King in tearful attendance. I always marvel at the compassion of Daddy King, who attended to his family with a tenderness that is rarely displayed in men. Over the years, as his family increased, with marriages, some of which you will see in this book, Daddy King received us all with love and joy.

Dad's children were close to his heart, as were his grandchildren. As daughters-in-law, Coretta and I felt little distinction. Dad often went shopping with Coretta or me. He often stopped by our homes to visit and eat and play with our children. He enjoyed dropping in on Coretta for hot, homemade vegetable soup and cornbread.

When I was pregnant with Alveda, Dad would come by our house every day with a bag of Lays potato chips, to "check and see how we were doing." The Lays plant was right around the corner, and Dad knew how much I enjoyed the chips.

I can remember when I first started calling him "Dad." Shortly after A.D. and I were married, we were at the "big house" for dinner. Mama King had everything laid out beautifully and the food was wonderful. I called Dad "Reverend King" at the table during this family gathering. He replied, "Baby. You call me Dad. I will be better to you than your own father would have been." Truly, Dr. Martin Luther King, Sr. was like a father to me, and better than the deceased biological father I never knew.

Dad was there throughout our lives until his death. On most Sundays, after Martin and A.D. were killed, Dad would take us all to a cafeteria for dinner after church. There would be fifteen of us at least, and he'd pay the bill. He enjoyed having his "family" together. Mama King usually had her camera along. They tried very hard to keep the family together.

I can remember when A. D. curtailed his dreams of entrepreneurship and accepted the call of God on his life. One day, at home, A. D. began acting very strangely. He was having a two-way conversation with an invisible source. He was saying things like, "Yes, what is it you want me to do? I'll do it. I hear you." I was very concerned because I couldn't get him to stop or to explain who he was talking to. I called Daddy King and expressed my concern. Dad said, "Don't worry, baby. He's just answering the call." Later, when I read the story of the prophet Samuel, who heard someone calling him in the night, and he finally understood it was the Lord, I began to understand what happened to my husband. Although he would have been a very successful business man, God had other plans for him.

Over the years, Mama and Daddy King attended every installation service for my husband's ministries. Daddy King was very proud that his sons were preachers.

As the years went by, my dear husband was invited to pastor four unforgettable congregations: Mount Vernon Baptist Church in Newnan, Georgia; First Baptist Church Ensley in Birmingham, Alabama; Zion Baptist Church in Louisville, Kentucky; and finally Ebenezer Baptist Church as co-pastor after the death of his dear brother, Martin. During his life, in its many facets and phases, A. D. formed lasting friendships, among them brothers in the cloth. Rev. B. J. Johnson is godfather to our son, Vernon. There were E. H. Dorsey, Carl Moncrief, Nelson Smith, John Porter, Rev. Kirby, Otis Moss, Leo Lesser, Earskine Lewis, Dick Gregory, Georgia Davis, Lukie Ward, Aretha Franklin, Cassius Clay (Muhammad Ali), his "Ace" Fred Bennett, Sunshine, Bernard Lee, Hosea Williams, and many more.

Throughout the days of the Civil Rights Movement, our lives were colored with relationships with people who the world recognizes as celebrities. I guess we are celebrities as well, although I have never sought the limelight. It was not uncommon to know personalities like Harry Belefonte and Miriam McKeba, who in those days performed at concerts to raise money for the ongoing Movement. In their respective books, my sister-in-law Coretta, and my nephew Dexter speak of many of the wonderful, dedicated artists who shared their remarkable talents in support of the cause. I will be forever grateful for the spirit of unity and love that caused people from all walks of life to give their all for the common cause of freedom in those days.

My life as wife, mother, and first lady has been challenging, interesting, and motivating. Even though my college matriculation ended, as did my plans to be a French major and an interior decorator, I had few regrets. A. D. was a strong protector and provider. He sheltered me, pampered me and loved me. We always had the very best of everything. Even though the early days of our lives were clouded with segregation, we enjoyed vacations, movies, fellowship with friends, house parties. Bid-Wiz was a big card game in the King family. Even the relatives from Detroit were big experts in the game. Whenever there was a gathering, the cards flew in fun.

When A. D. and his siblings were growing up, their parents took them to wonderful places. They believed in living well. That legacy passed on down to every generation. Even today, our children, grandchildren and great grandchildren enjoy the card games, travel to exotic places, movies and wholesome recreation.

Of course, I don't want the readers to even think that our lives were all fun and games. It's just that everyone reads about the tragedies in the historic tomes. Yet, the times of peril were so real, and if God had not been with us every step of the way, I guess we would have been frightened to death. Even in the height of the death threats against his life and the threats to his family, A. D. shielded us as much as he could. He was a buffer through the storms.

My husband was a wonderful leader and organizer. People flocked to him during the days of the Movement. He was a people's man. Everybody loved my husband. He was charming, vibrant, full of life. He kept us all so secure in his circle of love and protection that I am still thankful that I didn't have to face some of the horrors of the time. I know that A. D.'s strength came from God. I am just so thankful that God sustained us.

A. D. was especially adored by the ladies. Old ladies, young ladies and in-between, he always had a smile and a twinkle in his eye to make them feel special. Yet, knowing that I was his special lady, his wife, his true love, made everything alright. I never felt insecure about our relationship. I was Mrs. A. D. King, a loved and cherished wife.

What can I say about the relationship between A.D. and M.L., "the sons of thunder," as they were called by family and friends? Of course, if they were the sons, Daddy King was the Thunder. From his pulpit, he taught, admonished and preached the Word of God. "Make it plain" was one of his most favorite phrases. Dad was a dynamic, "fire-ball" preacher, a Civil Rights leader, a community icon and a wonderful father. Daddy King's influence was so predominant in the lives of all of his children. He was a wonderful role model for his sons. As young boys, on into adulthood, they mimicked their father's preaching style, his mannerisms, his stylish clothes, his bigger-than-life effects. They had encounters with racism, and Daddy King always taught them that they didn't have to be treated as second-class citizens. Dad was slow to take a back seat, and would often refuse to do business in racist situations. He was a man not only concerned with the outward image, but with the inner strength and character for which his son Marin would one day be renowned.

Daddy King was a polished, handsome man. He was well read, well learned, and he feared God. His sons were very handsome and polished as well. They had strength and compassion. They were the "cream of the crop."

In great part, their mother Alberta was responsible for teaching them about love and compassion. Their great-grandmother Jennie taught them to think, and to develop keen vocabularies. The three siblings had the best of everything. They lived in a beautiful home, full of luxuries that many blacks were not exposed to in those days. They read and traveled, and listened to fine music. They had tutors for music and languages, and history and the arts. They dined on fine china. They wore the best clothes.

People still talk today about how Alberta King rode to school in a chauffeured limousine when she was a child. She was the only child of a very affluent family. She maintained that fine lifestyle throughout life. Of course, when she married a preacher, things toned down a bit. Yet, Alberta, Dad's "Honey Bunch", insisted that her husband and children should enjoy life. They had beautiful cars. They Kings were well exposed to the best in life. They made sound investments in the business world. They were talented people. They were frugal and good stewards. They were generous to a fault, and supported charities and the church. Daddy and Mama King instilled these values in their children, and the legacy continues.

To say that Martin and A. D. were close would be such an understatement. Their lives were so parallel in so many ways. They looked alike as well. A.D. was taller, and had a deeper voice. His skin tone was fair, Martin's a richer brown. A.D. was a practical joker, but both men were funny, and made jokes all the time. M.L. loved my cooking, and would visit often before he was married.

Coretta is a good cook as well, and was a lovely hostess throughout her marriage to Martin. All of the women in our family have been good cooks and lovely homemakers throughout the generations. We are known for our gracious hospitality, our love of beauty, and our fierce regard for our children and family members.

People always remark that my sister-in-law, Coretta, and I look alike. A.D. used to laugh about how he and Martin as young boys had always said that they would marry women who looked alike—with long hair, little waists, and big legs. I suppose that Coretta and I would have fit those descriptions as brides. What is remarkable is the similarity in resemblance among our children, even though they are cousins rather than siblings. It makes a good conversation piece. People remark about the resemblances all the time.

A.D. and Martin were preachers, following after their father, grandfather, and Uncle Joel. As young men, prior to their ordinations, they used to have "whooping" contests, competing with their homiletics to such an extent that they would draw a crowd. What a sight to behold!

After they accepted their respective pastorates, they would visit each other, and preach in each other's pulpits. They were remarkable preachers, full of fire and truth. They both loved the Bible, and delighted in preaching the gospel.

A.D. and M.L. were also partners in the civil rights movement. When Martin marched, A.D. was often there at his side. In Birmingham and Louisville, and other cities, Martin relied on A.D. for strategy, organization, and leadership in those movements. They were often praised and maligned as well. They were lauded and ostracized. In most cities, they were either received as heroes or "rabble rousers and outside agitators." What many don't remember is that many blacks as well as whites resented Martin's going against the status-quo. People were generally comfortable with racism, and if not comfortable, they adapted. Few wanted to rock the boat, so to speak.

For the most part, I lived in the background. I do remember one occasion where I was riding on a city bus, alone. My husband and children were not with me. This was before Rosa Parks and Montgomery. When I got on the bus, I refused to go and sit in the back. I knew that I was a human being, and should be treated with dignity. The bus driver stopped the bus and said that he would "kill my black a--"if I didn't either go to the back of the bus or get off. For a moment, I started to rebel, and then remembered my precious, beautiful family waiting for me at home. I stared at the bus driver without a word and got off the bus. Needless to say, I was a major supporter of Rosa Parks when she made her monumental decision to keep her seat and her dignity.

Still, for the most part, my husband and I agreed that if our children were to have any sense of stability, it would be good for me to remain in the home, and allow him to go to the front of the battlefield. Together, we instilled in our children the same values of freedom, equality and human compassion that he and Martin espoused from their pulpit and picket lines—back when America grappled with her social conscience and searched for her soul. I believed that we were a team, me at home and him out in the streets. A. D. was free to support his brother, as he had done all of his life. For all of the years of the Movement, A. D. was there for Martin, and more often with him.

A.D. was there in Memphis when Martin was shot. He had gone there the night before to "help my brother," he said as he left home.

When Martin died, A.D. was heartbroken. He would sit quietly at night, and cry because he felt so alone. He was forever grieved, because he loved his brother so very much. A.D. was a man of compassion who loved with a passion for life and humanity. The loss of his brother was devastating.

Even though I have missed my husband sorely, I often wonder how he would have taken the deaths of his mother, Alberta, and our two children, Alfred and Darlene. Mama King was shot in the tragic incident at Ebenezer, and Alfred and Darlene died in separate jogging incidents. Each of these incidents took a heavy toll in my life. I have often cried because A.D. wasn't there to help me through it, while at the same time I was glad that he didn't have to be here to suffer the pain. What a paradox.

When Mama King was shot while playing the organ at Ebenezer, I was there in the congregation. When the ambulance came, God somehow allowed me to be the only person to ride in the vehicle with her. It was Mama King, Jesus, and me. I will never forget it.

On the way to the hospital, my eyes remained fixed on her. She gasped one time, and pressed her hand to her face where one bullet had penetrated. Although they worked on her for quite a while in the emergency room, I believe Mama King died in the ambulance when she gasped that one last time. This was such a tremendous loss that I never expected to suffer even more tragedy.

The drama would continue to unfold. My precious children, Darlene and Alfred, died while running on the track. Darlene was there for exercise. A few years later, Alfred, a sports buff, was working out. A lady who passed him by, while he was lying on the ground looking up at the sky before his last fatal lap, paused to ask him what he was thinking about. She later told us that he said, "I'm asking God to help these tired old legs make it around just one more time."

Al was in his mid-thirties, yet he was tired. I have often believed that the stress of the civil rights movement and the burdens we were all required to bear were just too much for these two dear ones. A.D., Martin, my dear mother, Bessie, Mama King, Darlene, and Al—how much I miss them. I miss Daddy King, too. His passing was the only death not linked to tragedy. Yet, he was sad at the end as well.

My husband's death was a tragedy unto itself. He died on our son Alfred's sixteenth birthday. He was found in our pool at home, with a bruise on his head and with no water in his lungs. I was out of the country at the time. Efforts to retrieve medical reports proved fruitless because we were constantly told that the records were lost, or had never been recorded.

There had been several attempts on my husband's life, prior to his death. Our home and church had been bombed. We lived under the constant threats that were so prevalent to many of that era. Daddy King continued to say until his death, "They killed my boys." He was convinced that both sons had fallen as victims, martyrs of an era of violence and hope.

I miss my gentle giant. Still, somehow, we made it through. We learned, in the words of Daddy King, to "thank God for what we have left."

In this book you will see pictures of our family, of the civil rights days, of our ministry. See our family through our eyes, hear our story in the voice of the writer of this saga, my daughter, Alveda.

Sons of Thunder explores little-known but provocative episodes of the Civil Rights Movement, in large part through the remembrances that A. D., Daddy King and I shared with Alveda. A. D. died at 38, just 15 months after the assassination of Martin. I agree with others that my husband's death was part of the overall evil that plagued the nation at that time.

In many instances, truly in most, I was in the background and on the sidelines, yet I was there. As the wife of a major participant of a most significant part of history, I remember many events.

Alfred and I were married for nineteen years. It often seems as if those short years spanned many lifetimes. This is our story, and the story of our family, the Kings of Georgia. It is a story of powerful egos clashing within the Movement's top ranks, of the Movement sputtering yet succeeding in spite of itself.

Our lives have been stormy, God-inspired, romantic and often adventurous. My life with A. D. is part of this story. I am forever grateful to God for sending me this very special man, Reverend Alfred Daniel Williams King, I. He will be forever treasured in my heart of hearts. The good Lord gives, and receives back unto His own. To God be the glory, the honor, and the praise.

Mrs. Naomi Ruth Barber King

PROLOGUE

The old man might just make it this time. He's been talking about dying for as far back as I can remember. Stories have it that he never thought he'd live to be fifty, much less eighty-four.

In fact, I can recall Granddaddy telling me how he saw me in a dream three years before I was born. I was his little "white grandbaby," with very fair skin and strawberry blonde hair. Granddaddy said he saw me in my crib, reaching out for him, when he was at his lowest ebb (just one of many low ebbs he was to have as time passed on). And something, most likely God, told Granddaddy to hold on, because this baby would need him. (You may have heard him tell one of his favorite sayings: "I'm goin' to go on and see what the end's gone be." Granddaddy's been going on and holding on for as long as I can remember.)

Into this legacy I came, the first of eleven grandbabies and three great-grandbabies who loved and needed Granddaddy until the day he went to meet his Maker. And I was born feeling that my sole purpose for coming into this world was to help Granddaddy rise from his low ebb, to give him the strength to live. This feeling was so strong. I felt my life so linked to Granddaddy's that I thought I'd die the moment he died.

Granddaddy did live for many years. He lived through the deaths of his sons, his wife, and granddaughter, wondering all the time why God kept him alive. He got tired and weary over the years, but he kept on pushing. Most of the family wished that Granddaddy would never die. But of course, nobody lives forever.

Three weeks before his death, the Old Man was admitted to Crawford Long Hospital in Atlanta. (I was the first to start calling Granddaddy "Old Man," when he became seventy-eight. He reveled in his old age, pointing with pride in his white hair, years before he was even sixty. Other family members began accepting his old age, although it meant accepting the fact that he was human, with human limitations. Soon, others started calling him "Old Man," too.)

Granddaddy was admitted to the hospital, diagnosed as suffering with congestive heart failure. Although he'd gone through rough episodes before, we knew this one was serious when the doctors announced to the newspaper: "Dad has suffered a heart attack." This was the first time Granddaddy's illness had been defined as such. The strangest thing about this day in October was that while autumn refused to come to the city (the leaves were still green on the trees), winter pressed heavily on the heart of the old ram who had weathered so many storms.

Most of the family was in absolute shock. They'd seen Granddaddy recover so many times before. This time, it looked like he just wasn't going to make it. Aunt Christine (King-Farris, Granddaddy's only surviving offspring) and my brother, Rev. Derek Barber King, brought Granddaddy to the emergency room. Aunt Chris had carried Dad to the hospital before as well. Prior to these last two events, it was always I who brought Granddaddy to the hospital.

How Granddaddy hated going to the hospital. He'd be lying in bed, in a cold sweat, panting for breath, and fussing all along, "I'm not going. You hear me, Veda? Ain't nothing wrong with me. Just call Bridges."

Invariably, Dr. Bernard Bridges and Aunt Chris would both be out of town or otherwise inaccessible, and it would be me locking horns with the lovable old ram. (Many remember Granddaddy as a stubborn, determined, albeit fair-minded, loving man. Such adjectives remind me of the ram. Granddaddy was born in December under the sign of Sagittarius, the sign of the ram. Before I gave up the study of astrology [I accepted Jesus and the sign of the cross instead] I called Granddaddy Ram, in acknowledgement of his astrological sign, his having been born in December. Years later, I abandoned interest in astrology, taking the sign of the cross of Jesus as my guide.)

I would never take no for an answer from Granddaddy. I've been standing up to the old fireball since I was "knee-high to a grasshopper." "Granddaddy, you are going! Now raise your legs so we can get your pants on."

During the last few months, Granddaddy was hard to lift when he was ill. So we'd call an ambulance and rush him off to Hughes Spalding Hospital. The first time, my children's nurse, Nerissa Neal, was there to help me. The second time, my husband, Cliff Beal, M.D. was on hand.

The next to the last time Granddaddy went to Hughes Spalding, my brother Derek, his pregnant wife Janice, my son Jarrett, and Cliff and I watched the ambulance attendants load him into the ambulance. I jumped into the front seat with the drivers and rode to the hospital with Granddaddy. But the fact that he was really sick didn't stop him from fussing, "Don't you stick those needles in me. I mean it, girl." The medics were in awe of Granddaddy, amazed that he could be so near death, yet so full of spunk.

I told the medics to take Granddaddy to Hughes Spalding Hospital. Granddaddy had always been one to support black institutions (banks, restaurants, etc). Spalding was an excellent facility with several black doctors on staff. In later years, the hospital would be remodeled and expanded, and would become a children's hospital. Back then, it was a political project for the black community.

I was one of the political activists, a state legislator at the time, who helped raise several million dollars to "Save Hughes Spalding." There was a need to encourage blacks to use and appreciate black facilities and black medical expertise. So why not take Daddy King, a major supporter of black institutions, to Hughes Spalding? And if a black facility and black doctors were good enough for Dad, then, aren't such services good enough for anyone? Somehow, during those days, I was always the manipulator, always looking for an opportunity.

Granddaddy was pleased to know that Spalding wasn't going to close. He enjoyed the special love and attention from the nurses, as well as the fond, yet professional treatment from the doctors.

Since Dr. Bridges was no longer on the Hughes Spalding Medical staff, his heart specialist, Dr. Calvin McLauren, admitted Granddaddy. Granddaddy was especially glad to know that Dr. McLauren had trained under his personal heart specialist, Dr. Hurst, a member of the Emory Hospital medical team.

I once heard Granddaddy say to McLauren during a medical examination, "You and Graham (Dr. Jimmy Graham treated Granddaddy for arthritis and rheumatism, and had admitted Granddaddy to Spalding the time before when Granddaddy showed signs of heart failure during a routine office visit) are doing a fine a job. My grandson-in-law is a doctor, too, you know?"

Since I was the apple of his eye, Granddaddy only chuckled at the accusations from friends and family that "Veda is just looking for attention again. You can't let her use you like this, Dad. She wants you in Spalding because she wants some publicity for the hospital and herself. And she's using you to get it. Doctor Bridges isn't even on the staff. You need to go to Crawford Long so that Dr. Bridges can treat you."

As it turned out, the hospital did get some publicity and Granddaddy got better. It was not until he mismanaged some medication prescribed by Bridges that he became ill again.

There was one really interesting experience during one of Granddaddy's hospital episodes. He was wheeled into Spalding's intensive care unit, too sick to realize where he was at the time. But shortly after the IV medications were administered, Granddaddy became alert and responded with his unfailing concern for others.

Beckoning for the nurse, Granddaddy asked as she approached his bed, "Who is that poor soul in the bed in that other section?"

Surprised that Granddaddy hadn't heard about the illness of a relative, the nurse raised her eyebrows in an expression of anxious concern, "Why Daddy King, that's your daughter-in-law Naomi's mother, Mrs. Bessie Bailey."

The nurse was properly startled at Dad's response, "Naomi's mother? Well, I'll be damned."

Granddaddy survived that hospital tour. It wasn't long, though, before he had another episode and was rushed to Crawford Long Hospital. Shortly after Granddaddy was admitted to the Crawford Long ICU, Aunt Chris started calling the family. My phone rang at six thirty Sunday morning. Aunt Chris seemed very subdued. Anxiety and anticipation made her voice sound heavy. "Veda, we've had to bring your Granddaddy to the hospital. Dr. Bridges says he might not make it this time."

I sat straight up in bed and pushed Cliff. "Wake up! Granddaddy's dying."

Cliff woke up immediately. "What? Where is he?"

Our younger children, Eddie and Celeste, were spending the weekend with their cousin, Mi-Mi. My oldest, Jarrett, had been staying with Granddaddy, during recent times of illness. Cliff and I had only ourselves to get ready. We arrived at the hospital in twenty minutes.

At the hospital, the medical team was working frantically over Granddaddy's inert body. I went to the door of the ICU and was denied entry. I turned to Cliff. "You're a doctor, they have to let you in. Go to him and let him know he's not alone here. You're family."

Granddaddy was first, foremost, and always a family man. I knew he'd have a fear of dying in a cold, clinical environment with no family to hold his hand. Cliff gained entry to the ICU, and told us later that he let Granddaddy know that the whole family was in a room nearby.

The family gathered in the family waiting room. There was Derek and Aunt Chris. Aunt Coretta (Scott King) came in. Angela (Christine's daughter) came in with her father, Isaac, Sr. My brother, Reverend Vernon King, came soon after. Isaac, Jr., Dexter (Scott King), and Bernice (Coretta's youngest) rounded out the quiet, solemn group.

Over the hospital intercom, we heard the announcer call, "Code 99, ICU." We saw technicians running toward the unit with IVs and electric paddles. Uncle Isaac broke our anxious silence.

"Maybe we should all pray." Angela's face was swollen and streaked with tears; Isaac Jr.'s eyes were red and swollen. Dexter's face was red. Aunt Coretta was pensive, as was Aunt Chris. Neither was crying, each giving most of her attention to her grief-stricken children.

I stood to join the group, not sure if I wanted to pray for Granddaddy's recovery into his life of constant worry, duty, responsibility, loneliness, and pain. Maybe it would be better if God could take the Old Man to his bosom and rock him there for eternity, or at least long enough for him to shed the trials of life.

We joined hands and stood together, and Derek started to pray. I don't remember his words, but it was something to the effect that God shouldn't let Granddaddy die because we weren't ready yet. Granddaddy was still needed here on earth.

I think God and Granddaddy heard the prayer. While we were praying, the alarm message stopped on the intercom. As soon as the prayer was over, Dr. Bridges rushed out of ICU and exclaimed, with tears rushing down his face, "He's crossed over. Dad's crossed over."

For a moment, everyone was in shock. Crossed over? What did that mean? Had Dad crossed over into glory?

Bridges sensed our bewilderment. "No, it's a miracle. We were just going to administer the paddles. Then all the vital signs registered close to normal. He's recovering!"

It was a miracle. Everyone fell to his or her chair in joy and relief. God had wrought us a miracle. Granddaddy wasn't going to leave us, after all. Aunt Coretta went back to the phone where her daughter Yolanda (Yolanda King) had been holding since the prayer began.

My mother, Naomi, and my brother, Alfred, arrived just in time to hear this good news. How relieved they were. They, along with Jarrett, were going to take Granddaddy's death harder than the rest of us would. These three spent more time with Granddaddy over the last two years than any of us. Mom would run errands and go over and cook for him often. Al would drive for him, and run errands. And Jarrett slept in the room with him, caring for his comforts. And their special losses made the thought of losing Granddaddy too hard to bear.

On his sixteenth birthday, Al had discovered our father, Alfred Daniel Williams King, dead in our home's swimming pool. He was hit very hard with that tragedy. Then, my grandmother, Alberta Williams King, was shot in church while playing the organ. Al had been Bigmama's favorite grandson (she left her message of love for him in her will). Granddaddy was Al's last anchor.

For mother, Granddaddy was father and father-in-law. Mother's real father died soon after she was born, and Granddaddy always held out loving heart and hands to her. Since Mother had just lost her mother, Bessie, having buried her a few months before, this was an especially difficult time.

For Jarrett, the old man was Great-granddaddy, Granddaddy, and Daddy, too. Since my divorce from Jarrett's father, Jerry, Granddaddy has helped spiritually, financially, and emotionally to fill the father-figure role for Jarrett. Jarrett was Granddaddy's first great-grandchild, a fact that Jarrett and Granddaddy were mutually proud of. It was going to be hard for Jarrett to adjust to this loss.

Just as Mother and Al came in, the doctors gave us permission to visit Granddaddy one at a time. Being Granddaddy's kin, having his traits of stubborn determination, we were determined to ignore the rule of one at a time. Several of us crowded in next to his bedside.

Granddaddy told each of us almost the same thing. "I'm with you for a few more days, but I won't be here long."

Most of the family would not believe him.

Derek stood by the bed, rubbing Granddaddy's big, once strong, now weak, cool hand. "You can't go yet, old man. You owe me two more years."

Granddaddy just gave a faint smile, and answered in a hoarse, whispery voice, "Two years, huh?"

Jarrett chimed in, "No, at least six, Granddaddy."

Added sensitive, hopeful Angela, "At least ten, Granddaddy."

Granddaddy only smiled. "Maybe a few more days." Everyone took that to mean that Granddaddy would keep holding on like he'd always done. Except me—slipping into his room while everyone else was outside in the waiting room, I kissed him on his dear, smooth, unwrinkled brow and tried to keep the tears from my eyes and my voice.

"Is that right, Old Man? You gonna leave us?" I asked him if he was tired. He nodded yes. "It's okay, Granddaddy. If you want to stay, we love you. If you want to go on home, we love you, too."

For the next few days, Granddaddy was in the hospital. Aunt Coretta, always perceptive to the needs of others, knew that Dad would want constant company. She helped us to work out a round-the-clock routine so that Aunt Chris wouldn't feel the need to keep a twenty-four-hour vigil.

The newspapers took pictures of Aunt Coretta carrying a brown paper sack, rushing from her car into the hospital. She was bringing some of the vegetable soup that Granddaddy had often eaten at her house. That same day, she whispered to me across his bed, as I prepared to settle into my watch. "I think he's dozing. He's afraid to sleep, you know. Afraid he might . . ."

Aunt Coretta was probably on the right track. Granddaddy didn't want to die in his sleep while in the hospital.

The most interesting thing about all of this is that Granddaddy got sick on a Sunday. He was ready to die on that Sunday. Granddaddy turned his face to the wall like Nebuchadnezzar, ready to meet his Maker. Yet at the call of his family, Granddaddy must have prayed for a reprieve. His beloved family was so sad, needing so much reassurance, that he couldn't leave those needing so much, so suddenly.

And so, God and Granddaddy gave the family three weeks. We all had three weeks to come and sit around his bedside and assure him and ourselves of the love and gratitude for his constant strength and devotion.

Those last few weeks were a home going time for Jarrett and Granddaddy. Jarrett had been going through adolescent turmoil, needing a break from me and the problems of living through a broken marriage and subsequent remarriage. So he soothed his spirit, and snuggled close to Granddaddy during those weeks, sleeping in the same bed with him as he'd done so many years before. For many weeks after Granddaddy left us, Jarrett wouldn't come home, needing instead to stay close to where Granddaddy had lived until he could let go.

It wasn't just Jarrett who gave Granddaddy constant attention during those last weeks. I think the Old Man got more attention from his family in those final hours than he'd gotten in many years.

Even little Eddie took time away from TV to talk to Granddaddy when he called. "What you doing, Eddie Beal?" I think Granddaddy was looking for one more preacher to carry on his legacy; that he was hoping that Eddie might just be the one. Eddie is a big talker, and he always wanted me to tuck him in at night so he could say his prayers.

During those last days, Granddaddy had two visions, which amazed everyone. The first was about the baby Derek and Janice were expecting. Granddaddy told Janice, "You gon' have a boy. They gon' have to take it. You can't have that baby. They'll have to take it."

Then, two days before Granddaddy died, he had another vision. He shouted for Derek so loud that he woke up Janice and Jarrett. Derek jumped out of bed to see what was wrong. Granddaddy was sitting up, eyes glowing.

"Get up! You got a church! They called, you got the church."

Derek had been trying to get a church for several months. Granddaddy wanted Derek to have a church, real bad. His was a legacy of preachers—two were gone, someone had to take their place.

The next day, Granddaddy told Derek, "That was a dream last night, son, but the second week in December, you'll be going to take your pulpit."

True enough, Derek got a call two weeks later. Tabernacle Missionary Baptist Church in West Palm Beach, Florida, wanted him to come the second week in December. They wanted Derek to be their pastor. Just like Granddaddy said. (Martin, Jr. is remembered as a prophetic dreamer. This gift is dominant in our family line. Like Martin, Jr. and Granddaddy, many of us have dreams and visions. The Bible says that in the latter days, "old men will dream dreams, and young men will have visions."

Our family is gifted with both dreams and visions. The "gift" appears in many of us in every generation, and doesn't discriminate as to gender.)

Angela and I reflected the day after Derek got the news. Granddaddy must be like Abraham, a favorite of God. God knew that Granddaddy really wanted to know that his line would continue in the ministry, so he opened up heaven's door and let Granddaddy see into Derek's future.

The other vision was true as well. Remarkably and amazingly (several weeks after Granddaddy died), Derek and Janice had a boy, Derek II, weighing over eight pounds at birth. The baby's head was so large that he couldn't push out of the birth canal. The doctor, Jim Freemont, called me away from Janice's labor bed. Derek was in Florida preaching for his new church. Mother and I were at the hospital with Janice, helping her through her labor. Freemont looked over the x-rays and remarked, "She can't deliver, I'll have to take it."

Thank God that Derek and Janice were living with Granddaddy at the house during those last days. Not just because they had a chance to share in Granddaddy's visions, but Granddaddy would have been so alone if Derek, Janice, and Jarrett hadn't been living there when it was time for him to depart from earth.

Granddaddy and Bigmama built their large, split-level home for family. When Aunt Christine married Uncle Isaac, they lived at the big house until their home was built. So it was with Cliff and me. And finally with Derek and Janice.

Once, Cliff and I were looking at the nighttime soap opera *Dynasty*. Cliff laughed at the storyline. "Why does Blake Carrington have such a big house, and insist that his whole family live with him?"

I chuckled and answered with another question. "You ever heard of Martin Luther King, Sr.? Same story, my dear."

Of course, we were not on the level of the Carringtons. We were middle-class blacks. Yet, it was a comfortable lifestyle. In the midst of all of this, I had to put some private demons to rest.

Sometimes, I felt like Granddaddy was controlling—very much like Blake Carrington. Each man wanted to keep his whole family up under him. Granddaddy took me from Mama and Daddy when I was only two because he said he needed me. It felt like Mama and Daddy just gave me away. For years, I was too immature to understand that Granddaddy was most likely acting out of concern for my parents and me. They were young, and knew very little about caring for and supporting a baby. He was getting older, and may have needed some inspiration in his life. I finally realized that in his own way, Granddaddy was looking out for everybody.

Granddaddy was always looking out for everybody until the day he died. During those last few weeks, I didn't have a great need to visit him every day. I'd seen or talked to him almost every day of my life. He used to write me letters when I was in school, to send me money and his love. I think I wanted to let go of him a little, while he was still alive, hoping that it would make his dying easier to accept. He was my granddaddy, and my best friend. I knew he needed time with the others, and they needed him. I'd been pretty selfish with him all my life. It was time for me to let others have a chance to spend time with him. There was so little left.

Eight days before Granddaddy died, a very poignant episode came to lighten the sadness. Saturday evening, Cliff, the children and I went to get Jarrett to take him to a party. We blew the horn, using Granddaddy's signal when we got there: toot-toot-toot-toot-toot-toot-toot-toot. Jarrett called out of his bathroom window (the same window Granddaddy had used for more than twenty years to watch his family come and go from his driveway).

"Granddaddy wants you!"

Celeste was fussing. "Let's go, Mommy. We'll miss Punkin's birthday party."

But I got out of the car and went in. Granddaddy was sitting in his rocking chair. "I need a ride, can you help me?"

It was on the tip of my tongue to say, "No, I am in a hurry and the kids would be disappointed if they missed the party." But then, something reminded me of all the times I'd asked for Granddaddy's help. He'd never said no.

"Sure, Old Man, just hurry and let us help you get dressed. I have to take the kids to a party."

In keeping with his character, Granddaddy was ready to defer to the pleasures of the children.

"That's okay, I'll find somebody else to take me."

I couldn't stand the look of rejection on his face. I covered up my emotions with a gruff voice.

"We're gonna take you, and that's it. So hurry up and let us dress you!"

Cliff, Jarrett, and I dressed Granddaddy and got him to the car. We were halfway across town when I asked why he was going to Ebenezer on a Saturday.

Granddaddy seemed befuddled. "Why, isn't this Sunday?"

Granddaddy was ready to go to Homecoming Services a whole day early.

By now the kids were screaming, "Take us to the party!" Their noise was getting on Granddaddy's nerves. "Just take me to the (M.L. King) Center, I'll ride with Christine."

I started to tell him that Aunt Christine wouldn't be there on a Saturday, but I decided to humor him. When we got to the Center, Aunt Christine was there, but she was driving away, and we couldn't get her attention.

Granddaddy decided to go to his all-time favorite restaurant down the street, The Auburn Rib Shack. When we got there, Granddaddy decided to get out and go in. Celeste was outraged.

With the arrogance and inconsiderateness of a six-year-old (I can remember being just as asinine myself) she demanded, "Mama! We are going to miss Punkin's party. Just leave Granddaddy at the Rib Shack."

By this time, I'd had it. I broke into laughter. Cliff was amazed. He couldn't see what was funny. I tried to explain.

"This is wonderful. Things like this only happen in the movies. The kids don't realize how lucky they are to be able to spend time with this great old man. He's acting ridiculous. You're acting like a fool. This is really crazy."

We all went into the Rib Shack. Granddaddy ordered Brunswick stew, ribs, and apple cobbler, and promptly began to flirt with the girls behind the counter. He decided that he'd let us go on to the party and he'd stay there. He was adamant until I called Aunt Chris, who insisted that he come home. We finished our last meal with Granddaddy and dropped him at Aunt Chris' and went on to the party.

A few days later, Celeste insisted that I take her to see Granddaddy. Maybe she was feeling a little sorry about how she'd acted. Maybe she sensed that she wouldn't have many more times to see him. She put her little hands on his neck and gave him a massage. Granddaddy said her fingers felt real good.

That same day, while we were visiting, Granddaddy called me to his side. "Somebody's been stealing my money. I have to sleep with my pocketbook under my pillow. And my will, they're after me about my will."

I was so mad. There were people in and out of the house all the time. Granddaddy was sick, tired, lonely, and depressed. And he had to worry about somebody coming into his house, stealing his money. I remember thinking then, maybe he would be better out of all of the bull.

And in a few short days, he was. On Sunday morning, Granddaddy got up and got ready for church. I called that morning.

"Hey, Old Man, how ya' doing?"

His voice, though shallow and weak with panting and shortness of breath, seemed happier than it had in days.

I was concerned, but not overmuch, when he said he was going to church. "You sure you feel like it?"

His voice regained that strength and melody that brings tears to my eyes when I hear it on tape today. "Yeah! I may even preach!"

I chuckled and got ready to hang up the phone. "See if you can get Jarrett up and tell him I said he should go to church too!"

Jarrett did get up and went to church with Granddaddy that day. Aunt Chris drove them. They went to Jasper Williams' church. For some reason, Granddaddy liked Jasper a lot.

When they came home, Jarrett went off with friends. Granddaddy sent his young protegé, Edward Buggs, for some Popeye's chicken. He told Derek to go and get some Lanacane from the drugstore. Janice recounted those last hours to me.

Granddaddy and Aunt Chris were in his room when he called Janice in. "I want to give you some money."

Granddaddy told Aunt Christine to count the money out. She said, "Dad, you don't want Janice to have that much money on her lying around the house." He answered, "I'd rather she have it. If I don't give it to her, somebody else will just come in and steal it." (Someone had been stealing Granddaddy's cash from his wallet and stealing his checks from his bankbook, forging his signature and cashing the checks.) Janice thanked Granddaddy, then went to her room. Aunt Christine followed Janice and counted the money out.

After Granddaddy ate his chicken he felt sick. "I feel one coming on. Get me to bed." Somehow, Aunt Chris got him to bed. He started feeling shortness of breath and he gasped, "Help me with my breath."

Aunt Chris came over to the bed. "How can I help you, Dad?" She went to get some water. When she came back, there was a rattle in his throat. Aunt Chris called Derek. He came into the room, his portable phone up to his ear. Janice came, too. They looked at Granddaddy. He said, "That's Janice."

Then, Granddaddy's eyes were rolling back in his head. Derek dropped the phone, "Call an ambulance."

Aunt Chris said, "What's the number? 911." Then, Aunt Chris ran downstairs. Janice picked up the phone and called emergency and Dr. Bridges. Derek started CPR. Isaac, Jr. came into the room, looked at Derek and Granddaddy and went to join his mother at the bottom of the stairs.

Janice was holding Granddaddy's hand. She said she felt life leave it. Derek kept up the CPR until the ambulance arrived. The attendants took him away. Aunt Christine and Isaac, Jr. returned to the room. Isaac dived for Granddaddy's pillow, maybe to get Granddaddy's personals to give to his mother for safekeeping. But Janice and Derek already had Granddaddy's wallet and checkbook.

Derek was furious. Isaac hadn't stayed to help with the CPR, but he was there to pick up Granddaddy's things. "That's okay, Isaac. Don't touch it. We'll take care of it."

Granddaddy had always told Janice to get his wallet, diary, and checkbook if anything happened to him. It was all pretty territorial. Everyone wanted to be in charge. I guess things were pretty tense, and everyone was reacting the best way they knew how.

Granddaddy was pronounced dead shortly after he arrived at the hospital. Cliff and I were out shopping. When we got home, his mother Sally Mae rang the phone. "Why didn't you tell me Granddaddy was dead?"

I thought she was playing a joke, chastizing us for being gone all day. "What? Sally Mae. Be serious."

She was. Granddaddy was gone. I felt guilty as hell. I hadn't thought about Granddaddy since I'd talked to him that morning. Where was I when he needed me? Out having fun. I wanted to die. Granddaddy had never deserted me, but I'd left him alone at his time of death. The old feeling came back for a moment. Would I die, too? Was the bond that strong? Surely not. I wanted to live, then. But I wasn't so sure I could make it without Granddaddy.

At the hospital, the medical staff let family come to see Granddaddy's body. Lying in a bed under the covers, his hands and face exposed, he looked so peaceful, like he'd been kissed by angels and welcomed into God's arms. I kissed Granddaddy. I guess others did, too.

Jarrett said he had a vision (remember, the gift is predominant in our family). He was crying and asked God to let him see Granddaddy one more time. A bright light appeared and Jarrett saw a figure that looked like Granddaddy, and he was joined by other three figures. They looked at him for a moment, and then they were gone, with the light.

Of course, Jarrett is an actor; Granddaddy was real proud of Jarrett's talent. And as an actor, Jarrett has a vivid imagination and a big streak of creativity. Somehow, I don't believe this was imagination. I believe it was real. Maybe Jarrett needed assurance to know that Granddaddy had reached the light of God and the love of Bigmama, Daddy, and Uncle M.L. (Martin Luther King, Jr.). But where was Darlene (my sister who died many years back)?

But, we are a family of seers. Granddaddy had visions; Uncle M.L. had dreams. Jarrett's vision could be real, too.

Some may argue that Granddaddy could have lived longer if he'd accepted the pacemaker that Dr. McLauren wanted him to wear. But when Granddaddy's sisters—Cleo and Woodie—couldn't talk him into wearing the pacemaker, they said they gave up.

Granddaddy was tired, a man full of days just like Job in the Bible, according to brother Derek's eulogy of the Old Man. He missed his wife, Alberta, and his sons A.D. and M.L. He missed his granddaughter Darlene, and old friends like Bennie Mays. And Granddaddy had a need to see his Maker. He had a need for peace and contentment. He'd looked forward to it while living a full life. After eighty-four years of joys, sorrow, mountains and valleys, Granddaddy was longing for home. And though he's gone home to Glory, he'll be Sons of Thunder. Knowing that his love and spirit are alive and well makes missing him a little easier to bear.

CHAPTER ONE

How to tell the many delightful, nostalgic, funny, sad, triumphant, and joyful remembrances of the legacy of the King family? There have been greater challenges in life, but none so enjoyable. Where to begin?

It all started long before I was born, but I guess a good point for me to start is right before my entrance into the world. The family was up in the air because Daddy (Alfred Daniel Williams King, I) was going to marry Mama (Naomi Barber). They'd been dating since she was twelve and he was fourteen. In later years, Daddy would tell me that he'd always known he'd marry Mama.

But knowing was one thing; having to was quite another. Mama's mama (Bigmama Bessie) was an old-fashioned, superstitious lady. Bessie was happy to have Mother courted by a member of the King Family. Why, wasn't Reverend Martin Luther King, Sr. pastor of Ebenezer Baptist Church, the very church on Auburn Avenue that was growing every day? And Reverend King's wife, Alberta Williams King, was daughter of the successful minister who had passed the church on to Reverend King.

Success and religion, what more could a young lady hope to attain? And young A.D. was kind of cute, too. Not too tall, about 5'8." Bright-skinned for a colored man. And he dressed real well. And he could talk faster about most things than anyone else; Bessie knew. That young man was going places. And he could take "Neenie" and Bessie with him, Bessie reasoned.

A.D. was a little older than Neenie, and Bessie wasn't so sure that being a preacher's son was protection enough from the temptations of sin. So when Naomi was old enough to go out on dates with A.D., Bessie would warn her,

"Now, Neenie, you make sure that A.D. is wearing a raincoat when he tries to kiss you."

Needless to say, Neenie, young, naive, and innocent didn't know what a "raincoat" was, other than the knee-length, hooded piece of outwear that people wore when it was raining outside. I must confess that it took me a few minutes (years later, after the "pill" had swept society by storm) to figure out why Bessie had figured that Daddy would have to wear a raincoat to kiss Mama.

Mama says that when she'd ask Daddy about the raincoat, he'd roar with laughter. But he never bothered to explain the need.

So Daddy didn't bother to wear a raincoat when he kissed Mama. And Daddy married Mama, during her first year in college.

And months later, I was born. I guess Daddy never wore a raincoat during the whole time he was married to Mama. Because soon after I was born, Al came along. Then there was Derek, then Darlene, and finally Vernon. Mama says that if Daddy hadn't died when he did, there would probably have been another child. Daddy always said he wanted six children.

Right after I was born, Granddaddy and Bigmama came to the hospital to see me. Daddy was there, and smiling, he said, "Girl, that baby's skin is so white. You better be glad she looks like me, or I'd have said she belongs to the milkman." She didn't know what to say to Daddy. I did look like Daddy, though. Some say it was just like he spit me out. I had his big head, full lips, broad nose, and eyes that were slightly slanted. In later years, Daddy would tease me, "You look just like me, girl, only you're a lot prettier." I thought Daddy was handsome, with his charming smile and the deepest cleft in his chin. His hair was slightly wavy, and he wore it very short for many years. He dressed with flair, and had such a personality that he seemed to say to world, "I don't give a damn—I'm gonna have fun." I was secretly proud to be like Daddy, though sometimes I'd wish I looked more like Mama, since she was so pretty.

Mama was just as surprised to hear what Granddaddy had to say. Granddaddy looked at me and said to Bigmama, "There's that baby, Bunch." That's when he told Mama how he'd seen me three years before, in a dream.

For the next several years, I was Mama and Daddy's baby, and "Baby" to Granddaddy. I went to live with him and Bigmama in the big Queen Anne house on Boulevard. There was a tall, mahogany staircase, French doors to the dining room, tall, built-in bookcases, and a real clothes chute spiraling down from the upstairs bathroom to the basement.

Mama and Daddy lived at the Williams family home on Auburn Avenue. Today the house is the Historic Martin Luther King, Jr. Birth Home. Back then, it was a big house shared by two families. Mama, Daddy, and my brothers and sister lived upstairs. The Goosby family lived downstairs. I visited every week, and spent the night sometimes.

But I usually felt like an outsider. My brothers didn't help me to feel any better. They'd say I was adopted. I didn't even look like them, with my pale face and red-gold hair. I had the big King head, the Williamses' full, beautiful, africoid lips and nose. I even had Mama's and Bigmama Bessie's big hips and legs and high Indian cheekbones. But my skin color was off. I used to cry because I was so much lighter than everyone else. I felt like an alien until Darlene was born. She was even lighter than I. Years later, we found out that the blood of Granddaddy's Irish grandfather caused fair-skinned babies to pop from generation to generation.

The story of our Irish ancestry is a romantic account that has been recounted and recaptured in various ways over the years. Granddaddy's sister, Aunt Woodie, once told it to me this way:

"Our grandmother was a freed slave. She had a dark, lovely, ebony complexion, and was very close to her African ancestry. Our Irish grandfather met her and fell in love with her. He wanted to marry her, but whites couldn't marry blacks back then. They started north to get married, but something happened. Maybe they didn't have enough money or something. Anyway, they jumped the broom and stayed together. Our daddy, Jim King, was one of their children. He looked half-white, which is why bright-skinned, red-headed babies like you pop up in our family most generations. We don't talk about it much, because mixed babies were always something to sweep under the rug and not talk about."

This was always such a romantic story. A mixed marriage, controversial at the time, which resulted in generations of Kings who would fight for the same human rights that were denied this couple so long ago.

At any rate, our family is full of varying skin hues. We have the African and Irish bloodlines, as well as Native American ancestors. You can see these ethnic groups reflected in our family. Aunt Woodie was a light coffee brown, Granddaddy was slightly darker. Aunt Cleo was an exotic, rich, red-skinned woman. Uncle Joel was dark brown. Daddy was fair-skinned, Uncle M.L. was coffee brown, and Aunt Chris is a rich brown, more like her mother.

My daughters Celeste and Jennifer and youngest son John have the same fair skin that I have, with red-gold hair, while their brothers Jarrett, Eddie, and Joshua are a beautiful coconut color. I appreciate God's gift of multi-colors now. Such variations are common in any black ethnic family. I appreciate that fact now, but I didn't when I was younger. Before my sister, Darlene, was born, I was the only one with fair skin. My brothers would taunt me, saying, "We don't know where you came from. You must have been adopted, you are too pale." With all of my brothers' teasing me I was really glad to get back to Granddaddy's house.

One evening, there was a dinner party at Granddaddy's house. Mama said I was still a baby, just learning the fine art of social etiquette (for potty habits). Aunt Christine said she toilet-trained me. It seems like everybody had a hand at the task.

On this particular evening, during the party, I did a number in my pants. Since everyone seemed to be so pleased when I produced this feat in the pot, I thought it might be nice to share the accomplishment with the guests. I grabbed up a handful and ran straight to Granddaddy.

Mama said Granddaddy heard the patter of my feet coming toward the table, saw my outstretched hand, and held out his big brown hand. "What you got there, Baby?" I proudly dropped my trophy into his waiting palm. I must confess that I might have been hurt and surprised when Granddaddy didn't respond with his usual smile and praise.

He opened his fist, sniffed, rolled the little balls around in his hand and exclaimed, "Well I'll be damned, it's hockey!"

Mama insists that's the way it really happened. Granddaddy used to laugh about that story after I grew up. And until the day he died, whenever I offered Granddaddy anything, he'd look and it, and ask what it was before he'd accept it.

There were often parties and meetings at the big house on the hill. There was room for my cousins Clara and Betty Ann to live there too, since Daddy was married and living away. Uncle M.L. was in school, and later married Aunt Coretta and moved to Alabama to take his first church, so he didn't live there either. So the doors were always open for family.

For a short while, my brother Al lived with us too. If I was Granddaddy's pride and joy, Al was Bigmama's heart. He could get anything from Bigmama, just by giving her his crooked grin. But he didn't stay with Bigmama and Granddaddy as long as I did. When he was six, he announced, "I'm going home to stay with my Mama." And true to those same words, he lived with Mama until he died.

There are too many stories to recall and record at this time. Like the time Granddaddy took me with him to Detroit to meet his family. His sisters Woodie, Cleo, and Lenora were different to me from the women at home. They hugged and kissed like everybody else. But they didn't have the same soft, southern accents. And they wore fancy hats and hairdos. They were crazy about Granddaddy; he was a brother who could work miracles with advice, money, and business contacts, and most importantly, with love. They were glad to see Granddaddy. And Aunt Cleo took a fancy to me.

As I noted earlier, Aunt Cleo was an exotic-looking woman, with beautiful, rich, golden brown skin, huge breasts, full lips, and a wonderful sense of humor. She birthed eight children, and has always had a house full of grandchildren. She seemed to adopt me as one of her brood.

Aunt Cleo said I was a very vain child, even though I was fat as a pig. (I ate everything in sight. Mama said I must have been suffering from too much of everything—love, attention, material things. And I never seemed to have enough. I wondered if it was a case of having too much, or not having enough. Living away from my parents and brothers and sisters caused me to wonder if they really loved me. But looking back, I guess I did have too much, of everything. And it spoiled me rotten.)

Aunt Cleo said even though I was fat, I thought I had the prettiest legs in the world. I never wanted a bump or scratch on those legs. I guess that's why God let me get a long ugly scratch one year, and varicose veins that get worse each time I have a baby. The veins never kept me from getting pregnant, though. I'd always wanted six children. Maybe because Mother had five, and I wanted to top her. Maybe because Daddy wanted six. Maybe because my sister Darlene wanted six, and never lived to have one. And maybe I felt that I have a responsibility to replace those who are taken from the family, with a new life. At any rate, I have been blessed to be the mother of six, and the grandbabies keep coming. I am truly and wonderfully blessed.

But my thoughts of having babies were far in the future during those early days with Granddaddy. Those were the days of thinking Granddaddy was almost as wonderful as God; that if he couldn't solve a problem he could just call God up, and have God fix everything.

I thought that Granddaddy was the handsomest man alive. He may have been a bit vain, too. Granddaddy had a real big head (the King head that causes so much pain when mothers are birthing King babies); smooth, unblemished skin the color of almonds, honey and Irish coffee mixed together. He had very shapely legs, almost as pretty as a lady's. And his nose was slim at the bridge and slightly flared at the nostrils. He had the prettiest set of false teeth, and silky white hair with little black streaks running through it.

Granddaddy always smelled good. He used lots of talcum powder (men's or ladies'; he bought whatever he smelled on someone else and liked). And he smoothed his hair down with tonic and put on stocking caps to keep it smooth. He used tweezers to pluck hairs from under his chin, and rubbed lotion all over his body to keep his skin from drying out. He had wonderful skin all of his life.

One day, I was bragging to Cliff about how Granddaddy kept himself up. Cliff wouldn't even put lotion on his hands in cold weather to keep them from chapping. I wanted to choke him when he raised his eyebrow and grinned, "Don't you think he carried all that stuff a little bit too far? I'm a rugged sort of man myself."

I punched Cliff in the arm. "Are you calling my Granddaddy a sissy, just because he like to fix himself up?" Cliff only laughed. "Anyone alive knows if there was a real man in this world, it was your Granddaddy." I decided to forgive Cliff, and not choke him.

Granddaddy did care about his appearance. He took great pride in wearing beautifully cut suits and wonderful hats for every occasion; and he made a conscious effort to smell good. His friends used to tease him, suggesting that he was trying to cover up the smell of the plough and mule.

He liked for Bigmama, Uncle M.L., Daddy, and Aunt Chris to look good too. They were a beautifully dressed, well-groomed family. And Granddaddy took great pride in Aunt Chris' talents as a seamstress.

Aunt Chris spent all of her life being a model daughter. She is a very accomplished seamstress. Granddaddy often boasted about her creative outfits. She was a major soloist in the church choir. She graduated from Spelman College and completed her graduate studies in New York at Columbia University. She was the first black woman to enroll in the Graduate Business Program at Columbia. Although there was no overt action to force her out of the program, Aunt Chris finally changed to education, because, in her own words, "I was black and a woman. This was unheard of at that time. They did nothing to help me and everything to discourage me."

However, that experience at Columbia did nothing to stanch Aunt Chris' business acumen. She started out as an elementary school teacher and worked to become a professor at Spelman College. She was the finance director at the Martin Luther King,

Jr. Center for years, founded the King Day Care Center, and watched over its management for years. She traveled to London and Paris with Bigmama and Granddaddy before she married Uncle Isaac. Bigmama and Granddaddy raised her to be a lady.

As a little girl, I was jealous of Aunt Chris. After all, she got to be Granddaddy's real daughter. And she was pretty. And she wasn't fat. She did everything right. She never talked too loud. She never walked too fast. She'd never burp in public. I'd been guilty of all of the above and more. And I always felt that Granddaddy wasn't quite pleased with my behavior. Years later, I would start out on a path to become scholar, politician, writer, and anything else that would earn me a star in Granddaddy's book. But during my younger years, I was determined to get attention in the most negative ways possible.

I was allowed to romp, yell, act out, have my way, and eat too much. Why didn't Granddaddy insist that I be a lady, too? I guess that by the time I was born, Granddaddy had met his major objectives in life. He had a big house, a wife with high social standing, an accomplished daughter, one son who was starting in the ministry, and his younger son would be whipped into shape soon enough. Time now for indulgence. The time was to spoil me, lavish me. I became an absolute brat.

Everyone accepted the fact that I was a brat. I was the family pet imp. Granddaddy even nicknamed me "Pest." During the car trip from Atlanta to Marion, Alabama, to Uncle M.L. and Aunt Coretta's wedding, I was restless. I've never been able to ride in a car (or plane or boat, for that matter) without getting motion sickness.

I was real little at the time, and kept insisting that Granddaddy stop the car for water or the bathroom or to let me stretch my legs. Mama said Granddaddy finally got so tired of my complaints that he turned around and yelled, "Veda, you are a living pest." The name stuck. Even today, Mama will get tired of my antics and say, "Go home, Pest." (When Celeste was born, I passed the name on to her. I got tired of holding the title alone. She can play some pretty interesting tricks too. Sometimes I would call her Pessie, until I realized that I was transferring my frustration to her. Of course she didn't like the misnomer.)

Just before Uncle M.L. married Aunt Coretta, he brought her home to meet Granddaddy and Bigmama. They were all surprised because they knew that Granddaddy wanted Uncle M.L. to marry the daughter of a prominent Atlanta businessman. As quiet as it's kept, a few other ladies were hoping to become Mrs. King, Jr. too. In fact, over the years at least three ladies have told me, "I almost became your aunt."

At first, Granddaddy was determined not to like Aunt Coretta. And he surely was not going to accept her as his new daughter-in-law. So what if she was studying in Boston to be a fine singer? He already knew whom he wanted his son to marry.

But just as it was to prove time and time again, Uncle M.L. had a mind of his own. And just like Daddy, Uncle M.L. was going to choose his own bride. And so he came, with Coretta on his arm, to the "mountain." (Granddaddy did sort of look like a mountain in his younger days. While not tall in stature, he managed to appear to tower over everyone.)

Granddaddy was cordial enough when he greeted Aunt Coretta. But he didn't hug her. And Granddaddy always had a habit of touching, hugging, and patting on the shoulders. He was a touchy-feely kind of man.

He didn't hug Aunt Coretta. And she kept her distance too. As usual, I ignored Granddaddy's chilly attitude. I thought Aunt Coretta was pretty. She had legs like my Mama. She was as tall as Mama. She looked a lot like Mama. I ran to her and hugged her legs. I couldn't say Coretta. So I said, "Co-Co." Aunt Coretta says she remembers my little hands squeezing her, and Granddaddy's chill starting to thaw. If I liked Co-Co, maybe she would be all right.

The name Co-Co stayed with Aunt Coretta. Next to Corrie, Co-Co became a pet name for Uncle M.L. to call Aunt Coretta. Granddaddy and Aunt Coretta became very close over the years, and remained so until he died. He accepted her with joy and blessed their union, which bore much fruit.

So now, Granddaddy had two country girls for daughters-in-law. Mama had been born in Dothan, Alabama (although Bigmama Bessie brought her to Atlanta when she was a very little girl). And

Aunt Coretta was from Marion, Alabama (her daddy, a prominent businessman in his community, owned his own dry goods store, a fact Aunt Coretta was very proud of). It was funny how life had a way of turning out. Granddaddy, a former country lad, had journeyed to the city to find a city wife. His sons, city bred, found they had a taste for country women.

But there is nothing "country" about Mama or Aunt Coretta. Mother's voice has never even had a trace of a southern accent. She has a flair for creative cooking and interior decorating. Daddy always kept Mama dressed up like a big doll. (Mama said one day Daddy came home unexpected and she had on a robe with a little hole in it. He took one look at the hole, poked his finger in it, and ripped the robe off Mama. She was real careful not to wear torn things again. He hated safety pins too, so she spent a lot time mending things.) Mom graduated from high school, and was making honors at Spelman College, where she was majoring in French before she married Daddy. She often sang at concerts for his church functions.

Mother was usually reserved, though. It was like she was remembering that her mother was a domestic worker, and she felt like she was never quite as good as Aunt Chris, or even Aunt Coretta. I would get mad at Mother, wondering why she didn't go to dinners and parties and other functions unless Daddy made her. Sometimes, Daddy wouldn't take no for an answer. "You're my wife, dammit. Not some mouse. Now, get dressed!" Mama would put on some of the beautiful clothes he'd buy for her to wear, and rise to the particular occasion, but she wasn't really comfortable moving about in society. She didn't break out of her shell until long after Daddy died, after Granddaddy's death, in fact. Then she explained, "I never wanted to upset your Daddy and Granddaddy, so I kept my feelings to myself. Now they are gone and I have no one to account to for my actions." Mama has finally come into her own, but she lacked this confidence and independence gained over the years in those early days.

Aunt Coretta was a lot different from Mama. From the very beginning, she made it clear that she was an independent, accomplished woman. Of course, she had finished college when she married Uncle M.L., and I imagine that gave her a base for personal pride and security. She was a couple years older than Martin, and seemed to take pride in her maturity. And her family had their own business back in Marion. She was a very intelligent, cultured lady.

Even at an early age, I admired beauty and culture. I wished I were prettier, like Mama, Aunt Coretta, and Aunt Chris. And Bigmama was classy as well. They smelled good, they dressed beautifully. They spoke softly. But they didn't appreciate the really good things in life. They couldn't kick off their shoes and run barefoot through the mud. They couldn't wiggle out of their too-tight girdles in church (though I did one Sunday when Bigmama insisted that I wear one because my behind would shake when I walked).

Bigmama had a big sense of humor sometimes. But she didn't always appreciate some of the things Granddaddy would do. Like the time he brought home a pet monkey for me. She wasn't very happy about the pet. "King! This is ridiculous. Nobody has a monkey in their house. It will tear up my curtains."

Granddaddy only grunted. "Let the girl have the monkey. You don't like dogs."

We kept Pete, the monkey, until in my impishness I gave Bigmama a reason to insist that he had to go. I pulled Pete's tail and he bit me. That's all Bigmama needed. "See, he'll give the child rabies. I don't know what's worse, the monkey or you. You give Veda everything she wants."

Granddaddy did give me just about everything I wanted. I had only to ask, and whatever I desired was made possible. Especially food. Granddaddy liked to eat just as much as I did. He'd go around thinking up things to eat, and say, "You want a hot dog?" Of course I was ready to eat whenever the occasion arose. We'd go to the old curb market on Edgewood, where they sold fresh meats, fruits, and vegetables. He'd buy a few things, and then we'd stop at the deli-window outside and have hot dogs and ice cream. Another favorite hangout was the Planters Roasted Nut Shop, downtown. Hot, greasy Planters Peanuts were wonderful. By the time we got home, though, we'd always be ready to eat again. We had great fun on eating sprees.

Another time, Granddaddy bought a rooster, a hen, and some chickens. It was just after he and Bigmama moved into the big house in Northwest Atlanta. The neighborhood was very posh; the house was very modern and elegant. When Bigmama saw the chickens, she was very upset. "People will think they're in the country, King. Get rid of those things."

It was pretty gory to see Granddaddy wring the chickens' necks. When he gave them to Bigmama to cook for dinner, she wouldn't. Granddaddy did. He was the only one with stomach enough to eat them.

Another time, Granddaddy agreed to keep Aunt Woodie's French poodle. She wasn't able to take him back home to Detroit, following a visit. Bigmama hated dogs. She was already disgusted with the two dogs Granddaddy had insisted on putting in her back yard. They wrecked her flower garden, and she didn't like to go past them to get to her fence in the vegetable garden.

The poodle, John F., was really kind of cute. He was spoiled, though. He thought he was a person. He was used to sitting on couches and chairs and eating with the family. Bigmama was not about to have a dog living in her house. Bigmama locked John F. in the basement; it broke his heart.

When John F. finally got out of the basement, he was as upset and depressed as a person might have been. He growled sadly, hung his head, and slowly started up the stairs. He looked around to see if he had an audience. He looked so bad that Bigmama was slow to make me catch him before he could make it to her bedroom. We followed him. In the master's bedroom, John F. went out of the glass doors to the terrace. He sighed as if hopelessly sad, and then took a suicidal dive off the terrace. He hurt his legs. Granddaddy realized that John F. wouldn't make it if he stayed at the house much longer. As soon as he was well, Granddaddy sent him home.

Granddaddy brought another dog home. Tappy was Mama Lillian's dog. Mama Lillian was Granddaddy's secretary. She ran his office at church and she used to help Bigmama with Daddy, Uncle M.L., and Aunt Chris when they were little. Bigmama would sometimes travel with Granddaddy, and Mama Lillian would mind the house and the children until they came back. Mama Lillian used to help Mama and Daddy with us.

When urban renewal tore down her home, Mama Lillian was forced to move from her family house near the church. Granddaddy helped her to get a new house. She got a little dog, Tappy, to keep her company and to be a watchdog. Tappy had a loud bark, and he was a tough little dog. But he was too small to fend off a bully dog. The mean dog bit Tappy's stomach out. The animal hospital patched Tappy up pretty well, but Mama Lillian was too hurt to keep him. So Tappy came to live with Granddaddy.

After Bigmama died, there was some speculation among the church members that Granddaddy would marry Mama Lillian. But Granddaddy fooled everybody. Although he dated a mature widow named Mrs. Juanita Toomer (a long-time friend of Bigmama's), and a lady very close to my age, Granddaddy didn't remarry. He had a few romantic interests (he even flirted with a local TV news anchor lady), and I think he missed Bigmama too much to even consider remarrying. Some of the family didn't want him to remarry.

Bigmama knew how to keep Granddaddy happy. She was a very warm, loving, sexy lady with a sense of humor and more than a little intelligence. She had her college degree, and she was an heiress in her own right. Her father and mother left her money and property. But she never rubbed her holdings in Granddaddy's face.

Bigmama taught school while her children were younger, but she ran her household at the same time. By the time I was born, there was no need for Bigmama to work. She did church work and other volunteer work to keep her active mind busy.

Bigmama always greeted Granddaddy at the door wearing a caftan or something pretty. And the pots from the kitchen would be smelling good. Granddaddy had no way of knowing that sometimes, Bigmama got home just twenty minutes before he did, threw the pots on high heat, jumped into a house dress and set the table just in time to be ready as he walked in.

Theirs was a beautiful marriage. They would argue, but I don't think he ever hit her. He could break her heart with words, though. Granddaddy loved to say "damn." Bigmama hated cursing. She would actually cry if he said "damn." And if he said "mess," Bigmama would go to their room with a headache.

Once, after one of his cursing scenes, Bigmama clammed up, refusing to say one word. Granddaddy couldn't help pushing her a little. "I suppose you'd prefer someone with a little class, like my friend Bennie Mays?" Bigmama wouldn't dignify his accusation with a comment. When Bigmama wanted to punish Granddaddy for something, she would just stop talking to him. (Although I think she did have a crush on Dr. Mays. She was always talking about how handsome and polished and well-spoken he was. My mother and many other women thought Mays was handsome too. I preferred someone down to earth, like Granddaddy.)

Granddaddy couldn't stand it when Bigmama refused to talk to him. He was the kind of man who needed verbal and physical affection.

Sometimes, when Bigmama wouldn't talk to Granddaddy, I would climb up in his lap, pat his face, and feel sorry for him. He couldn't help it if he was a grouchy bear sometimes.

Bigmama would often tease Granddaddy about being stiff and rigid sometimes. At home, Bigmama would tell me how she used to dance and play music with her friends before she married Granddaddy. After she married him, she had to lead the life of proper preacher's wife.

I asked her if her life wasn't much the same as it was when she was living with her Daddy and Mother. "Oh, no. I had fun when I was a young girl. My mother was very pretty, and enjoyed nice things. And she let me have little parties and things with girlfriends. We would talk and tell jokes and have the best time."

Bigmama knew how important it was for girls to know how to sing and dance and have other social graces. She used to buy me the prettiest dresses and fix my hair in long braids with pretty bows. We'd go on shopping sprees to Rich's, Davisons, and Zayre's. (Bigmama didn't really care if she was shopping at a first-class store or a discount store). She bought whatever she liked, from whatever store had it.

After we shopped, we'd have lunch. In the early 'fifties, we'd have to eat in Rich's basement because blacks weren't allowed in the Magnolia Room—Rich's class restaurant.

Bigmama didn't like being treated like a second-class citizen. If her money was good enough to buy clothes, her money was good enough to buy her a seat in any restaurant in the store. I learned to feel the same way. After Uncle M.L. and his movement boycotted Atlanta stores, Bigmama and I started having wonderful chicken potpie in the Magnolia Room. I had to use my best table manners then. Bigmama tried to make a young lady out of me. When I was ten, she even sent me to charm school.

When I was old enough, Bigmama gave me a book, *For Girls Only*, which told all about the female cycle and the male and female reproductive systems. Bigmama said it was silly for a girl to not know what life was about. She was amazed that our school was taking sex education out of the curriculum because parents didn't want their children to know about "such things." So I grew up feeling comfortable discussing sex with the women in my family.

Bigmama was a buffer between Granddaddy and Aunt Christine. Granddaddy wanted Aunt Chris to be perfect. He really didn't even want her to go out on dates. The only acceptable beau in Granddaddy's eyes was a preacher that didn't quite turn Aunt Chris on. Daddy and Uncle M.L. used to threaten their friends who would try to date Aunt Chris. "Don't try it, man, the old man will take your head off." They used to follow Aunt Chris around to make sure she didn't have secret dates.

No wonder Aunt Chris grew up to be reserved. Sometimes, she seemed to be downright stuck-up. Granddaddy and Bigmama taught her to be such a lady that she really didn't know how to have fun. She'd turn up her nose at my antics.

But I can't help wondering if Aunt Chris didn't secretly wish she didn't have to be so reserved. I mean, she's a highly spirited, creative, sexy person, but she always had to be on her p's and q's. Granddaddy wouldn't give her an inch, and he gave me miles of freedom. I could run to him, with skirts flying, jump onto his lap, kiss and hug him, and he never seemed to mind how boisterous I became. And when I managed to do something nice, he'd pat me on the head and smile.

Aunt Chris had a jewelry box full of little tokens from admirers. On Valentine's Day she would always get several boxes of candy. Bigmama would insist to Granddaddy that Aunt Chris had a right to lead a normal life, to go out to movies, and go dancing and things like that.

Aunt Chris and Granddaddy had a row about her dancing one day. Aunt Chris had made a lovely dress to accentuate her tiny waist and her ample bosom (she and Bigmama had the largest bosoms. Aunt Chris's daughter Angela inherited them too). She slipped into the dress shortly before her escort was to arrive. I was spread out across her bed, with my chubby legs crossed at the ankles, swinging behind me.

"What you goin' to do, Aunt Christine? Show me!"

Aunt Christine whirled around the room with an imaginary dance partner. Just as she completed the turn, Granddaddy came to the door.

"Christine King, what are you doing? I know you're not dancing, because preachers' daughters don't dance."

Granddaddy wasn't going to let Aunt Chris go out that night, but Bigmama, with her gentle persuasive ways, convinced Granddaddy that Aunt Chris hadn't done anything wrong. After all, hadn't Granddaddy danced with Bigmama before they were married?

Aunt Christine's eyes twinkled with surprise. Her Daddy had danced? Impossible! Granddaddy looked a little sheepish. "Well, don't do too much dancing, girl."

Uncle M. L. never needed a buffer. He was Granddaddy's heir and could do little wrong. This wasn't the case with Daddy. Bigmama often had to intercede for Daddy. Somehow, Daddy had inherited the family trait of the alcohol demons. Granddaddy's father, James Albert, used to drink. One day, while in his cups, James Albert slapped his wife, Delia. Granddaddy, the protector of the family even then, defended his mother. His Daddy promised never to hit his wife again. Granddaddy wrote about it in his book. He would say that the reason he never touched liquor was because of what it did to his father. Daddy and other members of the family, including myself didn't escape the curse so easily.

Sometimes, when Daddy was frustrated, and would take a drink, Bigmama was the only person in the world who could console him and bring him away from the drink and back to himself. She was their "Mother Dear," and with tenderness and compassion, Alberta kept the demons at bay, and taught her family to love in the face of adversity.

That is the beauty of the King family legacy. Daddy King and Mama King were true romantics at heart. They loved each other, and they loved and protected their children. And in the midst of all the trials and tragedies, there was always the love and romance.

CHAPTER TWO

The story of Martin and Alberta's courtship was old-fashioned and sweet. Young Reverend King had been attending church and Reverend Williams was grooming him to be an assistant pastor. Young "Mike," as Granddaddy was called in those days (he would change his name to Martin after the birth of his first son), wanted to court young Alberta. The preacher's daughter was pampered and sheltered and it was difficult to get a moment alone with her.

One night, when the family was heading for prayer meeting at the church down the street, Alberta asked to stay home with a headache. Her mama offered to stay at home with her, but Alberta thought she'd be okay with a cool cloth for company.

Shortly after the family left, Bigmama felt better. She got up and stirred around until it was time for them to come home. Then she got back into bed.

Her mama and papa came home. "How was the meeting?" Her mother felt her brow for fever, and finding none, smiled. "Fine, dear. Reverend King was there, but we told him not to come by, since you're not feeling well."

Miss Jenny was a little surprised when Alberta didn't seem too upset. "Weren't you expecting him?"

Bigmama fanned herself a little, "I'll see him Sunday, Mother. Right now, I'd like to go to sleep."

About an hour later, the lights in the Williamses' family home were turned off. A shadow slipped past the front yard and around to Bigmama's window, which was open to let in the spring breeze.

Granddaddy slipped into the window and got his first, real private kiss from Bigmama. When I asked him if he did more than kiss her, he said, "Go on, girl!" He did admit that he was glad to find out that she was a passionate lady. He'd been a little concerned, since she was an only child. He was scared that Bigmama would not want many children, either.

After they were married, Bigmama told Granddaddy about the miscarriages her mother had suffered from. She said she was lucky to be there herself, and that having been an only child, she was looking forward to a large family.

Granddaddy was too glad to comply with her wishes. From their union came Willie Christine King, Martin Luther King, Jr., and Alfred Daniel Williams King.

So the roots of Granddaddy's dynasty were firmly planted. He'd gotten his society wife, an heiress, in fact. He'd gotten his father-in-law's church (after serving for four years as the assistant pastor). The members had learned to love Reverend King, the young fireball preacher who could whoop and sing, and who had married the preacher's daughter. When Reverend Williams died, Ebenezer was proud to call Reverend King their pastor.

Granddaddy and Bigmama lived in the Williamses' family home for many years after Reverend Williams died. Bigmama's mother, Jenny Williams, lived with them until she died.

Granddaddy helped to deliver his children in that house. He told me about it when I was pregnant; his voice was close to tears of compassion. "I felt so sorry for your grandmother, Veda. She worked so hard to birth those babies. And as I helped, hearing her groans, I thanked the Lord I was a man. I'm glad it's easier for you women today."

Bigmama never talked too much about labor and delivery. But, when I was carrying Jarrett and asked her if I should breastfeed, she did admit that breastfeeding wasn't all peaches and cream. "Veda, sometimes my bosoms would be so full of milk, and they would hurt so much that I felt like going out and paying somebody to just drink the milk." I thought the story was funny. Granddaddy didn't at the time Bigmama was having babies, but he learned to laugh and talk about the story later.

Granddaddy told me a funny little story about the days during Bigmama's pregnancies. One day, she was craving something, he couldn't remember what. She sent him to the store down the street. On his way down the street, Granddaddy had to pass by this lady's house that he'd been trying to avoid. The lady saw him coming, ran and got her shotgun, came back to the door and aimed it straight at him. When I asked him why, he looked so innocent. "I can't imagine why the woman would want to shoot me." I told him I was glad she didn't since Bigmama was waiting for him to come back from the store.

Granddaddy had another funny story that he told at the same time. "There was another lady, who I used to visit before I married your Bigmama. I used to go by after church meeting and have a milkshake. She could make the best milkshakes. When she heard I was going to marry your Bigmama, she invited me over. I went, expecting to have to explain because I just figured she'd be mad. She didn't seem to be. In fact, she made me a milk shake. After I finished it, I got sick as a dog. I think she poisoned me." I thought the story was so funny that I got Granddaddy to tell it often, especially in dinner parties and family gatherings.

As the years went by, Granddaddy remembered his promise to himself that he had made on the long walk from Stockbridge, Georgia, to Atlanta with his shoes on his back, so he wouldn't wear holes in them. He had his city wife, his big church; now he was going to have his big, fine house.

With savings and income earned from investments, Granddaddy bought a house on a hill on Boulevard, a street that overlooks downtown Atlanta today. He bought his little mansion from a man named Dr. Burney, and took his family there to live. After years of living in a house owned by his father-in-law, then his wife, he felt good to be buying a house of his own.

Granddaddy was proud of his house. He was proud of his family. And he was proud of his church. He was living in his glory—respected in the community and making a little money (enough to invest in some things of his own).

As Granddaddy's sons grew older, he decided that it might be time to start molding his dynasty into a legacy. He was a good preacher. The membership was growing—the choirs were some of the best in the city, thanks to Bunch (his pet name for Bigmama—he called her Honey Bunch when they were courting). Maybe his boys could become good preachers. Then he could pass Ebenezer on to them like Reverend Williams had passed it on to him. What a blessing it was to have sons.

Daddy and Uncle M.L. grew up hearing Granddaddy preach. College and graduate training were just a matter of formality in their lives. Of course, refined, cultured sons of middle-class families went to college. But all the real training they would ever need to follow Granddaddy's chosen vocation was to be gotten from watching and hearing him preach.

Granddaddy was a fireball preacher. He would take a text from the Bible (like the story of "The Least of These" [Matt: 25-40] where the people wanted to feed Jesus and wash his feet, but had neglected to attend to the needs of the needy they met every day). Then, he would lay out the story, pick some analogies from the lives of his members, and finally end the sermon with a song and a story.

By the time he got to his parable or story, Granddaddy would be panting, sweating, blowing, gesticulating, and bellowing in a strong voice (a technique called whooping).

A story I remember was the story he told about the old country doctor that people would come for miles to see because he had a healing touch. "The old doctor hadn't been to a fancy college. He got his degree from a mail-order school. But he had a healing hand. People would come from miles around to be cured. And the old doctor would go to those who couldn't come to him. People kind of grew to think that the old man would never die. He became an institution." By this time, Granddaddy's music in his throat would be getting stronger and stronger. "One day, people came to see the old doctor. But he wasn't there. There was a new shingle over his door." Granddaddy would pause here, to let the members move to the edge of their seats. "That sign said . . ." his voice would quaver and tremble. "That sign said . . . that sign said STILL IN BUSINESS JUST MOVED UPSTAIRS!" People fanned and shouted and joined the church in droves.

One Sunday, when I was a little girl, after such a story, Granddaddy took a flying leap off the pulpit. Mama Lillian and Mrs. Auretha English in the choir stand almost fainted. Bigmama missed her cue to start playing his song at the organ. As the tails of his flock tail coat settled around him (looking like the wings of a great swooping bird coming to rest), Granddaddy sang one of his favorite "ditties" (familiar tunes accompanied by foot patting and hand slapping, with or without instrumental accompaniment), "Amazing Grace."

The members were ecstatic. Some shouted, some swooned, and many visitors joined the church. And Granddaddy was building a foundation, a legacy to leave his sons.

Granddaddy's act was hard to follow, but his sons were up to the challenge. They'd enjoyed their young manhood, their times of studying and all types of part-time jobs, and their friendships with fellows of their circles and fellows from the neighborhood. Daddy and Uncle M.L. never learned to be bourgeois. They enjoyed the lives of high social standing, the travels, the private schooling, and the middle-class girls.

But M.L. and A.D. never lost the common touch. They were just as at home in the pool halls on Auburn Avenue (where they often enjoyed a cigarette and a beer with their friends), as they were in the halls of Morehouse (and Harvard for Uncle M.L.). They were ready to roll all of their young life experiences into ministerial channels.

They knew how to give a good whoop, sing a good song, and call a good text. They even made little jokes about who could whoop the best—which could write the best sermons. Uncle M.L. would say, "Aw man, just pick a topic. Once you've heard one good sermon, you heard them all. Just a little practice and a little creativity could make any topic your own."

They just needed a little nudging. Daddy and Uncle M.L. didn't want to think that they had to preach just because

Granddaddy wanted them to. After all, there were other things they could do. Daddy was a pretty good refrigerator salesman. In a few years, he could own his own store or something.

And Uncle M.L. performed remarkably well in school; he was quite a scholar and orator. He could be another Benjamin Mays or something. (Heaven forbid. Granddaddy loved and admired Bennie Mays as mentor and friend. He even took Bigmama's small hints and comments about thinking Mays was so handsome and polished in his stride. But his sons were going to be preachers, after him!)

Uncle M. L. took a church in Montgomery, Alabama, in the mid-1950s shortly after he married Aunt Coretta. For a short while, it looked like Uncle M.L. was falling into his Daddy's mold as required.

Daddy was little more reluctant, being somewhat rebellious and resentful of the fact that his life was being programmed. He did finish Morehouse, where he was also a swimming champion. The thing is, Daddy wanted to be a businessman, not a preacher. Preaching was okay for M.L.—after all, he was the old man's namesake. But Daddy meant to plan his own life.

But, as has been said before, Granddaddy was a strong man, and Daddy succumbed to pressures, and took his first church in Newnan, Georgia, in the late 1950s.

For a while, Granddaddy was happy. He had two sons as preachers, who could come and be his co-pastors, and finally take over as pastors of Ebenezer when he went to take his final rest.

But God and history had other things in mind. In Montgomery, Rosa Parks refused to give up her seat on a bus. The civil rights movement began, and Uncle M.L. and Daddy were no longer just preachers. They were religious civil rights leaders. There are so many analogies concerning the parallels of their lives. Uncle M.L.'s home was bombed; Daddy's home was bombed. Uncle M.L. went to jail, Daddy went to jail. Uncle M.L.'s life was threatened, along with his family's; Daddy's life and his family were threatened as well.

I remember Hosea Williams talking about the Selma March, and how Daddy faced the beating with bravery and reminded them of his brother's message of love and non-violence. So often, Daddy would quote his brother, his father, and the Bible in days of violence, unrest, and uncertainty. Daddy was very close to his brother Martin. He was often at his side at marches and meetings.

When Uncle M.L.'s home was bombed in Montgomery, he and his family moved to Atlanta not long after. Somehow, the two brothers found time to be together, and to bring their families together. We were always very close in those days. In Atlanta, Uncle M.L. agreed to serve as co-pastor at Ebenezer, but he was not often in town. He was usually in jail, or being stabbed or being beaten with billy clubs and snapped at by dogs when he wasn't leading marches or sitting in at lunch counters. Granddaddy never could quite understand why Uncle M.L. couldn't leave the dangers of the movement behind—and come home to preach.

When Uncle M.L. was at home, he was a good preacher, though. He could preach and sing too (he loved the song, "Precious Lord"). One of his favorite texts was Matthew 5:44: Love your enemies. His most famous "Mountaintop" sermon, which stirred the soul of the world, was taken from Deuteronomy 32:48-52 in the Bible—the story where God allowed Moses to see the Promised Land before he died.

When Uncle M.L. preached his most famous "Mountaintop" sermon, people didn't really get the analogy, at first. They thought he was talking about God and Moses. But he was really talking about God and himself. God took Uncle M.L. to the mountaintop. "I may not get there with you, but I want you to know today that I've seen the Promised Land! Mine eyes have seen the glory of the coming of the Lord!" Uncle M.L.'s eyes glowed with the light of God's power. People were inspired. God had taken Dr. King to the mountaintop; He'd shown him the Promised Land. People cried, their hearts swelled, they felt the glory of God.

"Here comes the dreamer, let us slay him and we shall slay the dream." This story in the Bible proved that dreams don't die. Uncle M.L. died, but his legacy continued. Granddaddy's legacy was to continue too.

After Uncle M.L. died, Daddy came to Ebenezer as co-pastor. He'd had a church in Birmingham during the heart of the movement there (our house was bombed in 1963). After Birmingham, Daddy took a church in Louisville, Kentucky, where he preached and led the open housing movement. We came back to Atlanta when Uncle M.L. died, so Daddy could help Granddaddy with Ebenezer.

Daddy was a good preacher too, and he knew the power and Glory of God. One of his favorite stories was about Jesus and the disciples as they embarked on a journey at sea—"Oh yea of little faith," Matthew 8:26.

Daddy could be so descriptive with the story—about how Jesus was asleep and the disciples woke him up. "Can't you just see him? The man was tired; he'd been out casting out demons, helping the blind to see, the lame to walk. Raising the dead. And he just wanted a little rest." Daddy would slump a little here for effect. "But what did the disciples do? A little storm blew up. You know about storms. The winds and waves of life can scare you; make you want to lose your cool. Yell at your wife, burn your husband's dinner. Even make you take a drink, sometimes." (Daddy sure knew about that.) By now the church was full of Amens. Daddy would switch over to Mark 5:39. "The faithless men needed only to call on the power of God to still the storms, but they had little faith. They were scared. They wanted to call on somebody who they could see. So they woke Jesus up. I can see him now, waking up and seeing the elements crashing all around the little boat—wondering if that was all they were worried about. 'PEACE, BE STILL.' Then I can see Jesus going back to sleep as the disciples glory in the miracle of the quiet waves. Jesus can quiet life's storms." Daddy would whoop to the shouting members and bring the congregation and new members home to the music, "Peace Be Still."

Granddaddy had the satisfaction of knowing that he'd raised two fine preachers. They didn't live long enough to fulfill his legacy. They both died as a result of the civil rights movement. And Granddaddy was left alone, with Ebenezer again, with no son to pass it on to.

Bigmama convinced Granddaddy that he had to retire because he was getting up in years. I don't think age was bothering Granddaddy as much as the crushing loss of his son. But, Granddaddy succumbed, and asked his board of trustees and deacons to call a co-pastor.

They called Reverend Otis Moss, a wonderfully spirited minister from Ohio. Moss was a close family friend, too, and Granddaddy and Bigmama were sure that the transition would be a smooth one.

Reverend Moss stayed six months, and found that he missed his congregation in Ohio and that Ebenezer missed being pastured by Reverend King. Moss gave the congregation back to Granddaddy and went back home.

Bigmama wanted Granddaddy to try again. The church called Dr. Joseph L. Roberts, Jr. Granddaddy decided to retire, rather than share the pulpit. Roberts was to come in 1975. Bigmama liked Dr. Roberts and was looking forward to working with him. But she was shot at the organ, playing "The Lord's Prayer," before Roberts was ever installed.

This was another crushing blow for Granddaddy. No sons to preach, no wife to play the organ. He let Roberts have Ebenezer—Granddaddy attended services fewer than six Sundays every year until he died.

But Granddaddy never stopped loving Ebenezer. He kept close contact with the members—they never stopped calling and visiting him. Ernestine Kelsey would bake him a coconut cake every year for his birthday. Mrs. Jefferson would send fresh rabbits for Mrs. Walker (church member and housekeeper) to cook. Deacon George Howell was always available to drive, as were Deborah and Rose Sturgis. Deacon Sims and Deacon Horton would do anything for Granddaddy. So would Reverend Fred Bennett (anytime, day or night). Yolanda and Ada Gordon made sure he had fresh fish often. Reverend Smith brought vegetables. Then there were Louis and Sarah Reed, and Jethro and Aretha English. I must stop the list here for lack of time and space.

For several years, Granddaddy still kept office hours at the church to attend to correspondence, calls, and the like.

Mama Lillian, Granddaddy's secretary of forty-seven years, retired when Granddaddy did. The church gave her a beautiful retirement dinner, "I Remember Lillian."

When Granddaddy decided to continue office hours as pastor emeritus, no funds were provided for a secretarial replacement. Granddaddy paid a church member to do the tasks. She would tease Granddaddy about chasing her around the desk during dictation. I think it was the other way around, with her flattering Granddaddy, just to boost his ego. As were most of his members, she was devoted to Granddaddy, who had always been a father figure for her. Granddaddy paid her from his personal funds, to type his sermons and his letters.

I also thought something should have been done to keep Granddaddy from climbing so many stairs to his office. Granddaddy's arthritis and knee problems were getting progressively worse, and climbing nearly thirty concrete steps two or three times a day wasn't as easy as it had been in younger days. Uncle Isaac always said that Granddaddy needed the exercise, because the doctors wanted him to remain active. I think the sedate walk around the block with Janice or pretty neighbors Yolanda, Yvonne, and Judy Swells was much more enjoyable for him. Granddaddy would have enjoyed a little elevator chair like the one he'd ride in up to the sanctuary on Sundays.

Granddaddy was also concerned about his grandsons Derek and Vernon getting positions in churches. Derek had a degree from Morehouse, and a master's in theology from Colgate Rochester. Vernon was coming out of Morehouse. Tim McDonald retired as assistant pastor of Ebenezer, but two other people were called to share the assistant pastorship. Granddaddy's secret dream of seeing his blood in Ebenezer's pulpit was not to be realized, at least not now.

A year before Granddaddy died, Dr. Roberts and the board of trustees presented a building plan to the church members. (The church can't always accommodate the large crowds that flock in on Sundays to worship at the place where Dr. Martin Luther King, Jr., and Sr. once preached. History draws visitors.) They wanted to build a large edifice on the property near the existing building. The new building, "The New Horizons Sanctuary," is right across the street from the "Heritage" building today.

Back then, I felt that people would not flock to the new building as they did to Ebenezer. They came to the old church because they were looking for history. And I knew that it would break Granddaddy's heart to see his church turned into a museum (Heritage Hall was being used for weddings and funerals.)

But, Granddaddy had something to look forward to. Although his church might become obsolete, his sons were dead, his wife was gone—he had two grandsons who could whoop and sing like their Daddy, and could bring in the fold just as Granddaddy could.

Derek and Vernon joke just as Daddy and Uncle M.L. used to. They compare each other's tapes, to see who can whoop the loudest. They have their preaching contests, and they use a couple of stories that Granddaddy passed on to his sons and from the sons to the grandsons.

One goes like this, "I used to cry because I had no shoes, until I met a man who had no feet. Glory to God, thank God for what we have left."

The other story is about people who think they're too good to shout, and how a man and his mule could be a good example for them to follow. Somehow, Granddaddy never completely got away from mules. "There was a man who would go around shouting. He was never ashamed of the gospel. People would see him on the street and say 'Fool! What you got to shout about? Your wife is dead, your house is burned down, and your children don't know you. All you got left is that dumb old mule. And yet, you go around praising God.' The man would look, and start telling them about how he had food to eat, clothes to wear, the sun, the moon, and the sky. He got so happy. 'Let me tell you about Jesus. Hold my mule, I'm going to shout right now!'"

Granddaddy, Daddy, and Uncle M.L. loved to tell about Jesus. Derek and Vernon have picked up the legacy. Martin hasn't accepted the call yet, but he can preach too, which he proved at Granddaddy's memorial service. And Dexter has a way with words. And my children and grandchild show signs of having the gift of ministry. Before Granddaddy died, I left Ebenezer, searching for a deeper experience with the Holy Spirit. Since then, I have accepted the call of the evangelist and prophet, a road less traveled in our family.

So, Granddaddy went to sleep knowing that his dream was still alive, his legacy continues—he's still in business, just moved upstairs.

CHAPTER THREE

At the beginning of the 1960s, it looked like Granddaddy's plans for his dynasty were going to be realized. Daddy was soon to accept a pulpit in Birmingham. Uncle M.L. was home as co-pastor of Ebenezer. Aunt Christine was getting married. Granddaddy and Bigmama were moving into their new home (having been forced away from downtown by urban renewal). There was just one little problem, the civil rights movement.

Aunt Christine felt the effects of her brother's crusade for freedom in a way my brothers, my sister, and I could sympathize with. Uncle M.L. and Daddy were encouraging everyone in their congregations not to buy from segregated stores. This was one of the first "Black Christmas" holidays, with a moratorium on shopping.

Of course, I had always been a bit different about Christmas. When I was a little girl, about three or four, Mama says, I kept asking Daddy if there really was a Santa Claus. I didn't believe it. How was a jolly, fat, white man going to climb down our chimney? It was too little. Then too, even though we could talk with someone dressed up in a red and white suit, did that really mean he could produce everything that I was asking for? Well, the night before Christmas, Daddy and Mama were invited to a party.

They put us to bed early, with our neighbor downstairs to baby sit. Daddy told Mama, "Let's get the things put out before we go." I had been playing sleep, crawled out of bed on my belly, quiet as a mouse, to the living room behind the big chair. When Daddy pulled out the big bag of toys, I jumped out from behind the chair and said, "Ah ha, see! I told you there's no Santa Claus." Daddy was outdone. Mama was hiding a giggle behind her hands. Daddy said, "Oh hell. Just leave them out to play with. They know anyway."

So traditional Christmases didn't mean the same to me. That didn't mean that I didn't expect presents every year, though. So the "Black Christmases" and "Black Easters" (no new dresses for girls and suits for boys) were a major challenge.

That first Black Christmas meant no Christmas toys for us, and no wedding gown for Aunt Christine.

Aunt Chris had finally surprised everyone with an announcement of marriage. Her girlfriends and interested observers had written her off as an old maid, since most of the men in Atlanta's social circles had been scared off by Granddaddy, Daddy, or Uncle M.L. Granddaddy seemed hellbent on approving a preacher or nobody for Aunt Chris.

The interesting thing was Aunt Chris didn't seem perturbed at all about her lack of a husband. She was young (in her late twenties), very attractive, and she had a career that she enjoyed (teaching). She enjoyed sewing, reading, traveling—her life was interesting enough not to worry about finding a man for the sake of having one.

Then, a young soldier, Isaac Newton Farris, came to town. He found a job at *The Atlanta Daily World* newspaper. He met a friend, Lewis Reed, who invited him to worship at the church where he was a member—Ebenezer Baptist Church. Isaac went and enjoyed the service. A few weeks later, Reed invited Isaac to see him marry Sarah Atwater (who would later become the second secretary for the church). After the wedding ceremony, there was a dinner-reception at Lillian Watkins' house, across the street. Isaac was invited, and he went alone.

When Isaac walked in the room, a sparkling, laughing young woman immediately caught his eyes across the room. He sought out Reed and pulled him away from his young bride. "Who is that?" Reed, anxious to get back to Sarah, looked to where Isaac's eyes were glued on Christine. "Oh, that? That's Christine King, the pastor's daughter."

Christine was not alone. Her escort for the evening was a young minister (who met her Daddy's approval), Reverend Porter. Porter (who loved food) smelled chicken and made the biggest mistake of his life, leaving Christine alone. Porter headed for the kitchen. Isaac headed for Christine.

Not many days later, Aunt Christine brought Uncle Isaac home to meet Bigmama and Granddaddy. I thought he was the most handsome man alive. (I was ready to take the title away from Granddaddy.) He was about as tall as my Daddy, had gray eyes that would turn blue if he was near the sky, and green if he was near our green living room carpet. His hair was short, and he had a pretty head—and pretty teeth, and light brown skin.

Aunt Christine thought Uncle Isaac was handsome, too. You could tell by the way Aunt Chris proudly held on to Uncle Isaac's arm, that she was enjoying her "beau." And Bigmama seemed to be rather taken with him too. Granddaddy was not so quick to make his observations known. He asked Uncle Isaac a lot of questions, but he didn't tell Aunt Chris not to see him again. (As the years went on, Granddaddy let us know how much he really respected Uncle Isaac. When business decisions needed to be made, Granddaddy would call on Isaac. I think Granddaddy saw himself as a young man in Uncle Isaac. He saw that Uncle Isaac, a young man from a Missouri farming town, wanted a society wife, and that he had career objectives. And Granddaddy could relate to that.)

A wedding date was set for late summer. A courtship and engagement followed that would take Atlanta society by storm. Aunt Chris had parties and showers galore.

Uncle M.L. discovered an irritating skin disorder during this time. He and Daddy both had very sensitive skin. They had tried every shaving technique available, trying to find a way to shave without getting razor bumps and mild skin irritations. They finally resorted to "Magic Shave," a depilatory powder that, when mixed with water, smelled like rotten eggs. They used the product with some success

Right before Aunt Christine's wedding, Uncle M.L. broke out in a skin rash that Bigmama felt might be related to the "Magic Shave." It was then that she told me about the time Uncle M.L. went to a doctor who treated a dark, splotchy skin rash with a cream. Much to Uncle M.L.'s annoyance and Bigmama's dismay, the doctor said that he could not change the color of the spots, but he could make his face darker to match them. Uncle M.L. was so mad that he wanted to sue the doctor. (The man of peace was human, after all.) But he began to calm down as the dark spots began to fade. Bigmama was worried that Uncle M.L's dark rash would reappear, but the little irritation cleared up just before the wedding.

In the middle of Aunt Christine's wedding preparations came Uncle M.L.'s announcement about the store boycotts. People were not to shop at segregated stores.

There would be no problem for the bridesmaid's dresses. Aunt Chris was making them. But her beautiful wedding gown was on order from Rich's. What was to be done? The boycott could not be broken; there were too many people in the picket line who knew her face and Bigmama's.

Finally, Bigmama made a decision. Since the dress had been paid for prior to the boycotts, it could still be used—it would be picked up by Bigmama's close friend who worked for the store. Aunt Chris and Bigmama were on pins and needles. The lady was late getting back from downtown. When she arrived, she explained that she had gotten the dress from the bridal department, taken it to the restroom, squeezed into a stall, rolled the lovely garment into a small bundle, and jammed it into a shopping bag.

The dress arrived while Uncle M.L. and Daddy were out of town. The last hurdle had been jumped. The wedding was on. Aunt Christine had eight bridesmaids and two junior bridesmaids, my friend Phyllis Norwood and me. (We were too young for stockings and it was too hot for tights. So we went barelegged. But our dresses were like the grown-ups'. We felt like grown-ups too. I even forgot to be self-conscious about being fat for that day.)

My cousin Yolanda and my sister Darlene were flower girls. Aunt Coretta (just able to squeeze into her dress because she was five months pregnant with Dexter) was the matron-of-honor. Mother couldn't be an attendant because she was expecting, too (Vernon was coming), and Mama was too big to fit into a dress. Daddy dressed her up real pretty, and she was escorted to her seat on the front row, looking like a big, pretty doll.

Granddaddy proudly gave Aunt Christine away, as a crowded church looked on. Bigmama sniffled as Daddy and Uncle M.L. officiated at their sister's wedding.

The wedding photo album was beautiful. Bigmama would later receive as a gift from a well-known black female artist. Constance E. Nelson (who also presented the church with a beautiful portrait of Uncle M.L.) gave a picture of Aunt Chris in her wedding gown. It was reproduced in portrait size and hung in the living room of the house.

So the city girl had married a man from a Missouri farming town. The happy couple went on a honeymoon to Nassau, Bahamas, and returned home to live with Bigmama and Granddaddy until their home was ready.

By now, Daddy and Uncle M.L. were discovering that they had inherited their father's delicate stomachs. Dad would always complain about gas pains and queasy feelings in his stomach. Uncle M.L. developed nervous hiccups and a tendency toward indigestion. Poor Daddy got ulcers, and was forced to eat baby food from time to time. Deprived of the rich foods he enjoyed regularly, Daddy became as grouchy as a bear.

To top it all off, I was leaving Granddaddy and Bigmama to go and live with Daddy and Mama in Birmingham. Daddy and I got off to a head-knocking start. Every time he told me to do something, I would say, "I don't have to and if you try to make me, I'll tell Granddaddy." Daddy would counter, "Go ahead, just don't call him on my telephone."

I began to realize just how far away Granddaddy really was. I didn't learn not to play Granddaddy against Daddy, though. If I wanted Daddy to buy me something, and he wouldn't, I'd always say, "That's okay. My Granddaddy will buy it." And when Granddaddy would call, I'd ask for whatever I wanted, and it would soon arrive in the mail.

This didn't help Daddy's and Granddaddy's relationship too much, either. Since birth, Daddy had been trying to meet Granddaddy's approval, to make up for not being firstborn. Daddy always felt second best in Granddaddy's eyes. I don't think

Granddaddy was conscious in creating these feelings in Daddy. Granddaddy just had a way of being obsessed with carrying on the name and legacy of his family, and recognized the firstborn son of each family branch as the torchbearer.

(This same obsession was carried over to Martin as firstborn of M.L. and Al as firstborn of A.D. Dexter, Derek, and Vernon somehow always seemed to be aware of the elevation of their firstborn brothers in Granddaddy's eyes. Isaac, Jr., and Jarrett felt the effects of Granddaddy's obsession even more. Granddaddy was patriarch of their family; his name was King. They had Granddaddy's blood, but they did not carry his name. They bore the burdens of being part of the King family—the tragedies, the public criticism—but for Isaac, Jr., and Jarrett, removed from the base of their fathers' families, settled in Atlanta, under Granddaddy, they felt that life had somehow treated them unfairly, by taking away their birthrights by giving them names other than King. The fame and infamy attached to the name often eluded them.)

So now, Daddy was playing catch-up. He was the first to marry from his dad's family. Now, he would be the first to bring a son to the lineage in the next generation. He would prove himself. He was going to pull his family together, and prove to his daddy how successful he could be as a father and a pastor of a large congregation.

I wasn't going to make it easy. I would always fight with Daddy. I was rebellious, angry, confused. Why had I been uprooted not once, but twice? As a baby, I had been taken from the arms of my mother—the roof of my father—and given to my grandparents. Now, a few years later, I was being taken from my grandparents, and returned to my father's house.

I wasn't quite returned to my mother's arms. I was still a little angry with Mama, for giving me away. And now that I was living with her, I was angry with her for not caring that Bigmama and Granddaddy had let me grow to be a big, fat pig. Mama wasn't fat. She was slim and pretty. Everybody said so.

My sister Darlene wasn't fat, either. Although we had the same nose and face structure, somehow, Darlene was prettier. She and Mama had a special bond. Maybe it was because Darlene had been burned when she was two. Mother had turned on Darlene's bathwater in the bathroom of the old Williams family house on Auburn. She left Darlene in the bathroom, while she ran downstairs to the clothesline for a few minutes. She heard a scream, "I am hot, Mommy," and so she came running back. Darlene, her sash from her frilly dress having caught fire in the space heater next to the tub, was in flames.

Mama said she ran for a blanket, picked Darlene up, and rolled her up in the blanket. After smothering out the flames, Mama covered Darlene with Vaseline. Then Mama called the ambulance—when the attendants arrived a few short minutes later, they said Mama's quick thinking had saved Darlene's life. Darlene recovered after several weeks in Grady's burn unit. She had skin grafts for her back that had suffered third-degree burns. Darlene never recovered from the emotional trauma of the burns or the scars. (My brothers, with the cruelty of little children, didn't help. They used to call her "burnt-up bacon.")

Darlene and Mama were very close, and remained so until Darlene died, in a jogging incident, years later. I was jealous of their relationship, so I wouldn't allow myself to become too close to either of them. I missed out on the years of female friendship that so many women cherish. My little sister and mother were strangers who just happened to live in the same house with me.

I wasn't so friendly with my brothers, either. My little brother Derek liked to tease me about being fat. One morning, Mama Lillian (who had come to help us make the move to Birmingham) was cooking pancakes. Derek was in the kitchen eating. I smelled the food cooking, and went looking for my plate. Derek heard me coming and smiled. He really wanted me to be a playmate. I was rather surly. He jumped up and started running toward me down the hall. I bristled up, making my body look like a little tank. Derek ran into me, then bounced onto the floor and went sliding on his behind all the way back down the hall. He didn't try to make friends again, too soon.

I liked to play with baby Vernon, though, pulling his toes, sniffing his baby smell. Vernon was the only one not old enough to tease me about being fat. I was ten when he was born, and sort of felt like I was his protector.

I missed my protector. Where was my Granddaddy, who would always hear my problems and fill my every need?

During this time, Daddy tried his hand at old-fashioned discipline. Following one of my rebellious outbursts against his policy of clean rooms (I didn't like to clean my room. I was used to having someone clean up after me when I lived with Granddaddy. I was just plain lazy), Daddy decided to whip me.

I was so fat and husky, that I could wiggle away from his grasp. Daddy decided to hold me down with a kitchen stool. In the kitchen, Daddy told me to lie face down. He put the stool over my back, sat down, and proceeded to wail into me with his strap. After about ten licks, I decided that I'd had enough. I bunched my shoulder muscles. Mama was at the stove; she turned her head so that Daddy wouldn't see her laugh. I heard Mama giggle just as I bristled up, knocking Daddy from the stool. He was too amazed to continue the whipping. "I'll be damned."

Just as I was at what I thought was my lowest, Daddy had another idea. Maybe a boarding school would give me the discipline that I needed. He, Uncle M.L., and Aunt Chris had gone to boarding school, and now so would I.

Daddy consulted with Bigmama, and they came up with Boggs Academy, in Keysville, Georgia. I wasn't too thrilled with the idea of going away to yet another environment, but I really had no choice. Since I had to go, I figured out a way to get revenge on Daddy. I took all of his Johnny Mathis and Nat King Cole record collection. I didn't get to enjoy them, though (they were my favorites, too). Somebody stole them from my room.

At Boggs, I learned to sew and cook in home economics. I learned about all the religions of the world, which helped me to be a skeptic of my own religious heritage. After all, if God loved everybody, I reasoned, wasn't there religion beyond the Baptist faith?

Daddy and Granddaddy weren't too pleased with the letters I'd write home regarding my new religious discoveries. Granddaddy at that time was hung up on having everybody be a good Baptist. And Daddy was hung up on being everything Granddaddy thought he should be.

I wasn't pleased with Boggs. I'd caught an intestinal pneumonia bug and was dropping pounds (a blessing in disguise). My roommate Donna and I didn't always get along because she was as neat as a pin and I was as sloppy as a hog. I know I sound hard on myself, but that's how it was.

I missed home. I was ready for Birmingham or Atlanta (at that point, I didn't care which), and I couldn't get used to the country sounds of cows, birds close by outside, and roaches as big as my hand climbing on the inside of the walls.

When I went home for Christmas break, I'd lost twenty pounds. Mama was pleased. Daddy and Granddaddy didn't notice the weight loss as much as they noticed my espousing from religion class. I was full of questions, thought I knew all of the answers in the universe. Bigmama (she and Granddaddy came to Birmingham for a Christmas visit) didn't have too much to say. She was too busy checking out Mama's excellent housekeeping to notice me much. Bigmama was a generous mother-in-law, and enjoyed sharing with her daughter and daughters-in-law. Having been an only child, she also enjoyed her growing family. She became a stickler for family portraits, and was responsible for us sitting for family portraits over the years. All in all, it was a season to remember.

We didn't get many presents that year, either. The stores were still being boycotted. We had family dinners, carols and a tree, and we enjoyed the things Bigmama and Granddaddy had brought with them. I was mad because Al and Derek tore the head off the only doll I'd received. They took the doll for playing baseball, using the head for the ball and body for the bat. (Years later, Cliff and I got in the biggest argument when he wouldn't let me get a doll during a vacation to Acapulco. I wanted the doll to place on my bed. He said a grown woman didn't need dolls, that they had enough of dolls when they were girls. I didn't get to play with dolls when I was a girl.)

Soon, Christmas break was over. Bigmama and Granddaddy went back to Atlanta. I went back to Boggs. By spring break, I'd lost fifteen more pounds. I didn't go home because I wanted to visit a friend. By the time Mama and Daddy saw me at the end of the quarter, I'd lost a total of fifty pounds. For the first time in years, I wasn't fat. I wasn't happy, either. I remember during my last semester at Boggs, I had an encounter with God. I was lying in my bed, alone in my room. I heard an audible, deep voice ask, "Are you ready to die yet?" Admittedly, I was morose and sad, and didn't think I had anything to live for. Yet, I knew that there was more ahead of me in life. I remember, to this day, answering, "No. I want to have children." That was a turning point for me. I finally got my parents to hear me. Mama and Daddy let me leave Boggs. I didn't have to return.

In Birmingham, the next year, 1963, I was learning to socialize with other children. I'd never been around many children until my experience at Boggs, so for the most part, accustomed to spending my time with adults and saying and doing whatever I pleased. Now, I was making friends. Two girls. Jocelyn Lewis and Yoland Beard really seemed to like me. At age twelve, I was ready for spin-the-bottle, if that's what it took to be part of the group, but I wasn't so sure that I liked the idea of some boy putting his mouth on mine.

Just as I was learning to play games, dance, and make friends, strange things began to happen. A man started following me home from school. He was very strange-looking, and as I walked home each day, for three days, he was just across the street, walking as fast or as slow as I did. On the third day, he started to cross the street. I took off running and rushed home to tell Mama. She called Daddy. And Daddy called "Ace" his friend, Reverend Bennett.

Reverend Fred C. Bennett was a rugged-looking man who had short wavy hair, and skin that looked like he never wore lotion. He had a pretty smile, though, and Daddy really liked him. He'd brought Bennett home for dinner one day, and said to Mama, "Look Neenie, I found this man. I like him. He's going to be my Ace." Daddy and Bennett called each other "Ace" from that day on; Bennett became a major field marshal and security man for Uncle M.L. and Daddy in the movement.

Bennett was so good at security that Daddy felt safer with him than with the Birmingham City policemen. Daddy asked Bennett to tail me and see what was going on with the man who I said was following me.

On the fourth day, the man followed me again. Bennett jumped out from behind a bush and caught him. The man had a knife. Bennett took the knife. I never saw the man again after that day, but Bennett and I became good friends. He'd saved my life. I had a new defender.

Not long after that incident, our house was bombed, along with several other homes and a hotel owned by A.G. Gaston, a civil rights leader of the community. Soon after, so was a church, killing some little girls that I went to school with.

There are many accounts of the bombing of our home. My friend, investigative reporter Jeff Prugh, has compiled my favorite account. It follows:

SATURDAY, MAY 11, 1963. It was a typically springtime afternoon, the eve of Mother's Day. Birds chirped, flowers bloomed, children played in the streets.

In a sense, Birmingham breathed huge sighs of relief, barely 24 hours after city hall grudgingly agreed to desegregate certain public accommodations if the coalition of activists led by Martin Luther King, Jr., Ralph Abernathy, and A.D. King, among others, would call off their protests in the streets.

For six weeks, with seemingly the whole world watching, Birmingham had turned into a cauldron seething with hate and violence embodied in TV images of Commissioner Eugene "Bull" Connor's police turning firehoses and attack dogs on black citizens. As protests mounted, so did arrests—with hundreds of marchers, including countless schoolchildren and, briefly, Martin and Ralph Abernathy, filling the city's jails.

The tide of public sentiment nationwide had begun to tilt in favor of the movement, but Birmingham—a blue-collar town controlled from Pittsburgh by U. S. Steel, and where steel mills belched plumes of smoke—remained stuck in a time warp. Old values didn't go quietly. Hard feelings abounded in a city better known for heat than light. A combustible changeover in the city's form of government—which would soon force "Bull" Connor and others out of power—did nothing to soften tensions of the moment. It seemed to pour kerosene on a smoldering fire.

Birmingham had not yet earned its derisive nickname, "Bombingham." That was about to change.

IN A GRASSY field owned by the steel mill, Alveda and Alfred lay on their backs, gazing skyward at the blue kite they flew, its white tail serpentining in the breeze. Alveda would one day recall how delightfully strange it felt to be alive on this day. For the moment, the cacophony of death threats and angry phone calls to A.D. King's family house in Ensley, a community a few miles west of downtown Birmingham, seemed galaxies away.

A.D. King continued planning and strategizing, as usual. Naomi went on a routine shopping foray, picking up special tidbits for her Mother's Day meal. Their smaller children played in the backyard. The housekeeper, Minnie McCloud, lived down the street. She didn't come in that day.

At about 9:00 P.M., Naomi put the children to bed. A.D. came in a bit later, had a snack, and went to bed. He didn't sleep but sat up poring over scriptures for tomorrow's sermon. In the den nearby, Alfred lay on a sofa, watching a war movie on television.

Naomi stayed up late and set the dining room table for tomorrow's dinner. At almost 11:00 P.M., she lovingly placed her fine crystal and china on the polished mahogany table covered with fine lace and linen. Behind the table, on the breakfront, china plates on tiny gold stands graced the room, glistening with painted pictures of Jesus and his mother Mary. Satisfied with her preparations, Naomi crossed into the living room and sat on the sofa.

The night seemed eerily calm, especially after so many weeks of civil unrest. Naomi stared at the picture window, a conversation piece admired by the community and parishioners who had provided the pastor and his family with a fine parsonage—a modern ranch home, on a half-acre corner lot, with a handsome front lawn and fenced-in backyard. The picture window spoke of the affluence and esteem of the young minister's family.

Then, suddenly, almost as in a tableau, the big window oddly cracked in a jagged, diagonal pattern from an upper corner. Naomi stood transfixed, her ears all but assaulted by the loud war film that her 10-year-old son, Al, watched in the den. "I don't remember hearing a sound in the front room—just seeing the window crack," she recalls. "It was so strange."

A.D. strode into the front room, telling Naomi, "It's too quiet. Something doesn't seem right." But in a split-second, he, too, observed the buckling window. Sensing danger, he hastily gathered Naomi in his arms and swept her out of the front room.

Just as they reached the den, a frighteningly massive explosion blew out the front wall of the house, picture window and all, spraying shards of glass and debris. "We looked back, and half our house was gone," Naomi remembers. "There was a big, dark, gaping hole where our lives had been."

Alveda, then 12, recalls that the soundtrack of exploding bombs in the war movie had kept her half-awake. "Suddenly I heard Daddy shouting, 'Get out! It's a bomb!'" she said. "I jumped up, grabbed my robe, a navy and white Christmas gift from my Bigmama (her grandmother, Mama King), and began running. Darlene was in the bed sleeping. Daddy yelled for Derek, Mama grabbed Vernon and we all headed out the back door through the garage." As the family began climbing over the back fence, a chubby Alveda struggled mightily to escape, only for her bathrobe to snag—a moment she savors lightheartedly now, more than 40 years removed from the terror and chaos of that Saturday night.

A few minutes later, Naomi returned to the front of the house and surveyed the devastation. A Birmingham police car drove up before anyone else arrived, she said, and a solitary officer got out of the car. He walked toward Naomi and said nothing, she remembers. "He didn't ask if anyone was hurt," she said. "He didn't ask if we were okay. I asked him, 'What are you doing?' He was kicking about in the debris with his toe. He didn't answer—he just kept kicking and searching."

As the officer walked toward the house, Naomi said to him, "If you're going in, I'm going in, because I don't know what you will do." She said she followed him inside, and again, he said nothing, just kicking the debris with his toe.

In the street outside, pandemonium erupted. Neighbors alighted from their houses. More police cars arrived. There were whites who had no other reason to cruise through a black neighborhood at that hour of night, driving by, heckling, jeering, spewing hateful threats. Some in the crowd picked up rocks and boulders from the debris and hurled them at the cars, breaking windows. Police, wielding nightsticks, pushed through the crowd.

An officer brandished a club in Alveda's face, yelling, "Get back to your house!"

At that instant, A.D clasped the officer's arm forcefully and pulled it back. "If you hit her, you'll draw back a nub!" A.D. screamed, using slang for threatening to cut off the officer's arm. As Alveda recalls, "That wasn't so nonviolent, but I guess he could be allowed to be upset just then."

A.D. King and his family didn't yet know it, but the black-owned A.G. Gaston Motel, the downtown headquarters for Martin Luther King, Jr., and his brain trust during the Birmingham campaign, had been bombed, too. Some theorized that whoever planted the bombs that night were looking for Martin, who stayed either at the motel or at A.D.'s house when he visited Birmingham. As it turned out, one bomb gutted the Gaston Motel's Room 30, where Martin had stayed—but too late. Martin had returned home to Atlanta for the weekend, eluding what he would write in his memoirs was an attempt to assassinate him.

The next day, Mother's Day, President John F. Kennedy appealed for calm and ordered 3,000 troops to the outskirts of Birmingham on stand-by alert. In September, the president would speak out again in the wake of the most infamous of all Birmingham bombings—one that killed four black schoolgirls on a Sunday morning at the Sixteenth Street Baptist Church, an explosion heard 'round the world.

Meanwhile, Naomi and A.D. King returned on Mother's Day to the shambles of what was their house, accompanied by Alveda. A.D. quietly walked the nearby streets, asking neighbors if they'd seen anything suspicious. In the dining room, where the table Naomi had set the night before lay in ruins, she observed in the debris the reproduction of the face of Jesus on a plate that had shattered. "I picked it up," she recalls. "His wonderful face was intact."

Naomi searched for the other pieces and put them away. She would one day glue the plate back together.

OUT OF THE ashes of the bombing at A. D. King's residence would emerge one of the most compelling—but least told—stories of America's civil rights era, all but left for dead in history's graveyard. It is a story of our police, courts, and press—how they were cozy with each other, but not necessarily with the people of Birmingham, which Martin Luther King, Jr., in 1963 had denounced as "the most segregated big city in America."

It's a story, too, of two Americans—one black, one white—sons of the Deep South, their lives changed irreversibly by fate. Both men would remain essentially strangers. But as their separate lives briefly cross paths, these two Americans share an unrelenting social conscience for which they would, in different ways, pay a staggering price.

One is Roosevelt Tatum, 39, black, apolitical, a laborer who had briefly attended Miles College in Birmingham and whose sudden, figurative "15 minutes of fame" would be intense, and his life sadly all too short.

The other is Dan Moore, 40, white and outwardly a cigar-chomping prototype of a Southern cop, but also a modern-day Don Quixote who, behind the scenes, would be scorned and rebuked by powerful men who, like Moore, had been sworn to uphold our laws.

About all Tatum and Moore have in common is that they are fathers and contemporaries who had served their country during World War II. Tatum toiled aboard a navy minesweeper in the Pacific; Moore lost a finger to a mortar-shell explosion while on army patrol in Germany.

Roosevelt Tatum and Dan Moore would, in their own ways, stand up and cry "foul" in pursuit of justice, only to find misery, disillusionment, betrayal by the very government they had once dutifully served while putting their own lives at risk.

SIX WEEKS AFTER the bombing of A. D. King's house, Roosevelt Tatum comes forward on June 22 to tell A.D. an extraordinary story—that while he walked home late on the night of May 11, he saw a Birmingham police vehicle that would be identified in a U.S. District Court document as car 49, stop in front of the house.

Tatum, according to a statement taken by authorities and which I would obtain 13 years later, said he stood near a streetlight not far away and saw two uniformed officers plant and throw the bombs that demolished the front of A.D. King's house and blasted a crater on the front lawn.

A.D. King picks up the phone. He calls the local office of the FBI, which sends two agents to interview Tatum. Three days later, on June 25, Tatum is flown to Washington, D.C. There, Tatum, according to a U.S. government document, repeats his story about the bombing to Rep. Emanuel Cellar, a New York Democrat who then was chairman of the House Judiciary Committee; Assistant Attorney General Burke Marshall, head of the Justice Department's Civil Rights Division, and unidentified officials of the FBI.

If what Tatum says is true, he becomes the only known eyewitness to any of the nearly 40 post–World War II bombings of Birmingham homes, businesses, and churches amid the struggle to end segregation in Alabama's largest city (population 340,000).

His statement to authorities is excerpted: "One uniformed policeman, about 5 feet 10 or 11, medium build, got out (sic) the car, walked behind the car to Rev. King's house. He walked to the front porch, at a moderate pace, stooped and placed a package at the right side of the steps . . .

"Policeman then ran back to the car, got in, (and) driver of police car tossed something out the window of the auto, which later was found to have been an explosive of some kind, approximately 2 or 3 feet from the sidewalk directly in front of the King residence.

"In about 2 to 3 seconds there was an explosion, possibly dynamite. A second explosion went off, and the uniformed policemen in car #49 had returned to the scene, as if they were investigating . . ."

In the light of hindsight, is it possible that the police officer who Naomi said arrived at the house moments after the bombing—asking no questions, but sifting the debris with his toe—was one of those two uniformed officers that Tatum said he observed? Was this officer searching for incriminating evidence and hoping to remove it from the scene?

Meanwhile, the FBI gives Tatum—having returned from Washington to Birmingham—a polygraph on July 3. His story implicating the police is not made public until August 21, the day after a bombing of the house of Arthur Shores, a black civil rights attorney. Once again, rioting against police ensued.

Local U.S. Attorney Macon Weaver issues on August 22 what he says is an "unprecedented" statement about a case under investigation. In a Birmingham News story banner headlined "'False charges' brought attack on police," Weaver says Roosevelt Tatum—whom he identifies not by name but by his race—lied, adding that after the third polygraph question, Tatum signed a statement saying he had made up the story, which Weaver said had incited the riot on the night of August 20.

(A handwritten statement obtained by me from the Justice Department through the Freedom of Information Act and purportedly signed by Tatum in handwriting that differs sharply from that in the rest of the statement, said he had gotten drunk that evening. However, nowhere in other documents obtained by me, particularly those recounting Tatum's journey to be questioned by federal authorities in Washington, is alcohol consumption by Tatum alleged or an issue in his account of the bombing.)

Tatum, in a news conference at A.D. King's house, sticks to his story. He said FBI agents "rigged" what he said was a test of the polygraph, instructing him to answer "no" to all questions, which he said related only to his children, not the bombing. When asked if he had an infant son nicknamed "Bronco," Tatum was quoted as saying, "I started to say 'yes,' but they told me to say 'no,' so I did."

High-ranking federal authorities, meanwhile, had clashed during July and August over whether to try Tatum's case in court or in the press, according to documents obtained through the Freedom of Information Act. In Birmingham, they wanted to prosecute Tatum for lying to a federal officer. But in Washington, they said that would be inappropriate since Tatum, through A.D. King, had approached the FBI, not the other way around.

One Justice Department official, however, did not object to Weaver's request for permission to tell the community that Tatum's story was "false." "If it is deemed appropriate to advise the community of the false accusation," Nathaniel E. Kossack, chief of the department's fraud section, wrote, "I would have no objection to the United States Attorney's making a statement."

It is impossible to know precisely what happened on May 11 and thereafter because some of the government's information conflicts. A document that says Tatum had been questioned on May 11 after the bombings and provided "no pertinent information" (again, there was no reference to alcohol consumption) adds that Assistant Attorney General Burke Marshall interviewed Tatum in Washington on June 25. In a telephone interview 14 years later, Marshall would tell me that he could not remember Tatum or his department's investigation of the bombing. When I advised Marshall that U.S. Attorney Weaver had told me in an interview that Marshall had approved Weaver's public statement saying Tatum's story was "false," Marshall replied, "That was sort of a jackass thing to do."

One who did remember was a black attorney who had been dispatched by Marshall's Civil Rights Division to Birmingham, there to interview Tatum. Years later, that attorney, Thelton Henderson, would tell me that he found Tatum's story believable and that he had said so in a report he wrote to his bosses in Washington, but to no avail. "I had told them something they didn't want to hear," Henderson said.

Curiously, not even the Justice Department of Attorney General Robert F. Kennedy—whose legacy would include championing social justice for minorities—could stop its runaway juggernaut in Birmingham from steamrollering toward Roosevelt Tatum.

AUGUST 28, 1963.

In Washington, D. C., on the steps of the Lincoln Memorial, Martin Luther King, Jr., delivers his landmark "I Have a Dream" speech that inspires millions: ". . . I have a dream that my four little children will one day live in a nation where they will not be judged by the color of their skin but by the content of their character." Among the crowd estimated at 250,000 that day was A.D. King, who had accompanied his brother to the nation's capital.

In Birmingham, on that very same day, hardly anyone notices that an all-white federal grand jury, in USA vs. Roosevelt Tatum, indicts Tatum for violating 18 U.S.C. 1001, making a false statement to a federal officer. Maximum penalty: a $10,000 fine and/or five years in prison. A local newspaper headline the next day: "Jury clears police of bomb charges."

Tatum surrenders voluntarily on August 30 at the U.S. Marshal's Office in Birmingham. There, according to then-Chief Deputy Marshal Dan Moore, Tatum tells a deputy he wants to talk to someone. "The deputy sent him to see me," Moore recalled. "Tatum told us his story, and we took a statement from him. I could see that he never had a chance. They wanted him out of the way."

Tatum, freed on $1,800 bond, prepares to go to trial on November 18, 1963, four days before President Kennedy's assassination in Dallas. But at the last minute, Tatum is oddly persuaded to change his "not guilty" plea to "guilty"—for reasons that his lawyer, Orzell Billingsley, Jr., would tell me years later that he could not remember.

At his sentencing, Tatum is scolded by U.S. District Judge Clarence W. Allgood—a conservative appointed by President Kennedy—and then ordered away to psychiatric evaluation. Tatum would serve about half his one-year-and-a-day sentence in federal prison in Florida. A handwritten note on a government routing slip conveys a sense of relief within the Justice Department: "This is the end of the infamous Roosevelt Tatum case."

Unable to find work upon returning to Birmingham in 1964, Tatum becomes depressed and relocates to New York, leaving behind a common-law wife and five children. He moves in with a relative and, according to friends, sinks deeper into depression and drinks heavily. He would die in 1971, at age 47.

DAN MOORE is a Purple Heart veteran of World War II who, in 1947, began a career in law enforcement. He is quiet-spoken but resolute, a family man who would become eternally idealistic about what our justice system should be, but cynical about what it is.

In 1963, Moore is chief deputy U.S. marshal for the Northern District of Alabama, headquartered in Birmingham, having earned pay raises, promotions, and citations of merit. As disbursement officer, he had complained about judges and marshals using office telephones for personal long-distance calls or cheating on expense accounts.

In June, while Roosevelt Tatum is being questioned in Washington about the bombing at A.D. King's house, Moore becomes incensed when he learns that his boss, U.S. Marshal Peyton Norville, and Judge Allgood participate in selecting the federal grand jury that would indict Tatum. In sworn testimony, Moore would say that he told a Washington-based official of the U.S. Marshals Service that his boss had bragged to him about putting his son-in-law on the grand jury.

A Justice Department examiner's report in 1964 would say, " . . . The jury box was one name short. The then-Marshal, Mr. Norville, knowing his son-in-law to be a qualified voter, wrote his name on a piece of paper and put it into the box. When the Marshal returned to his office he passed this information to the Chief (Moore) in an informal conversation . . ."

In 1964, Moore would be subpoenaed by an attorney who represented eight white supremacists and who had been tipped about Moore's allegations that U.S. Marshal Norville had told him he had placed his son-in-law on the grand jury. The eight members of the militant National States Rights Party had been indicted by the Tatum grand jury for disrupting efforts to desegregate some of Birmingham's schools.

After the attorney takes Moore's deposition alleging that the grand jury had been improperly impaneled, Moore is approached by Judge

Allgood, and, according to Moore, the judge tells him, "You've got me backed against the wall now. What the hell am I supposed to do?"

Moore to Judge Allgood, "Throw 'em all out! Dismiss all the indictments (including Tatum's)!"

Amid allegations that the grand jury was tainted, the judge drops charges against the whites—publicly citing "fundamental deficiencies" in the indictment—but the judge doesn't let Moore's testimony impugning the grand jury get in the way of the case the feds had built against Roosevelt Tatum.

Dan Moore continues to press for propriety in the federal courthouse in Birmingham. However, he becomes persona non grata. He refuses an offer of a lifetime pension of $3,971 a year ($331 monthly) if he would retire on the spot, after nearly 20 years with the U.S. Marshals Service, and claim what he says would be a bogus disability. He would describe the offer as "a crooked scheme designed to steal public money and to cover up what I knew about obstruction of justice in the Tatum grand jury."

Additionally, Moore is ordered to take psychiatric exams. Three psychiatrists find no mental illness. One describes Moore's behavior as consistent with that of someone who is "conscientious, sensitive, creative, and almost compulsively fair-minded."

Nevertheless, Moore is fired in 1969, accused of falsely alleging corruption in the federal law-enforcement system in Birmingham. Documents include harsh words from Judge Allgood, who had said he wanted Moore barred from his courtroom and was quoted as saying of Moore, "I wouldn't let him take a dog of mine out to water."

Moore's administrative appeals in quest of back pay fail after testimony about pre-1965 events is barred, thus blocking references to the Roosevelt Tatum case.

Dan Moore, like Roosevelt Tatum, does not work full-time again in Birmingham, except for a stint as a security guard. He and his wife Elizabeth, a career nursing supervisor, carry on to raise their three sons, one of whom becomes a U.S. Army helicopter pilot, another an army tank commander.

In 2001, Moore was bedridden but alert, talking at length about what he called the abuse of power and privilege in our public institutions. He remained a lifelong student of how government, law enforcement, and our press are supposed to work and where they fail us.

THE STORY ABOUT Roosevelt Tatum and events that swirled around the bombing at A.D. King's house would not likely come back from the dead had it not been for Dan Moore, whom I met in 1976, shortly after I started reporting in the South.

Dan Moore shared with me the troubles of Roosevelt Tatum even as he fought his own battles, having lost his job but never the admiration of his family or his own self-respect.

Roosevelt Tatum's closest friend, Morris "Eddie" Teasley, conceded he was skeptical when Tatum first told him his story of the bombing at A.D. King's house. "I asked him, 'Is that just a vision you got? Or a dream?'" Teasley recalled. "But Tatum said, 'No . . . this is for real. I've seen it . . . but I can't talk too much about it right now, man.'"

Teasley said Tatum told him he was forced to lie when asked if he had an infant son nicknamed "Bronco." "The boy (Tatum) knew the children's names," Teasley said. "If they said, 'Name the children,' he could have named 'em right down the line! He wouldn't have said 'no.' So, for that reason, I got to believin' some of the things he told me weren't false, see, because they tricked him on that. But why? (Pause) . . . But why?"

It was easy for me to conclude—after interviewing U.S. Attorney Weaver, Judge Allgood, and other principals who denied, lamely, that anything was improper, or those such as Assistant Attorney General Marshall who said their memory had lapsed, or others who didn't seem eager to talk—that instead of ordering our Roosevelt Tatums and Dan Moores to see psychiatrists, our government should be inviting them to lecture us on where our justice system breaks down and how it can be fixed.

Of all of my snapshot memories of this saga, perhaps the most heart-tugging occurred one morning as I sat with some of Tatum's family in the home of his aunt in Birmingham. Suddenly the front door swung open, and into the living room bounded a lean, handsome youngster in his early teens.

"Son," his mother said, "tell this man what your name is!"

He grinned and said, proudly, "Roosevelt Tatum, Jr."

Now it was clear—13 years after the government had wired up Roosevelt Tatum for that polygraph—that, yes, he did have a son nicknamed "Bronco."

***U.S. Marshal Peyton Norville** died of cancer in October 1963.*

***U.S. District Judge Clarence W. Allgood** was found dead in 1991 of an apparent self-inflicted gunshot, at age 89, at home in Birmingham.*

***Thelton Henderson,** former Justice Department civil rights attorney, is a federal judge in San Francisco.*

***Roosevelt Tatum** is buried in New York's Long Island National Cemetery.*

***Dan Moore** died in August 2001, clinging to what he said was "the constant hope that someday my name will be cleared—and Tatum's will, too."*

However, with A.D. King and Martin Luther King, Jr., having gone to their graves, we may never know why the movement never succeeded in pouncing on the crime and its aftershocks—and making Tatum's case, if not also Moore's, a cause celebre. A partial clue may lie in copies of letters from Tatum's Birmingham attorney, Orzell Billingsley, Jr., to Martin Luther King, Jr., repeatedly seeking payment of fees from the Southern Christian Leadership Conference for legal services rendered in USA vs. Roosevelt Tatum. The tenor and text of some of those letters suggest that Martin did not reply to Billingsley's letters seeking reimbursement. Could that be why Billingsley at the last minute decided not to go to trial—and thus changed Tatum's plea to "guilty"?

Surely this was a crime that showcased, as few others did, the horrors and hate, the fury and passion—and which cried out for justice, as few others did—during this unforgettable period of history.

That was Jeff's account, based upon research and investigative savvy. What follows now are my recollections, similar to Jeff's telling, but more emotional:

The night our house was bombed Mama was in the living room looking out of the front window (we lived in a ranch-style house, provided by the church. Everything was on one floor. The living room, guest bedroom, kitchen, and den were at the front. Our bedrooms were at the back). Al was in the den watching a war picture on TV. Daddy was in the bed, as were Vernon, Derek, Darlene, and I.

There was a big boom. At first, nobody moved, because we thought that it was Al, with the television up too loud. Then, a sixth sense (or God) told Daddy to go find Mama. Daddy ran to the living room, picked up Mama, who was staring out the big picture window in a daze, ran toward the back, and screamed at Al, "Come on, it's a bomb." He came past our rooms and said, "Get up, run out to the garage." We all got up and ran out, except Darlene, who was sound asleep.

I threw on a blue corduroy robe, ran out and tried to scramble over the back fence. My chubby behind got caught, and I was left swinging on the fence as Daddy realized that we'd left Darlene inside. He took off running and brought her out just as the second explosion rocked the foundations of the whole house, taking with it the front half of the house. The impact of the explosion knocked me off the fence. I saw my whole family, safe, and I think I fainted for a minute.

By this time, the streets were full of people. They were beginning to riot. A neighbor who lived across the street was insisting that he'd seen a police car pull up in front of our house just twenty minutes before the bomb went off. (Just two days later, the man disappeared, and we found out that the FBI had taken him away for questioning and had later had him committed to a mental institution.)

People were beginning to throw rocks at every car carrying a white face. After all, this was the home of their community savior. Reverend A.D. King had been leading the boycotts in Birmingham all these weeks—and he was the brother of Dr. Martin Luther King, Jr., (who was supposed to be visiting this very weekend, sleeping in the very room that was now blown to smithereens).

But the question was, did the bombers know that Uncle M.L. was supposed to be visiting at that time? And if so, who could have told them?

Mama's mind went immediately to our housekeeper, Mrs. Minnie McCloud, who lived just down the street. But Mrs. McCloud was mysteriously not at home (even though it was after eleven at night).

The shouted questions continued, while Daddy called out to the crowd, "Please, do not riot. My family is all right. We are safe."

A policeman came by with a billy club, trying to make a path through the crowd. He shoved me in the stomach. Daddy saw him, "Touch her again, and you'll be drawing back a nub."

I was enraptured. Daddy was my hero. He had saved me from a white, bully policeman. Daddy was magnificent, wading through the crowds, convincing everyone not to riot—to go home and cool off.

We went to somebody's house that night. I can't remember whose. Some of Daddy's deacons, Earskine Lewis, Eddie Prewitt, and others, stayed over to help Daddy watch the house.

The next morning, Mama was in shock. Her beautiful home with pretty curtains, wallpaper, pictures, and china was ruined. In the rubble of what used to be her living room, there was one thing left—a plate, part of a pair (Mary and Jesus), gleamed out from the debris. Jesus' shining face seemed to tell Mama that somehow, things would be all right.

We came back to the house to sleep. Mrs. McCloud had not yet been found for questioning. She disappeared mysteriously and she never was heard from again. Mama Lillian came to help us get the house back together.

One night, Mama's whole body started shaking. Every nerve was jumping. A doctor had to come and give her a shot, so that she could relax.

Another night, Daddy came home, the garage door came up, and went right back down (Daddy used his electric garage door control). Daddy came in Darlene's and my bedroom, and looked out the window, laughing. A police car sat there a minute, and drove away. Daddy had eluded another police trap. You see, back then, very few people had electric controls and remotes for their garages, at least not in our neighborhoods. I don't imagine that the police officers had them, either. They had no idea where Daddy went. Thank God.

It was about this time that Daddy decided that we needed to make a change. Within months, Daddy accepted a church in Louisville, Kentucky. Life in Birmingham was becoming much like life had been for Uncle M.L. and his family in Montgomery (after their home was bombed). We couldn't be sure when another bomb would be hidden somewhere, a threat to the whole family.

Granddaddy was in full agreement of the move. Louisville seemed to be a safe place, compared to Birmingham. And Granddaddy couldn't understand why Daddy had to be so involved in the movement anyway. He told Daddy on his last visit to Birmingham, "You and your brother are going to get your fool selves killed. A.D., why can't you leave it alone and be preachers? God's work is just as important, you know, and a lot less dangerous."

Daddy reminded Granddaddy, "Dad, you used to boycott stores in downtown Atlanta, years ago."

Granddaddy didn't want to hear of Daddy's rationalizations. "That was years ago, when things weren't so dangerous. And I wasn't running all over the country, leaving your mother with my children. And I certainly didn't go and get my house bombed. For God's sake, A.D., it was bad enough for M.L. to get in this foolishness. Now, you too? Try to act like you have some sense. Take the church, son, and preach."

Daddy did take the church in Louisville, and Uncle M.L. continued in Ebenezer's pulpit when he was home. Before we moved to Louisville, we spent a few days in Atlanta. We went over to Uncle M.L. and Aunt Coretta's house for dinner.

They had a big house on Johnson Avenue, in the Old Fourth Ward of Atlanta. Aunt Coretta would have preferred a house in another area, since the Old Fourth Ward was something like the ghetto. But Uncle M.L. wouldn't hear of it. He wanted to live in the area where he'd been born, and Johnson Avenue is just a few blocks from Auburn Avenue. And besides, Uncle M.L. and Daddy agreed that it would be hypocritical to live in fine neighborhoods while the people they were fighting for lived in the ghetto. (That's why our house had been on a ghetto street in Birmingham.)

Aunt Coretta had fixed the big, two-storied, wood-frame house real pretty, though. There was a nice fire place, with real bear skins for rugs in front of it. There were French doors opening onto the dining room.

The day of the family dinner, Uncle M.L. came home just as Aunt Coretta was seeing to making Granddaddy, Bigmama, and some other guests comfortable. "Corrie, where are my house shoes?" He wanted her to go and get them and put them in front of him so he could step into them.

Aunt Coretta looked like she wanted to tell Uncle M.L. to get his shoes himself, but I think she knew how much a chauvinist the man she had married was. She went and got the shoes, and he slipped them on.

Daddy was a super-chauvinist, too. Maybe it was a sign of the times. Granddaddy was not nearly as chauvinistic as were my Daddy and uncle.

We enjoyed the dinner, one of few such occasions when we all gathered together. Granddaddy was in charge. He called one of his family conferences, laid out his plans for what his family would be doing over the next few years. Daddy would go to Louisville. Uncle M.L. would continue to co-pastor Ebenezer, and when Granddaddy was ready to retire, Daddy would come back to Ebenezer, and be co-pastor with Uncle M.L.

Daddy and Uncle M.L. were quiet, as if they knew that history would not be so kind to the old man. But they let him have his dreams for that short time.

Early Family Portrait: A.D., Naomi, Al, Darlene, Alveda, Derek

Young Daddy King and family

Darlene and Derek with bride, Aunt Christine

King family, 1968

Christine, Daddy King, Coretta

Dad with grandchildren and great grandchildren

M.L. King's funeral

Bombing of A.D. King home in Birmingham

Prayer for safety and guidance—Birmingham

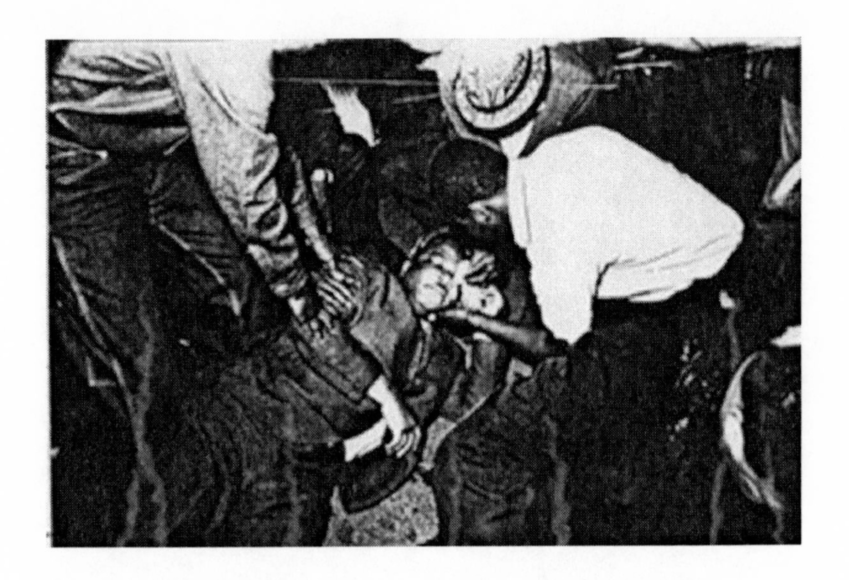

TO ANY SHERIFF OF THE STATE OF ALABAMA, GREETING:

By order of the Honorable W. A. Jenkins, Jr., one of the Judges of the Circuit Court, Tenth Judicial Circuit of Alabama, in Equity Sitting, as affirmed by the Supreme Court of Alabama, and the Supreme Court of the United States, and as reconfirmed by decree of Court dated October 19, 1967, you are ordered and directed forthwith to arrest, deliver and commit ____A. D. KING____ to jail in Jefferson County, Alabama, for a period of five (5) consecutive days, commencing on this date, or as soon thereafter as he may be apprehended by you, the said ____A. D. KING____ having been adjudged guilty of contempt of Court.

In accordance with the aforesaid orders of the Court, unless the said ____A. D. KING____ shall, at or before the time for his release from detention under the aforesaid sentence, pay into the Registry of this Court a fine, in the amount of Fifty Dollars ($50.00), you are further ordered and directed to retain the custody of the said ____A. D. KING____ for imprisonment for a period of twenty (20) days in lieu of payment of said fine.

Witness my hand this the 19th day of October,

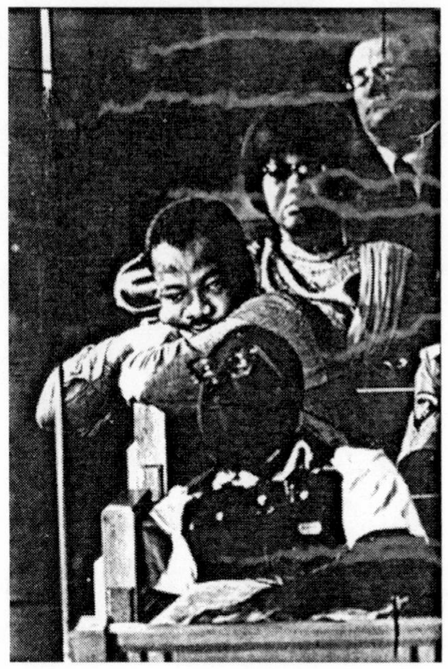

A moment of reflection

Strategy session

A.D. at a lunch counter sit-in

Poor people's campaign

Church Blast Is Shameful, Baptists Say

AUG 16 1968 E 7

The General Association of Baptists in Kentucky yesterday expressed "shock and shame" at Wednesday's bombing of Zion Baptist Church in Louisville.

A resolution adopted by the group's convention in Louisville said:

"We express our oneness with the Rev. A. D. King, the pastor of Zion, in his commitment to the complete freedom of the black people of this community and nation."

The association urged all pastors to support the voter registration campaign now under way in Louisville. "We call upon our total membership in Kentucky to qualify to vote in order to keep our state out of the hands of white racists," the resolution said.

Voter Rally Held Before Blast

Zion, at 22nd and Walnut, was the site of a voter registration rally Monday night, but police say they have found no connection between the rally and the Wednesday morning dynamite explosion.

The 642-church Kentucky association ended its 100th anniversary convention yesterday in Louisville.

The association's new moderator, the Rev. E. M. Elmore, pastor of Bates Memorial Baptist Church, 619 Lampton, said yesterday he plans to increase co-operation between the General Association of Baptists, a Negro group, and the Kentucky Baptist Convention, a predominantly white organization.

Missions and education will be emphasized, he said, with increased aid going to the group's main school, Simmons University, 1811 Dumesnil.

The association's first over-all budget, covering the main body and five auxiliary groups, also will be drawn up this year, the Rev. Mr. Elmore said.

At church bombing site—Louisville

Louisville ministry

the Rev. Andrew J. Young. "There was no sign of foul play."

THE REV. A. D. WILLIAMS KING

Formed local rights group

Louisville open housing

"As for me and my house we will serve the Lord."
The Legacy Lives On

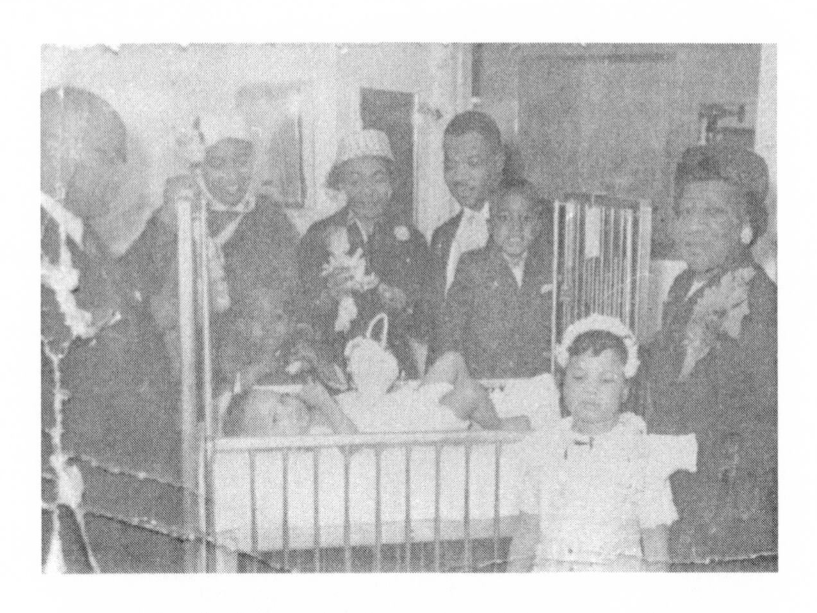

Our family learned early to smile in the face of tragedy,

Pretty Darlene, with such a spark for life.

Rev. A. D. King with congregation in Birmingham.

Musical Interlude.

Daddy and Alveda.

Daddy's girl got married. He died the next week.

Granddaddy, sister Woodie and her hubby Jerry
on a visit to Cliff and Veda's house.

Daddy King with Celeste.

Grandma Sally wants some meat on young Eddie's bones.

Rev. Vernon King, with wife Robin and daughter Victo.

Family Portrait at Aunt Coretta's Birthday Party.

John, Farris and Joshua.

Janice, Derek and Kyle.

Alveda and Mama Naomi.

Yolanda, Alveda and Grace.

Alveda King Beal puts Atlanta in fiction

By Actor Cordell

Alveda King Beal — college teacher, ex-legislator, political activist, actress, psychiatrist's wife, mother of four — has had still another calling.

She's a novelist, with two new books set in today's Atlanta, and she participated in the recent Georgia Romance Writers' fifth annual conference titled "Moonlight and Magnolias."

Now in the works is a book for non-fiction — an autobiographical tome about the people she knew in the grim days of the civil rights movement in the 1960s. Her two novels were published by Dream Books Ltd. which she and her husband Dr. Clifford Beal, have formed with the hope it will develop into a publishing outlet for aspiring and established Atlanta writers.

Whether the dream is fulfilled depends upon how much profit they will have on hand from the sale of her new books, "Images" and "The Arab Heart."

She began writing "The Arab Heart" in 1979 during her two terms as representative from the 28th district in the Georgia General Assembly.

It's the story of an Arabian prince who enrolls at Georgia Tech for training in technology to benefit his country.

"I was always curious about Arab culture, and became more interested when President Carter was getting [Egyptian Anwar] Sadat and Israel Prime Minister Menachem] Begin together for peace talks at Camp David."

Soon after completing the book, she was riding in a taxi from downtown to her home and discovered the driver was not only Arabian, but also a student, though at Georgia State University instead of Tech.

He agreed to read and critique the manuscript.

The changes he suggested were minimal, and he expressed surprise that she had written it without visiting Arabia, said Mrs. Beal.

While in Atlanta, the prince becomes involved with two women, one a white woman from Boston and one from Savannah whose father is white and mother black. The women vie to become his wife and live in Arabia.

"Atlanta is glamorous, interesting and exciting, and a suitable setting for romantic fiction," said the 35-year-old Mrs. Beal in the living room of her family's English Tudor-style home in the Bedford-Pine community.

As an author, Mrs. Beal has found an interesting peer group called Georgia Romance Writers and in August attended its fifth annual "Moonlight and Magnolias" conference. There she met Irene Vandercroit of New Hampshire, one of the leading agents in the field of romance fiction.

She took home a copy of "Images" and has written to Mrs. Beal with a favorable critique — but suggested that some sequences, such as the trip to the beach by the key character and a girlfriend, could have been made a bit more steamy.

Mrs. Beal, who is also active in the First World Writers organization here, is now at work on a third Atlanta-based novel, "Liane's World." Finding time for writing is difficult. A business communications teacher at Atlanta Junior College, she has a daytime sitter for Jennifer, 1; Eddie, 8, and Celeste, 9. When the family went to Hilton Head, S.C., for a vacation recently, she stayed holed up in their hotel suite writing.

The Beals also plan to produce movies here, the first being adapted from "Images," with filming starting next spring. She expects to play the aunt of the main central character in the tale of intrigue of the Atlanta modeling and big business world.

Her acting credits include the role of Leslie Ann Down's personal slave in the television mini-series "North and South." Her favorite of the plays she has performed in is "Tambourines to Glory" with Atlanta's Just Us Theatre, which gave her the opportunity to dance and sing.

But closer to her heart than her fiction is an unpublished autobiographical tome about the relatives and friends she has known in the civil-rights movement.

In her unpublished autobiographical book, she's being a stickler for candor.

She hasn't found time to confer with the people portrayed to obtain their sanction.

About another book, she takes issue with some of the editing done on her grandfather's "Daddy King, An Autobiography."

"It was written in first-person, but words like 'damn' and 'hell' were deleted, although that was the way he often expressed himself. Some people thought it unsuitable for a minister.

"My book is not any kind of expose, but I do try to present the people and events exactly as they are."

Her introduction to the civil rights travail came at the age of 12 in 1963 in Birmingham where her father, the late Rev. A.D. King, was pastor of a church. The parents and five children miraculously escaped injury when their home was bombed.

The latest King family tragedy came only last August when her brother, Alfred King, collapsed and died while jogging here, the same way her sister, Darlene, died 10 years ago.

Her brother Derek is pastor of a church in West Palm Beach, Fla., and the other brother, Vernon, is working toward a master's degree in divinity at Emory University. Her mother, Naomi King, works in the gift shop of the Martin Luther King Jr. Center for Nonviolent Social Change.

Son Jarrett, 16, who has had roles in several stage and television plays, is in the cast of "Leader of the Band," a movie recently filmed here.

Gwen Allen, Marietta: No, I think that it is going to be found illegal

Publishing Announcement.

INTOWN EXTRA, NOVEMBER 20, 1986

INTOWN PEOPLE

ACTOR CORDELL/Staff

DOUBLE DUTY: Alveda King Beal creates fiction at her word processor while babysitting with daughter Jennifer, age 1, in the upstairs family room in the Bedford Pine community.

Alveda King Beal puts Atlanta in fiction

By Actor Cordell
Staff Writer

Alveda King Beal — college teacher, ex-legislator, political activist, actress, psychiatrist's wife, mother of four — has had still another calling.

She's a novelist, with two new books set in today's Atlanta, and she participated in the recent Georgia Romance Writers' fifth annual conference titled "Moonlight and Mag-

ing Arabia, said Mrs. Beal.

While in Atlanta, the prince becomes involved with two women, one a white woman from Boston and one from Savannah whose father is white and mother black. The women vie to become his wife and live in Arabia.

"Atlanta is glamorous, interesting and exciting, and a suitable setting for romantic fiction," said the 35-year-old Mrs. Beal in the living

ta's Just Us Theatre, which gave her the opportunity to dance and sing.

But closer to her heart than her fiction is an unpublished autobiographical tome about the relatives and friends she has known in the civil-rights movement.

In her unpublished autobiographical book, she's being a stickler for candor.

She hasn't found time to confer

WHAT'S UP THIS W

Thurs. Georgia posed age bill chase o products will be discussed nett Rep. Charles Bann meeting of GASP Against Smoking Polluti p.m. at the Unitarian Church, 1911 Cliff Valley The public is invited to meeting. Information: 237

The "Christmas/Kwa Book Fair" continues thr day at West Hunter Lib Martin Luther King Jr. Local authors will be autograph books. There drawing for door prizes a jor credit cards are accep mation: 758-0811

The One Church, C Adoption Recruitment will be held with a 10 a.m. and 7 p.m. program at Baptist Church, 2174 Mar King Jr. Drive S.W. Any ested in adopting a child to the free programs spo the Fulton County Depa Family and Children Servi

The Congressional Beal

Beal Makes Bid . . . for Possible Dream

Alveda King Beal Seeks A Congressional Seat, Supports Jesse Jackson

Though her aunt Coretta Scott King and grandfather Martin Luther King Sr., have endorsed Mondale for U.S. president, Alveda King Beal has given her political support to the Rev. Jesse Jackson.

Ms. Beal, who is running for the 5th U.S. Congressional District seat of Georgia, formerly held by Andrew Young now mayor of Atlanta, said it is important that Blacks choose candidates of their own choice. "This goes for the King family as well. I support and encourage my relatives to remain politically active and to endorse the candidate of their choice... While I support the fact that my aunt and grandfather made these endorsements, I personally have given my political support to Rev. Jesse Jackson," Ms. Beal said.

Ms. Beal, a former Georgia state representative, told *Jet*: "Politically, we as Blacks are learning not to put all our eggs in one basket. We have now learned that there is not a very small minority within the Black community that can speak for all the Black vote. And Black people have certainly made that point clear and they continue to do so, every time they go to the polls."

She has attended fund raisers and award ceremonies in Jackson's honor and noted why she feels he is the best candidate for her. "His philosophy is [illegible] to mine (in terms of) education, unemployment, crime. He feels that the way to motivate people to stop committing crime in their neighborhoods is to give them hope, give them a sense of responsibility, give them jobs. And I certainly feel that," she said.

Reprinted from Jet Magazine, April 23, 1984

Inspired by the life, teachings and leadership of her uncle, Martin Luther King Jr., Alveda King Beal, a two-term state legislator, has qualified as a candidate to seek the 5th District Congressional seat.

Joined by her aunt, Coretta Scott King, grandfather, Daddy King, mother Naomi King, aunt Christine King Farris, other members of the King family and a host of supporters, Beal became the first candidate for the post on January 31, calling the date "the beginning of a possible dream."

See **Possible Dream** page 2

ATLANTA—State Representative Alveda King Beal visits shows her grandfather Rev. Martin Luther King, Sr. the papers qualifying her as a candidate for the 5th District congressional race. Watching are her mother Mrs. Naomi B. King and her aunt Mrs. Martin Luther King, Jr.

October 18, 2003.

Dr. Benjamin Mays, author, activist, educator and family friend. Mom and Bigmom thought he was so handsome. I was honored to greet him on a visit to the legislature.

Brothers in the struggle.

America's First Ladies, Rosalynn Carter and Coretta King,
take a little time to visit.

Daddy King and Aunt Coretta with President Carter.

Aunt Coretta and Daddy King with new legislator Alv.

At the Georgia Legislature with Kerry.

Jarrett greets President Carter.

October 13, 2003.

Groundbreaking for Morehouse King Chapel.

Groundbreaking for King Center.

Alveda at Dr. King's Portrait at Georgia Capitol.

CHAPTER FOUR

Just before Daddy took the church in Louisville, Uncle M.L. won the Nobel Peace Prize. Granddaddy was ecstatic. The civil rights movement had won this honor for his son. Granddaddy stopped fussing about Uncle M.L.'s work in the movement taking him away from the pulpit. After all, Granddaddy was still young enough to carry much of the weight of Ebenezer.

Granddaddy, Bigmama, Aunt Coretta, Daddy, Aunt Christine, and Ralph David and Juanita Abernathy went to Oslo, Norway, to see Uncle M.L. receive the award.

"Uncle Ralph" (we called him uncle, just like we called many of Uncle M.L. and Daddy's associates uncle during those days. We had a few aunts, too) and "Aunt Juanita" were a little put out because all of the attention went to Uncle M.L. as recipient.

Daddy said that there was a limousine caravan for Uncle M.L. and the whole group which arrived at the hotel to take them to the awards ceremony. The first limousine was for Uncle M.L. and Aunt Coretta. They, of course, invited Granddaddy and Bigmama to ride with them. When the Abernathys were not included in the first car, Aunt Juanita held back. The limousine caravan couldn't wait. If memory serves me correctly, I think they had to find their own way to the ceremony. Juanita was saying that if they couldn't ride with Martin and Coretta, they would walk. After all, her husband Ralph was just as much responsible for the efforts of the civil rights movement as Martin. By this time, the Abernathys were feeling just a bit unappreciated. Yet, as is often the case, history and the populace were fickle, elevating one personality to the pinnacle of a movement that was truthfully comprised of a sea of soldiers, committed to one cause. There were thousands of troops during the days of the movement, and hundreds of leaders and unsung heroes and "sheroes."

Of course, Uncle Ralph played an important role, all the way through the movement. When Uncle M.L. went to Montgomery, Uncle Ralph was a senior pastor of a prominent church, and an outstanding member of the Montgomery community. Uncle Ralph became friend and advisor to Uncle M.L. early, often going to jail right along with him, marching with him, working with him constantly.

Uncle M.L. always said, "Ralph is the best friend I have in the whole world." Uncle M.L. was thinking of Uncle Ralph and all of his contributions to the movement—and he was remembering all of the soldiers in his army when he accepted the award. Uncle M.L. accepted the award on behalf of everybody in his heart. And he expressed his appreciation by giving the total proceeds of $54,000 from the award to SCLC, to continue the work of the movement.

When people realized the depths of Uncle M.L.'s unselfish spirit, they joined the movement in masses. Those who couldn't physically drop everything and march off to protest for equal rights, sent donations.

SCLC now had financial backing. Aunt Coretta (while she wasn't so happy with Uncle M.L. for giving the whole cash award to the movement—how were they ever going to provide for their children if he insisted on giving every cent to the movement?) joined in the spirit of fundraising. She started traveling around the country doing freedom concerts. Her concerts did raise funds for the movement and were a much-needed outlet for her frustrated career as a professional classical singer. She had given up her dream of being on stage to be the wife of a preacher and civil rights activist.

Meanwhile, the awards ceremony over, Daddy returned to Birmingham and got ready to move to Louisville. Some of the members in Birmingham were sorry to see Daddy and Mama go. Daddy had been a good preacher, bringing in many members for the church. And Daddy had been a good motivator in the community. Things were stirred up now, time for action to continue. What would they do without their leader?

Other members were glad to see Daddy go. He and his brother, Dr. King, had come into their community and stirred things up, and now things were out of control. People, little children had died. Businesses had been shut down. People were being threatened. And all because of the name King. Good riddance to the Kings.

We left Birmingham for Louisville, with our station wagon packed, and anxiety in our hearts. Mama was leaving friends, and so were we. But such was the life of a preacher's family. You followed the call of God.

Granddaddy, Bigmama, Aunt Christine, and Uncle M.L. came to Louisville to see Daddy installed in the pulpit of Zion Baptist Church. Mama Lillian was there too, helping us through yet another transition. Daddy was installed in grand fashion. The church was large and beautiful. Built on a corner lot, Zion boasted a large, balconied blue and white sanctuary. And, most impressive of all, it had its own little prayer chapel, open twenty-four hours a day, right off the street. Saints and sinners could kneel and pray any time of the day or night.

There was a soda fountain and large kitchen in the basement of the church. The congregation was used to having Sunday dinners and the like. Daddy kept up the tradition of Sunday dinners, expanding the program so that each month, a different month club could sponsor the dinner. At our church, there were twelve birth-month clubs, where members came together each month to have a fellowship according to their birthdates. It was like home cell groups in a way.

Along with month clubs, Daddy initiated several other new programs. He gave a lot of attention to dealing with the youth population. Young families joined the church in droves. They were interested in the message of the Gospel, and the message of the day, "Men and women have a right to be free."

The civil rights movement came to Louisville. While segregation was not practiced in overt ways (schools and stores were already desegregated) there was a problem with "open housing." Blacks could not buy homes in white neighborhoods.

Daddy was quick to recognize the need for righting a wrong. He contacted Uncle M.L., and the troops came in. Daddy was left, for the most part, in charge of the organization. Uncle M.L. was traveling all over the country now, moving in after his troops came before, with information and motivators.

Uncle M.L. spared some of his troops for Daddy. Louisville met "Ace" Fred C. Bennett; big, loud-talking "leader" James Orange; funny man Dick Gregory; young Leon Hall; handsome J.T. Johnson; suave Bernard Lee; flower child Sunshine; loyal Cottonreader; and a host of other "freedom fighters." These were the lieutenants, often called "outside agitators" and rabble-rousers. They would come into town, set up at local homes and motels, and begin to organize sit-ins and marches. Dr. King would come to town later, and he would speak to the masses. People are familiar with famous leaders like Ralph Abernathy, E. Randall Osborne, Jesse Jackson, C. T. Vivian, Andrew Young, Joe Lowery and others. Yet, Daddy was also a chief organizer in those days, having been instrumental in the structure of the Birmingham movement; his leadership was accepted gladly in Louisville. Those were the days of the "freedom singers," and the coffee houses and the long days and nights of the battle for freedom.

Freedom rallies were held at the most interesting places, homes, churches, halfway houses, and street corners. And the young people adopted the movement.

Meanwhile, Daddy's family was settling into Louisville, happier than we'd ever been. Our first home, in a pleasant community, was a two-storied wood frame house. The residence was temporary, while the church was buying and remodeling a parsonage.

We children got a chance to attend our first integrated school system. I went to Louisville Male (and Girls) High School. Male was the first high school built in the city, and formerly was attended only by males. But when I started there in the tenth grade, black and white boys and girls made up the student body.

I made another startling discovery. I, fat Alveda King, was not fat anymore. Uncle M.L., while visiting, had laughed with Daddy when he said, "Brother, you'd better be careful. Veda's got big, pretty legs like her Mama. The boys will be after her soon!" I was slightly chubby, but people, most importantly boys, thought I was attractive. The boy next door, Tim Roberson, actually asked to be my boyfriend. He was my first real "beau." I was having a good time for once in my life.

Soon, our new house was ready. And for once (Daddy having little say in the matter since the church wanted to invest in some valuable real estate) we didn't move to the ghetto. We moved to a house near the river. The ranch-style house was pretty. Darlene and I shared a room with French provincial furniture. Al, Derek, and Vernon had a room together. (I stayed mad with them because I had finally developed Daddy's fetish for cleanliness. I refused to set foot in a dirty bathroom. They were forever pissing on the seats and the bathroom carpet. I spent a lot of time scrubbing our bathroom.)

When I was in a frenzy over having to share the bathroom with my brothers, Daddy would laugh and say, "Girl, you ought to be glad you don't live in France. When I went to Paris, the man and woman would have to use the same bathroom. I couldn't speak too much French (your mother is the language expert), so I tried to ask a lady in one of the shops where I could find a bathroom. I kept saying bathroom, not sure what kind of gesture to use. She kept nodding her head, and saying '*oui, oui.*' I thought she was saying wee-wee. Finally, I got so tired I shouted, 'Lady, that's what I have to do-wee-wee.' Thank God someone came up who could speak a little English. They told me where to find a restroom. When I got to the place, there were women squatting and men lined up against the wall. These were strangers, and you fuss about having to share with your brothers."

I laughed at Daddy's story, but I still didn't like sharing the bathroom. Don't enjoying sharing even today. Still, the new house was so pretty that I kept the bathroom and—wonder of wonders—my part of my room clean. I had gotten over my habit of throwing away dirty clothes to keep from having to wash them, too.

I left the boyfriend next door when we moved to the new house. I got a boyfriend from the church, Larry Acklin. Al started courting his girlfriend, Tina Ritchie. We were now teenagers.

I adored Larry. He gave me my first real, grown-up kiss in the church sanctuary (how sacrilegious) right under the picture of Jesus at meditation. It was on a Saturday. I was there with Daddy, who was in his office working on a sermon. I was waiting to take the car to the shopping mall. I got bored, and called Larry, who lived just around the corner.

Unbeknownst to Larry and me, Daddy's secretary (Kitty Johnson, who treated her big-bosomed daughter, Leona, like she was the Virgin Mary and Queen of Sheba rolled into one, would have died if she'd found out that her daughter had been stealing kisses with my best friend, Lamont Irvin) came to the church to reason and caught us kissing. She ran and told Daddy. I was on punishment for a whole week—no telephone.

There were a couple of unhappy moments at this time. I found out that Larry (who wanted intimacy, but went along with my pleas that I wasn't ready) had been sleeping with a white girl. The lady who helped with our house was a friend of the lady who cleaned the white girl's house. She found out from her friend that Larry had been sleeping over while the girl's parents were out of town.

I was heartbroken. I wanted to kill myself, and did take a whole bottle of aspirin (thank God, I only got a bellyache—it was a small bottle). Before I could seriously entertain the idea further, a school friend of mine really did kill herself. She was in love with a boy who was in the service and moving to Germany. Her family wouldn't let her marry him because she was in the eleventh grade. My friend was so unhappy about losing her love that she sliced her wrists and died.

I decided that I wanted to live. And that I could live without sex, and living without sex meant living without Larry. I got involved in school activities, and soon stopped fretting so much over the broken romance.

Life in Louisville was so interesting that I didn't remember to miss Granddaddy so much. He'd call every week, and I was glad to talk to him—but there were friends and experiences to fill in the gaps.

Daddy and I still weren't getting along. I was probably too much like him in temperament. Daddy meant to have his own way. So did I. We argued about allowance, clothes budget, dating age, dating hours, grades—the same thing that most teenagers argue with parents about.

But I had a secret weapon, Granddaddy. I was not yet above throwing in Daddy's face, "If you won't give it to me, Granddaddy will."

The congregation was growing—Daddy had something to write home and brag about. And he was a bonafide civil rights leader now. People came to him, asking him to lead marches. He appeared in news stories. Black politicians like State Legislator Georgia Davis sought him out for advice.

Daddy was in his prime. He had a big church and a big movement. The youth population adored him. I did too, but I never really wanted to admit it in words. I tried to express myself in deed.

I was dating Jerry Ellis now. It was a rebound romance with a cute young man, with the bowest legs I'd ever seen. Jerry had a part-time summer job working at the Audubon Country Club, a very elite place, whose members' faces were the color of the tablecloths. Jerry enjoyed the job and the tips. I thought it was about time that he took a little notice of what was going on in the real world. Like demonstrations and protest marches. I decided to have a little demonstration of my own at the country club. I drove up to the front door in Daddy's white Mustang. I was dressed to kill, feeling that I was as good as any of the white young ladies who were inside, having hamburgers and Cokes.

I asked for Jerry at the front door. The maitre d' said he didn't know him. I said, "Of course you do. He's a waiter." The man was so offended that his nose turned as red as any lobster they served there. "You'll have to go around the back."

I went to the back. Jerry was furious. The maitre d' had beaten me to the kitchen. "Do you want me to lose my job? Don't you care about the money I'm making? How do you think I pay for our little dates?"

Jerry didn't lose his job, but thanks to my persistence about blacks being free, he did start thinking a little differently about the movement. He even became involved in a small way.

A day before a major demonstration, Leon Hall, James Orange, and J.T. Johnson were sweeping the city, looking for warm bodies to line the streets for a march on city hall. Having a few marches under my belt, and being the daughter of a leader, I agreed to organize the students from Male High. Armed with handbills, I started through the hall, saying, "Come to the march tomorrow." The times and details were clearly visible and the flyers were hard to miss. The students took hold of them like wildfire.

We as students had been warned by the principal not to participate in the "antics" of these "outside troublemakers." He had insisted in a school rally that "Louisville has no race problems. These outside agitators have come to our cities to get you into trouble. Beware."

I, of course, ignored the warning. My daddy was no "outside agitator," and he was leading the march. My principal saw me on the second floor passing out the handbills. "Miss King, halt right there." Naturally, I didn't halt. I ran down the stairs and out the front door. Later, I was suspended for having "jumped out of the third, story window after inciting a riot." How ludicrous. How would I have survived the jump in the first place? Anyhow, I was able to marshal troops along the way.

My boyfriend Jerry, an officer in the ROTC unit, was out on the front steps drilling some of the troop members. I ran past him, saying, "See you later." As I looked over my shoulder, Jerry and his troops trained their bayonets at the principal as he ran out the door. The principal stopped and waved his fist in the air.

The next day, I was suspended from the English Club, from the track team, from the pep squad, and most importantly, from school.

Before the march, that next day, Daddy came to my school and stood up to my principal. The man turned red as a beet as Daddy waved his beefy hand in his face. "My daughter has done nothing wrong. And yet you accuse her of inciting the students to riot and then jumping out of a third-story window, when you tried to stop her? Where are the witnesses who will support this ridiculous story?"

Of course, there were no witnesses. If I'd jumped out the third-story window, I'd have broken at least half the bones in my body. The principal reinstated me for lack of evidence.

Daddy left me at school. As soon as school was out, I rushed home. Al was there and he and I slipped out to join the march. When Daddy saw us, he didn't make us go home.

We listened to the instructions about how to behave on a march. Many of our school friends were there, too. James Orange was walking back and forth, the proper field marshal, giving instructions. "If they hit you, don't fight back. This is a non-violent movement."

Uncle M.L. arrived, coming straight from the airport. He backed up James' statement. "No violence at any price."

We all agreed. We'd never come up against dogs, guns, water hoses (although I had been nudged by that billy club in Birmingham). Most of them had no notion of how violent and provoking angry segregationists could be. I, remembering the streets in Birmingham after our home was bombed, knew how it was, but I was swept away on the tide toward freedom.

During the march we were insulted, spit at, and heckled. We marched on. We reached the aldermen's chamber and went into the hearing on open housing. The decision by the council of aldermen was to uphold the existing policy. Whites had a right to say no to selling their homes to blacks.

That was our cue. We were going to sit in, spend days and nights in the chambers, if necessary, until the decision was changed in favor of open housing.

The mayor ordered the police chief to have all demonstrators removed. We lay where we were. Pandemonium broke loose. Al said a police officer made a move to step in his crotch. Al bit the man's leg and held on. All around me, friends and unknown faces were being dragged away. Daddy was being severely clubbed.

A policeman kicked me. I remembered the words of James and my uncle, "No violence at any price." I decided I could stand a little pain.

But then, an officer stomped into the stomach of my girlfriend, Renelda Meeks. I couldn't stand it. I went crazy. To stomp the pelvis of a woman, killing all of her future—the unborn of our race. I came up fighting and clawing. I wasn't as big as I used to be, but I didn't care. I would kill the monster.

I fought so hard that the policeman had to call his partner. "This is a wild one." They had me on the marble steps of city hall by then, and tried to throw me down those steps. I hung on for dear life. I fought, I kicked, I bit, I yelled. They shot me in the arm with some type of nerve gas. I didn't slow down. Finally, they threw me into a paddy wagon, where I passed out.

I woke up in jail. Mama and Daddy wouldn't come and get me out. "We said no violence. Now stay there and think about it."

Daddy was there to get me out the next day. My hero had saved me again. But we had few kind words to say to each other. "That's the last march you'll ever march in, young lady. What in hell's name made you fight like that? Your Granddaddy saw you on TV and blames me for getting you involved in this 'fool's mess'."

"Oh, Daddy. You men are all alike. It's okay for you to be a big civil rights leader, but the women need to stay home. That's what you make Mama and Aunt Coretta do." By now, I was learning to fight for my identity as a person. I was tired of the chauvinism that dominated Mama's life.

Daddy could do whatever he wanted. But Mama had better be perfect. I knew how he had people following her around, to see if she made secret dates and the like. Of course she didn't. Mother was faithful and loyal as a wife and as a mother.

Daddy and I got into a real argument on the way home. "You just think I'll have sex with some of your precious troops, don't you?"

He looked at me out of the corner of his eye and pulled the car over. "Veda, people are already saying that you are involved with one of the troops. Are you? Girl, I'll kill you."

"No, Daddy, I'm involved with them all, if you must know." Daddy hit me then. At that point, I admitted that I was still a virgin, and that some of my best friends actually were going with some of the troops. Some of them even got pregnant. I refused to tell who they were then and who the fathers of the babies were, and never have to this day.

I asked Daddy why it was okay for women to hang around the movement guys, and sleep with them. He said, "That's part of the movement, baby."

I kept remembering things that I'd seen and heard, like the time Daddy was trying to give a lady a ride home. She wouldn't get out of the car at her house, so Daddy brought the lady home in his car and left her crying in the garage. He wouldn't take her back home, and neither would Mom. I ended up taking her home. Daddy said he "couldn't get her to get out of the car." Something about he was trying to give her a ride home and she wouldn't get out.

Then, there was the time that a lady was flirting with Daddy at church. Mama saw the woman making her move. "She was rubbing her big chest up against the counter and batting her eyes at your father. He wasn't paying her any attention. Just as I walked in the door, the woman said: 'Rev. King, you are so blind. You just don't see anything.'" After church, the woman asked Daddy to take her home. Daddy said, "Dear, I can't take you home, but my wife will." Mama looked at them both, said: "Like hell I will," and jumped in her car and raced home. She was expecting Daddy to come home and raise hell with her. When he came home, he didn't say a word.

Then, there was the story Mom used to tell about riding in a car with Daddy, some preacher friends and their wives, and how a beautiful lady was walking down the street. Daddy yelled out, "Look at that stallion."

One of the other men leaned over to take a closer look and said, "Yeah, she's fine!" His wife slapped him so hard his glasses fell off.

These episodes bothered me so much, I tried to talk to Daddy about it.

"But do you and Uncle M.L. have girlfriends? People say you do."

"And people say you sleep with some of the troops and you say you don't. What is the truth, Veda? Listen, your Mama is Mrs. A.D. King, and will always be. Aunt Coretta is Mrs. M.L. King, Jr. and nothing will ever change that. You get that kind of respect from a man, girl, and you'll never need anything else."

Several of my friends got pregnant during that time. I didn't sleep with any of the men. It was mostly because of that conversation with Daddy. Then, too, Daddy would threaten them with dire consequences if they touched his daughter. And it was partly because I had a boyfriend. I was still a virgin, thanks to the Bible teachings of our family, and the strong men and women in our family. They taught me to value who I was as a person.

Daddy didn't mind me having a boyfriend, and he let me go out on dates. He would tease me, saying that he was going to drive me to my senior prom (I think he was trying to let me know that he was my best guy). But when the time came, he didn't. I rode with Jerry and another couple.

In my senior year of high school, while I was trying on my dress that I was to wear to Jerry's ROTC ball, a news flash came on the TV. Uncle M.L. had been shot. I fainted.

Daddy was with Uncle M.L. in Memphis, having gone the night before to "help my brother." Now, he didn't come home. He flew to Atlanta, to get Aunt Coretta and take her to Memphis. Then he flew back to Atlanta with the widow and his brother's body. Daddy was devastated. So much had happened. Daddy King's dream of a dynasty of preachers was crumbling. Public opinion, always fickle, was predictably reactive. Whereas many blacks had criticized Martin during the Movement as being a troublemaker, stirring up white violence, now everyone loved Dr. King. The public eye was on Coretta and her children. A. D. King, the slain hero's brother, was there at her side, silently grieving, strongly supporting.

Daddy held up beautifully through the days before the funeral. When dignitaries like Jackie Kennedy came, he made sure they got to Aunt Coretta's house safely. He tried to be his once carefree self, to make everybody think he was okay.

Daddy even took my cousin Clara and me, along with Reverend Bennett, to a hotel room at the Holiday Inn. (Bennett and Clara had just gotten married a short time before. Bennett had finally become part of the King family—for real—by marriage.) At the hotel room, Daddy knocked on the door. Two ladies, well-known in Louisville, down for the funeral, came to the door, dressed in flimsy negligees. They were expecting Daddy and Bennett to come alone. The women looked distraught, knowing that I knew them both very well. They were both married. They muttered something as I said hello. Daddy threw back his head and laughed. "Girl, always remember what a lady is, and what a lady isn't." I remembered our conversation of not long ago, about what kind of lady demanded respect. I think he was trying to show me something of life, in a real way.

This episode was something like a bizarre comic relief in the middle of a disaster. Daddy was having a hard time; yet, he was still trying to teach me. I will always remember his strength during those times.

Granddaddy was strong as well. Even though his co-pastor, his Nobel Peace Prize winner, his namesake was dead, he would try to hold the family together. Daddy, in his rage and anguish, turned to the bottle. Granddaddy was so overwrought about Uncle M.L. that he didn't have time to notice Daddy's pain.

The funeral came and went. The celebrities and the masses co-mingled, finding common ground in their grief. Yet, there was a big power struggle going on. Who would take over as head of SCLC, and the movement, for that matter?

Poisonous snakes that had pretended to be friends kept Daddy on the road to self-destruction. They threw women and liquor bottles at his feet. Daddy had only one thing in mind—to solve the murder of his brother.

Daddy never really thought about trying to take over as head of SCLC. He was too preoccupied with finding the killer of his brother, his life-long friend.

Aunt Coretta was receiving letters by the thousands, with condolences and cash contributions for her and the children. She needed the money, because Uncle M.L. had given most of the proceeds from his book publications and any other money he'd managed to come by to the movement. Some, seeing their meal ticket cut off with the death of Uncle M.L., resented Aunt Coretta's taking the money. "Dr. King would want SCLC to have that money. She's stealing the movement's money." Coretta was seeing to her family, as the contributors intended for her to. They shared in her loss, and wanted to help in some way. Somehow, most of the contributions were confiscated before they even reached the widow.

Aunt Coretta attended the SCLC board meetings, where talk of choosing a new leader was in the air. Some people admired Aunt Coretta for wanting to take part in the plans for what would happen ahead. It was her husband, after all.

Some people resented her courage. She was a woman, wasn't she? Why didn't she lead the women's movement, or something, and leave the movement to the men?

Harry Belafonte, close friend to Martin and Coretta, knowing that Coretta would have to have an outlet, said, "She ought to go somewhere and lead the welfare mothers."

The family was in turmoil at this time. Aunt Coretta's children were bewildered. They had never really known their father. They were hoping (in a way like Granddaddy) that one day, when the movement was over, their Daddy would come home, and be a regular father. This was not ever to be.

Bigmama was crushed. The child of her womb, cut down in his prime? Who would be next? She started looking over her shoulder, expecting to lose Granddaddy at any time. She would often say to him, "King, you need to get some security. Somebody's going to come into this church (Ebenezer) and blow your brains out."

We were all frightened. The threat calls that came to each of our households during Uncle M.L.'s lifetime (like: "We don't like smart niggers." Or, "Keep your nigger son at home, old man." And, "Oh, you're his brother, you're gonna be next.") kept coming.

Shortly after Uncle M.L.'s funeral, something happened that helped Daddy to decide what his course of action was to be. He was on his way to Zion one Saturday evening. Daddy usually spent a few hours at the church office on Saturday evenings, wrapping up his sermon for the next day—planning the service. For some reason, Daddy didn't go inside as he had planned. He parked his car and rode off with someone. I never asked him where he went. The light was on in his office; his car was in the lot. Someone thought Daddy was in the church.

A bomb went off, taking with it the pretty little side chapel on the same side of the building where Daddy's office was. The police were called. Daddy came up a few minutes after the explosion. It was clear what he had to do.

His father was alone in the pulpit, in Atlanta, devastated. His brother's organization, SCLC, was being torn apart by a power struggle. His life was in danger, no matter where he lived. Daddy was going home. He announced his plans at church the next day.

Again, Daddy faced a church that received him with mixed emotions. Some members were sorry to see Daddy go. He had brought prestige, new members, and the gospel to the pulpit of Zion.

Other members were glad to see Daddy go. The town had been torn apart, with demonstrations, rallies, and riots. And, worst of all, their beautiful church had been bombed.

Daddy and his family returned to Atlanta, to Granddaddy and Bigmama and to Ebenezer.

Daddy initiated many programs during the year following Uncle M.L.'s death. At Ebenezer, he started the weekly television show, bringing Ebenezer's message to thousands every Sunday morning. As in Birmingham and Louisville, birth month clubs were established as part of the church program.

The idea of the King Center, visualized as somewhat of a memorial library by Aunt Coretta (who had started a collection of writings, photographs, and other memorabilia in the basement of her home before Uncle M.L.'s death) was expanded by Daddy, who envisioned a multi-purpose complex of archives, administrative buildings, hotel, and amphitheater—designed for the purpose of carrying on the work of his brother.

Daddy worked feverishly that year, planning to build the King Center, preaching in his Daddy's pulpit—and trying to find out who'd killed his brother.

I was away, spending my first college days at Murray State University in Kentucky. When Daddy decided to move back to Atlanta, I had refused. I didn't want to leave my friends. I had no intention of going to Atlanta and Spelman College, where all the women in my family had gone before me.

Al probably would have stayed, too, if he'd been a little older. He had friends and a girlfriend in Louisville, so it was hard for him to leave.

So everybody left Kentucky but I. From September to December of 1968, I had little contact with my family, burying myself in a whirlwind of school activities at Murray State, trying to forget that I was a King, part of a major tragedy.

Daddy kept pressuring me to come home. I didn't want to. Finally, just before Christmas, he insisted that at the end of the school year I'd have to leave Murray and Kentucky and come to live with my family.

Once again, I rebelled. I convinced Jerry to marry me. I finally agreed to become intimate, just to spite Daddy. Instead of going home for spring break, I went back to Louisville with Jerry to get rid of my virginity and Daddy's hopes of getting me back to whatever plans he had.

Jerry and I went to the park in the Volkswagen his mother had given him for Christmas. And just like in the movies, we became intimate. A policeman came up to the car and opened the door just as we completed my initiation into the world of womanhood. The officer knew who I was. And he knew some people who knew Daddy. Somebody called Daddy and told him about the park incident. Daddy was furious. I had to come home as soon as the semester was over.

I agreed to come home if Jerry came with me. We were to be married whether Daddy liked it or not. Daddy finally accepted my stubborn decision. He asked Aunt Chris to pull together a wedding that Atlanta would not soon forget.

I took no part in the wedding plans. I was only getting married to spite Daddy, to vent my fears and frustrations the only way I knew how, by being difficult.

Jerry's mother was wonderful through all of this. She let me stay at her house on weekends, calling me "sister." I called her "Ninny" as all of her family did. I admired Ninny—she was a woman who had pulled herself up from a childhood of too many brothers and sisters, and too little resources. She and her husband owned their own house and were very independent and resourceful.

Daddy never really got to know Ninny (Helen Hatcher). When Jerry and I first started dating, Daddy paid very little attention, and never asked about his family. When I announced that I wanted to marry, Daddy said he wasn't so sure about me marrying so young, and someone from a family we didn't know very well. He'd heard that Jerry's mother had been "racy" in her younger days. And he asked if I wouldn't be happier with a boy from Atlanta.

I told Daddy that he sure had changed his tune, listening to gossip—because when the shoe was on the other foot, and people were gossiping about him, he considered it a sin and a crime. And he was talking about rumors that Helen was "racy." Why, if people believed half of the gossip that was always going on about him, he'd be as famous as a movie star. I knew that if he got to know her, Daddy would find out that Helen was a fantastic lady. But Daddy moved back to Atlanta before he ever really got to meet Helen. Mama and Granddaddy got to know Helen very well, though, and they loved her almost as much as I had grown to. (Granddaddy was always grateful to the love and attention Helen gave to her grandson, Jarrett. "That's a lady Jarrett will always be able to depend on.")

Aunt Christine bought my wedding dress for me. I didn't care what it looked like. By the time I arrived in Atlanta to try it on, the dress—size ten—was too large and had to be taken up. I had become anorexic during the last two years, carried away by the movement so that I rarely ate. Once I started losing, I liked the way I looked, and started lying to my mother about how often I was eating.

Even when Mother and Daddy returned to Atlanta, I didn't start back to eating. I was thin for the first time in my life. I loved it.

I went home to marry. To my amazement (nobody had bothered to tell me), Daddy was building a swimming pool in the backyard of the new A.D. King family home. It was a pretty little house in southwest Atlanta (Daddy would have preferred downtown, but urban renewal was forcing blacks away from the inner city).

Mama said they had looked at several houses, and that she had liked another house—bigger, but with less land—farther down the street. Daddy said he could handle the notes on this one, and he bought it. The purchase was a wise decision; the lot was the loveliest on the street.

My wedding day arrived. Daddy gave me away and Granddaddy performed the ceremony. Jerry's parents and family were there. Mama and Daddy finally got to meet Helen. Several of my school friends from Birmingham and Louisville came to be in the wedding. There was a big reception at Daddy and Mama's house, right after the wedding. The guest marveled at the lovely swimming pool. Some remembered that Daddy had been a champion swimmer during his Morehouse days. I remembered how Daddy used to take us kids to swim at Mosley Park when we were little, and how he would throw Mama, screaming, into the pool. I was feeling a little nostalgic as I looked at Daddy and that pool that day.

Daddy offered Jerry and me a honeymoon in Jamaica. Daddy, Mama, Vernon, Darlene, Aunt Coretta, Martin III, Yolanda, Dexter, Bernice, their Aunt Edith and her son, Arty, went away to Jamaica on a family vacation. Al and Derek had summer jobs and wanted to stay at home.

Jerry and I stayed in Atlanta. Jerry said he couldn't go away for a week because of the job he had just gotten at Sears. I went along with Jerry because I still wasn't comfortable traveling with my family.

Granddaddy arranged a weekend stay for us at the Marriott Hotel downtown. Bigmama had a bottle of champagne sent to our room and called about ten that night saying, "What ya'll doing?"

Jerry thought that was the funniest thing anybody could ask a couple on their wedding night. "Tell her we're reading the Bible."

Granddaddy presented us our marriage license in church the following Sunday. The next morning, as I was getting ready to go to work at the telephone company, I was surprised to hear Daddy's key in the lock. "What are you doing home? You're back a week early. Where's Mama?"

Daddy explained that he had to come back early and that Mama and the others would be back at the end of the next week.

The next few days were sort of dream-like. I was still honeymooning with Jerry. Daddy tried to be nice, but I could tell he was unhappy about the wedding, about Uncle M.L.'s death, about SCLC's falling apart, about not being able to get the family to go along with his plans for the new complex. And the strain of working with Granddaddy at Ebenezer was playing on him. Daddy was under a lot of pressure.

He was working on getting a new insurance policy that would pay for the house as well as securing benefits for Mama and the boys. He talked with the agent on Friday. He was to sign the papers the next Wednesday.

Daddy didn't get a chance to sign those papers. On Monday night, Jerry and I came home after having dinner out. We started up to the front door. I stopped at the front-screened window. Daddy was on the phone. I beckoned for Jerry to "shush."

"You can threaten me, you can keep calling me. But I won't stop. I am going to expose what I know." Daddy looked out the window and saw us standing there. "I got to go now. My family's coming in. Don't call back."

I went in the house and walked over to Daddy, who was sitting in the den. "Who was that?"

"Oh, nobody. How you two been doing?"

I looked at Daddy real hard. "You all right? You been drinking? You don't look like it."

Daddy said that he hadn't been drinking and that he might not ever again.

"What's that crazy man doing standing up on the hill, staring at our house, Daddy?" We had a strange family of neighbors right next door. They were white and looked like a cross between Germans and Georgia Mountain people. They rarely had anything to say to us, but the father would often stand outside and stare at our house. He didn't work, just seemed to be a handyman or something.

"Is he out there again?" Daddy stood up and started toward the kitchen door as if he'd look out. I headed for my bedroom, following Jerry, who'd already gone out.

Daddy came to our room in a few minutes. He looked at me for a long minute. Jerry was in the bathroom. Daddy sighed, "Veda, there are so many things I need to tell you. But you never want to listen to me or anybody. One day, you're gonna want to talk to me, and I won't be here."

I kissed Daddy, and gave him a little shove, knowing that Jerry would be out of the bathroom in a few minutes. "Aw, Daddy, we talk all the time, and we always will." Daddy shrugged, gave his crooked little lopsided grin, his dimple in his cheek and winked at me. Then he went down to his room and got on the phone.

But that was the last talk we were to ever have. The next morning, Jerry left for work at about five thirty. I got up at seven, and left thirty minutes later. At about ten, my phone on the switchboard rang. It was a telephone repair operator. My brother Derek was on the other end of the line. "Veda. Daddy is dead."

I dropped the phone. I ran out into the hallway. It was deserted. I fell to the floor. My Daddy was dead. Oh, God. Now I would never get a chance to tell him how much I loved him. I'd never get to fight with him again. Never get to talk with him about all those things he wanted to tell me. My Daddy—my hero—was dead.

Somehow, I got up from the floor and ran out the front door and caught the bus home. When I arrived home, fire trucks, police cars, and an ambulance were at the house. There was a crowd of people around, as well as news reporters.

I rushed toward the crowd, and ended up by the swimming pool. Daddy was lying on the ground, with people all around him. I knelt by his body, touched the ice-cold, clammy flesh. No life. I touched the indentation on his forehead, wondering how the bruise had gotten there. It hadn't been there last night. The firemen were pumping his lungs out. No water was coming out. I touched Daddy again, and screamed silently, "Come back." Then, a cold voice inside me said, "Why should he want to come back to this life of hell?"

I spoke aloud. "There is no water coming out. I thought when people drown, water comes out of their lungs."

The police chief stepped up and said, "Take this woman away, she's hysterical."

I wanted a comprehensive autopsy, rather than the routine one they did. But the police chief said I was too young, and that only my mother as official next-of-kin could order one. And she was in Jamaica.

The next day, the paper printed a report that Daddy had alcohol in his blood. But he had not been drinking that night before he died. He didn't go out. The report said he had died early that morning. Jerry and I (honeymooners) stayed up all that night and we heard nothing. Our bedroom was right over the pool, and our window was open.

Al had found the body in the pool. Daddy died on Al's sixteenth birthday. Al went into shock, and later became a recluse. His boyhood was over, and his manhood seemed frozen.

Mama, Aunt Coretta, and the kids came back the next morning. Mama was in shock, and when I insisted on her ordering an autopsy, she wouldn't listen. After forty-eight hours, there would be so much red tape that we might never be able to get an autopsy.

I tried to get Granddaddy to make Mama get the autopsy. Even he wouldn't listen. "My son is dead, Veda. Let him rest."

I couldn't rest. Mama said my cousin Toussaint Hill (Cleo's son) had been acting funny the day before my wedding. He kept walking around the swimming pool, saying, "A man went walking and drowned in his own pool."

I sought Toussaint out, trying to discover if he was being clairvoyant (a trait that runs in the King family—who are prone to visions, dreams, and the like), or if he had heard or seen something.

Toussaint was in shock, and was trying to drown his pain in the bottle. He didn't make any sense.

The police went to question the family next door. I followed. The young son said that he'd heard coughing and splashing at about three that morning. I wanted to scream that he was lying. Jerry and I were just a few feet above the pool, wide-awake, and we heard nothing.

Within a few days, that strange family packed up and left. The father had had a heart attack, they said. And they were going away.

We had the funeral; it was beautiful, with sweet songs, poems, and the eulogy. Granddaddy held up, the pillar of the family. Bigmama's grief was terrible to see. Both of her sons were dead within 15 months.

After the funeral, Jeff Prugh was working for the *Los Angeles Times*. Jeff came to town. He wanted to investigate Daddy's death. Jeff said he felt that there was an analogy between the death of the King brothers and the Kennedy brothers. Jeff needed a copy of the coroner's report. And he needed a member of the family to request that copy.

We went to the Medical Examiner's office, and asked for the report. We were told that there was no report. We insisted. We were told to come back another time.

I was still a little sad to be digging so deep into this matter. I told Jeff to try me another time.

Jeff came back almost a year later, still interested in the story. We went back to the medical records office and requested the records. We were told the records had been shipped to another place for filing.

We went to that location and were told that the doctor who did the examination of the deceased died before he had a chance to record his findings. "He would do so many routine autopsies in a day, then, he would wait, pick a day and catch up on his records. We're sorry, he died before he had a chance to record this one."

Jeff pursued the case for several years, and never got the report. Where had the reporters gotten their information from the day following Daddy's death? Was the information false—planted to keep suspicion from the real circumstances of the death?

Granddaddy began saying in public that both of his sons had been killed as a result of the movement. The cause of Daddy's death was never cleared up.

If the reader will accept this author's creative license once more, I'd like to share Jeff's account of Daddy's death with you:

"THEY KILLED my boys," Daddy King groaned to his loved ones, staggering through the kitchen door of the Southwest Atlanta home of his youngest of three children, the Reverend A.D. Williams King, Sr.

Daddy King—patriarch of a family who had been thrust onto the world's stage by the life and death of his firstborn, slain civil rights leader Martin Luther King, Jr.—learned to his everlasting shock and sorrow only moments earlier that A.D.'s body had turned up in the backyard swimming pool, dead at 38.

Like the Kennedy family before them, Martin Sr. and Alberta King—with their surviving daughter, grandchildren and others—sat heart-stricken at the loss of their second son, just 15 months after Martin Jr. died in Memphis from an assassin's gunshot heard 'round the world.

Outside the house, Police Chief Herbert Jenkins remained very much in charge as an ambulance, its red lights flashing and siren wailing, arrived and would soon carry away the body of yet another leader of "The Movement"—the bloody crusade in quest of civil rights for all Americans.

"Take this woman away!" Jenkins ordered his men at the poolside, where A.D. King's eldest child, Alveda, 18, knelt beside her father's body.

It was Monday, July 21, 1969—after a weekend that had made epochal headlines. The day before, Neil Armstrong and Buzz Aldrin walked on the moon. Two nights before, Senator Edward M. "Ted" Kennedy survived a car accident in which a 28-year-old companion, Mary Jo Kopechne, drowned off Martha's Vineyard in Massachusetts.

A.D. King's body, clad only in undershorts, had been found in the pool during the morning of July 21 by his eldest son, Al, who was observing his sixteenth birthday.

"Why is there no water in his lungs?" Alveda asked, nodding toward her father's body. "And why is his head bashed in and purple right there?" She pointed in confusion to the temple area.

That is when Jenkins ordered, "Take this woman away! She's hysterical!" Witnesses alongside the pool recalled that Alveda was not hysterical. Rather, she had been quiet-spoken and methodical as she asked questions.

Now she rocked back and forth on her knees, calling softly to her father, "Come back, Daddy. Come back." She rocked again and again until a voice in her heart asked, "Why should he want to come back to this life of hell?"

The circumstances surrounding A.D. King's death became all the more intriguing to his family and friends, inasmuch as A.D. had been an accomplished swimmer on the men's team at Atlanta's Morehouse College, where he graduated in 1960.

Above the terrace overlooking the pool, next-door neighbors gathered. The teen-age son of the neighbors' family would tell police that he had heard "coughing and splashing" at about 3:00 A.M. This information would not be included in the report by authorities, which said A.D. King had drowned and that there was no evidence of foul play. Nor would the bruises or lack of water in the lungs turn up in any medical report.

In fact, there would be no coroner's report. Years later, when as a Los Angeles Times reporter, I began investigating A.D. King's death and asked for Alveda's assistance in obtaining the autopsy report, we would encounter an assortment of excuses at the Fulton County Medical Examiner's Office.

At first, we were told that the records had been transferred and that it would take several days to locate them. To our dismay, we were ultimately informed that there was no official autopsy report by the medical examiner, Dr. Tom Dillon, who had since died.

When I asked to see copies of the medical examiner's notes, an associate replied, "There are no notes."

"Why?"

"Oh, Dr. Dillon had a bad habit," the associate said.

"What was that?"

"He kept those things in his head."

THE NIGHT before A. D. King's body turned up, Alveda and her husband of one week returned home from an evening out. Before entering the house, Alveda paused on the front porch, near a window, to eavesdrop on a telephone call her father was finishing.

"You can threaten me all you want!" A.D. told this person on the phone. "But I won't stop. I'm going to expose what I know. You killed my brother, and I'm going to prove it!"

A.D. hung up the phone. Alveda and her husband walked into the house.

"Daddy, who was that?" Alveda asked.

"Nobody, Veda. Just another crazy death threat."

A.D. had never wanted to involve his family in the danger that enveloped him. This danger had only intensified since the assassination of Martin Jr. After all, A.D. and his brother had been enormously close, sharing common traits of appearance and leadership, and although A.D. marched and preached on the front lines, he did so in the shadow of his Nobel Peace Prize–winning brother.

It had been A.D.'s destiny to work alongside his esteemed brother, serving with so much humility, courage, an unshakable faith in God and the heritage of his family, his people and humankind that he, too, would carve his own special niche in history.

Born into a family rich in tradition and prophetic vision, a son, grandson, and great-grandson of preachers, the Reverend A.D. King knew about leading toward fulfilling God's promise. He sprang from a bloodline of spiritual giants, as if pre-ordained to support and help lead the fight during the 1960s to bring dignity to millions of America's downtrodden.

A.D. never backed away from the call to non-violent protest—in Birmingham, in Selma, in Louisville, in Memphis, among myriad other venues across the racially segregated South—and he fulfilled his calling with grace and dignity. In 1998, at a remembrance in his honor at the Ebenezer Baptist Church, where he shared the pulpit with Daddy King at the time of his death, A.D. would be described as a "decent, generous, strong and gentle man—who loved life and people with a gorgeous and limitless passion." His zest for living was infectious. His laughter could light up a room. His love filled the universe around him.

Martin and A.D., blessed with strong, resonant voices, preached so persuasively that some friends dubbed them "Sons of Thunder." Some liked to compare Martin and A.D. with Moses and Aaron. Now it seemed as if neither, like the ancient leaders of the Exodus, would make it to the Promised Land.

Daddy King was distraught over the death of the promise, the passing of his dreams. Martin's dream of the promised land remained fresh in the wounded heart of his father, who had endured the past year and three months since Martin's assassination by clinging to his faith and love, relying on God's grace to shepherd him and his family through the rough-and-tumble storms. "Thank God for what we have left," Daddy King was fond of saying. Now, his second son, too, was gone.

NAOMI KING was still out of the country, in Jamaica. She had traveled there with her husband A.D. and their youngest children, Vernon and Darlene. A.D. had returned to the United States a few days early to sign insurance papers and to lead a picket line at an Atlanta linen supply business—both activities scheduled on the day he would turn up dead. Later in the week, he was to embark on a series of speaking engagements.

Now, officials were trying to determine whether the death was accidental or possibly suicide. "That's absurd," Alveda insisted. "How could he have been planning that meeting this morning if he were planning something like this? And how can it be an accident if his head is bashed on one side? There's no water in his lungs."

Published reports would later indicate that a high content of alcohol had been found in A.D. King's body. Alveda recalled in detail her conversation with him the night before the body was discovered.

"Daddy, you haven't been drinking, have you?" she asked. Alveda had often challenged her father about this habit.

"No, Veda. I'm not drinking. I'll never drink again."

A.D.'s voice sounded tired. He came across as very different that night, exuding determination on the one hand, and resignation on the other—a dual demeanor that was scary to his daughter.

For the past year or so, since the death of Martin Luther King, Jr., A.D. King had been everything for everybody. The responsibility was heavy and was taking a toll. "Uncle A.D." was there for his nieces and nephews, often picking them up and delivering them to swimming events and family outings. He was there for his father and mother, for his wife and family, for the movement.

A.D. was in Memphis on that fatal day—April 4, 1968—when Martin was shot. He had gone to "help my brother" in the crusade on behalf of striking garbage workers. Once Martin was gone, A.D. carried on as a leading strategist for the Poor People's Campaign, as a valued member of the board of directors of the Southern Christian Leadership Conference.

"There are a lot of things you're going to want to know," A.D. told his daughter on that final night. "You never listen, you know. But try to remember that the things we've been doing mean a lot—not just to us but also to our people," he added, referring to the civil rights movement.

Alveda had been involved in the movement since the bombing of their home in Birmingham, Alabama, in May 1963. Her daddy allowed her to attend the Children's March in protest of the bombing of Birmingham's Sixteenth Street Baptist Church on September 15,

1963—a crime that killed four schoolgirls and made headlines around the world. One of those girls had been Alveda's schoolmate.

Those horrific moments happened months before the start of a string of cataclysmic events. President John F. Kennedy would be assassinated in November 1963. His brother, Robert F. Kennedy, would be shot down in June 1968. Inevitably, comparisons would be drawn between the King family and the Kennedys, although no one could yet know how far those parallels would take both families.

"It's getting late, Daddy," Alveda remembers telling her father. "Let's talk again tomorrow."

With a sad kind of smile, A.D. replied, "That may be too late."

It was too late.

Yes, it was too late. Daddy left us just months after Uncle M. L. left us. I guess if I were to eulogize Daddy, I'd take the words from a program written for a memorial service in his honor:

"Alfred Daniel Williams King, Sr., was born July 30, 1930, the third child and second son of Alberta Williams King and Martin Luther King, Sr.

"It was the destiny of this second son to work side by side with his great and honored brother. And yet, the Reverend Alfred Daniel Williams King, Sr., worked with such humility, such courage, such an abiding faith in the cause of his family, his people and mankind, that he now stands forever in his own right as a hero and a good man.

"He was born into a family rich in tradition and prophetic in vision. His maternal grandfather was Adam Daniel Williams, second pastor of Ebenezer Baptist Church in Atlanta, Georgia. His father had assumed that pastorate and became a legend in the struggle of African-American people.

- Graduated from Morehouse College in 1960, completed his formal education with studies at the Interdenominational Theological Center in Atlanta.
- Pastoral career spanned from 1957 to 1969: Mt. Vernon Baptist Church in Newnan, Georgia; First Baptist Church of Ensley in Birmingham, Alabama; Zion Baptist Church,

Louisville, Kentucky; and co-pastor of Ebenezer Baptist Church in Atlanta, Georgia.

- Reverend King married his longtime sweetheart, Naomi Barber King. His children are Ms. Alveda C. King, Reverend Derek Barber King, Reverend Vernon C. King and the late Alfred D. King and Esther Darlene King.
- On April 4, 1968, Martin Luther King, Jr., was assassinated in Memphis, Tennessee. His younger brother, A.D. Williams King, had come to Memphis that day "to help my brother." After the passing of his brother, Reverend A.D. Williams King was everywhere he was needed. A faithful and valued member of the board of directors of the Southern Christian Leadership Conference and a leading strategist of the Poor People's Campaign.

"History thrust Alfred Daniel Williams King, Sr., into a most delicate and difficult position. He assumed that position with grace and dignity. He was a decent, generous, strong, yet gentle man—who loved life and people with a gorgeous and limitless passion.

"Reverend A.D. Williams King, Sr.'s contributions to his beloved church and family are legion, including a television ministry which lasted for 21 years, the Altar Call where people come to pray, and the expansion of the entrance to the Christian education building. He was indeed a giant in his own way."

Yes, Daddy was a giant, and he was my hero, and he was gone from this earth. Even today, I miss his energy and his love.

CHAPTER FIVE

What would Granddaddy do now? The first generation of his seed had been wiped out. Nine of his grandchildren were now fatherless. Granddaddy became father for us all. The years that followed were years for rebuilding, for Granddaddy and for the whole family. His sons were gone, he was tired, but he had no one to take over his pulpit for him.

Granddaddy's heart was hurting. Why had God given him this load to bear? But Granddaddy did not challenge God, he just asked for the grace to go on.

I was hurting too, and I didn't have the faith that Granddaddy had. In my pain, I had tried to find something to replace Daddy. And Uncle M.L., too, I guess. I got pregnant. Jerry wasn't real happy about becoming a father. He'd been talked into an early marriage. Then, I had become pregnant without even talking it over with him.

Jerry was away from his family, and he didn't understand his new family. I was acting strange during this time. I insisted that we get our own apartment. I knew that we couldn't keep living off Mama now that Daddy was gone. The income that he used to bring in (aside from the pension that the Ebenezer Church set up until Vernon was eighteen) was gone. Daddy used to get a salary from the church, and extra income from speaking engagements all around the country.

I didn't want to live with Granddaddy. I was feeling guilty about Daddy, having spent so many of my years proving that I loved Granddaddy more than Daddy. I now realized that I had loved my Daddy just as much. And I felt it would be disloyal to Daddy's memory to go running to Granddaddy, now that Daddy was gone.

And besides, Granddaddy had enough burdens to bear. His wife was heartbroken over the loss of their sons. He had to nourish and cherish her as he had never done before.

His church was pulling on him now, in a way that it had not done for the ten previous years when Uncle M.L. and Daddy had been there to help with ministerial tasks.

And Aunt Coretta was insistent on going ahead with the plans with the Martin Luther King, Jr. Memorial Center. Martin's work could not die, and the many factions at SCLC were pulling in so many directions that it looked like nobody could even remember what Uncle M.L. had lived and died for.

Granddaddy had to help everybody find a new lease on life. I felt proud of myself, I was carrying a new life, a light in the darkness, and I was going to give Granddaddy something to look forward to in this new low ebb in his life. It was just like history was repeating itself. I had been born when Granddaddy was at a low place. Now, I was carrying a new baby, when Granddaddy was lower than he had ever been.

Jarrett was born in 1970, looking just like Daddy when he was born. Of course, his looks changed later, but everybody thought it was a miracle (just the same way we would feel when Derek and Janice's baby Derek was born looking like Granddaddy fifteen years later). Granddaddy and Bigmama were ecstatic. Mama was, too. Here was a baby, a new life for our family to cherish.

Jerry and I tried to settle in Atlanta. We got a low-income apartment near Ebenezer (some of the new housing projects). Jerry worked, and I went to Massey Junior College to take Executive Secretarial Science. I worked part time as tour guide at Ebenezer, taking people through the church, to show them where Uncle M.L. had preached. We made a little gift shop in the church library, where people bought souvenirs and mementos of Uncle M.L.'s life and teachings.

Granddaddy started picking up weight in those days. People thought that he was always fat, but he wasn't—just a bit stocky. But he was unhappy, pressured now. And he ate. Bigmama tried to control his weight, and had a little success, but it was an uphill battle.

After Jarrett was born, I was fat. I had gained more than sixty pounds. Jerry was disgusted. Here we were living in a one-bedroom apartment, in a low-income neighborhood. He had been brought up with nice things, so had I. And I was unattractive. He got a girlfriend. She would call in the middle of the night, and I'd answer the phone. She'd ask to speak to Jerry, and he would tell her he would see her the next day.

Just when I was ready to file for divorce, Jerry was drafted into the army. He was glad; now he'd have a chance to travel, see the world. He'd always enjoyed the ROTC, and he felt the army was just an extension. I decided to tough the marriage out.

I was terrified. I didn't want to leave Atlanta and my family, and I didn't want to stay without my husband, alone in the apartment, with baby Jarrett.

I begged Granddaddy to do something. Granddaddy arranged for Jerry to be permanently stationed in South Carolina, with a clerical job. That meant I would still have to move away from Atlanta, but at least we would not be going to Germany, as the orders had originally stated.

Jerry and I started having problems. We pretty much agreed that we'd ruined his life. His big chance to travel and have new experiences had been ruined. And I was getting fat again; the baby was just an excuse. Where was the slim girl he had married?

Mama was helpful during this time. She tried to support and encourage me. But she was in Atlanta and I was living on an army base in South Carolina.

I was rebellious and unhappy. We were living in a trailer park. When Jerry wasn't on duty, he was off somewhere with friends, leaving Jarrett and me in the drafty trailer. Jarrett kept catching colds.

Feeling sorry for myself, I called Granddaddy. Bigmama snatched the phone from him. "Veda, enough is enough. You will give your Granddaddy a heart attack. He has enough to worry about. You insisted on this marriage, now work it out yourself."

I was working at the college there near the base. Jerry and I argued about money. He said I was making enough to help out with the expenses. I was helping out, but I was used to a certain lifestyle. We fought. I had had enough. I packed up with Jarrett, returned to Atlanta and filed for divorce.

Back in Atlanta, I decided to try my hand at being independent. I did ask Granddaddy to help me get an apartment and a telephone, but I worked and paid my own rent. I started dating other men.

I think I was looking for Daddy and Granddaddy in every man I met. I ran into an old family friend, just after I got home. His father and mother had been best friends with my father and mother for years. Granddaddy was disturbed about the relationship. He didn't like divorce (it was bad enough that I was getting one, but to be involved with a man who hadn't even filed for one yet was unheard of) and he wasn't sure where I was headed). But at least he was my friend, rather than my dictator, and we could talk about these things.

I was too wrapped up in my own life to notice what was going on around me. Granddaddy's hair was thinning a little, he grew heavier. He was tired.

Mama was working at the Center, feeling like an employee rather than part of the helm. My brothers were struggling along without Daddy, but they were having a hard time.

Darlene was going through some rough times, too. She dealt with her frustrations by taking Mama's charge cards and running them sky high on shopping sprees.

Aunt Christine and Uncle Isaac were becoming more involved with the Center. Aunt Christine was working with the bookkeeping. Uncle Isaac was working with merchandising and marketing of the gift items. Aunt Coretta was pulling together a multi-thousand dollar center, and the community was looking on with admiration and jealousy.

I became a little more involved with the workings of the Center, and started editing the newsletter. I helped with the King birthday celebrations.

Bigmama became involved with making the Williams family home, now the Kings' birth home, into a national historic site. She gave the deed to the M.L. King Center (which had changed from the Memorial Center to the Martin Luther King, Jr. Center for Non-Violent Social Change).

The Center's operations had expanded so that the offices were no longer located in the basement of Aunt Coretta's home. The Interdenominational Theological Center had provided space in its basement for the Center's offices.

Aunt Coretta was traveling across the country now, speaking and raising funds for the Center. I would often travel with her as secretary and companion.

Jarrett started spending a lot of time with Bigmama and Granddaddy.

Al, Derek, and Vernon leaned on Granddaddy more and more for financial and emotional support. Since Daddy's death, Granddaddy had been there for them, with money for school, clothes, cars, whatever. It hurt my pride to see them so dependent on Granddaddy, while my cousins had their parents for support. Mama, of course, did not have the resources of Aunt Coretta or Aunt Christine and Uncle Isaac. She was pressed to pay the house note and monthly bills, and to buy food. I was working, and had the house painted. I had a dishwasher installed in her kitchen, along with a double sink. Granddaddy shouldered the burden, and kept going on.

I became interested in politics. Andrew Young was running for congress. He didn't succeed with his first bid for the fifth-congressional seat of Georgia. I volunteered for the second campaign.

Reverend Bennett didn't like having me around the campaign. There was too much intrigue, and I was no longer safely married. But I kept going to the campaign office anyway.

My romance with my childhood friend suffered as a result of the campaign. He was not political, preferring to sit at his house and sip wine and philosophize about things. I wanted to be where the action was.

I met a man eleven years older than I was (I was twenty-two at the time). He followed me around the campaign whenever I was there. I was a little frightened of him, though, and I wouldn't give him my address or number.

One night, when I got home (I was staying with Mother again, having discovered that I was too lonely in my apartment), Jarrett, who was four now, was shaking like a little leaf. I asked what was wrong. Mama said Darlene had taken some aspirin for a sore throat. Jarrett, who loved the ground Darlene walked on (she was so good with kids), had followed her and finding the aspirin bottle, with the top loose (this was before they came up with safety caps) took the whole bottle full. They had rushed him to the hospital, had his stomach pumped and brought him back home. I asked why they hadn't called me; they said they had everything under control.

I called my friend Phyllis Norwood, and was able to catch her in town. She was a stewardess for Delta and had a flexible flight schedule. Phyllis met me at the hospital. I called my pediatrician, Dr. John Hall, and he rushed over, admitted Jarrett to intensive care, and started him on fluids. I was upset and feeling pretty guilty. If I'd been a better mother, staying home, and maybe even married, Jarrett wouldn't have taken the aspirin. Phyllis didn't make me feel a lot better; she also thought I should slow down.

Feeling sorry for myself, I went to the phone and called the man from the campaign. He invited me over for something to eat. As soon as Jarrett was asleep, I told Phyllis I was going home for some things. She and I left the hospital together. She went home, I went straight to Bob's (this isn't really his name) apartment. A relationship that lasted two years started that very night.

Bob was very devoted, but he was possessive, and sometimes threatening. When Jarrett got out of the hospital, Bob started helping me with him. Jarrett hated eating; in fact, Dr. Hall said he was close to being malnourished. Bob would cook up the best food, and talk to Jarrett and play little table games and coax Jarrett to eat.

Granddaddy didn't approve of the relationship with Bob, but Bob was helping with Jarrett. And Granddaddy was glad to see

Jarrett picking up weight. Granddaddy had been so desperate to get Jarrett to eat that he had his pharmacist make up the old formula he used to use with Aunt Christine when she was a girl (she didn't like to eat either)—Risman B was thick and horrible, but it did help a little. Bob was better than the tonic for Jarrett.

Bob was very worldly and sophisticated. He had been a celebrity athlete a few years ago. He swept me into a world that was totally strange and alien for me. For two years, I was in a daze, doing everything Bob told me to do.

He said that I should be more involved with the Center. I started spending more time there. He said that I should continue my college education and suggested journalism because I was a good writer. I enrolled in Georgia State.

Bob tried to get to know my family. He would go over and do errands around the house for Mother and go to Bigmama's and work in her garden. I was staying between Bob's apartment and Mother's house now.

Bob was very jealous. He started driving me in my car to and from work. (He didn't have his own car because he didn't keep a job. When he didn't have enough money for rent, he simply vacated one apartment and moved to another.)

My brothers didn't like Bob. They felt he had too much control over me. I couldn't get away. Every time I said the relationship was over, Bob would threaten to kill me.

While Bob and I were going through this crazy relationship, things were going on in the family. Bigmama was becoming more and more nervous. More and more visitors were coming to the church services on Sunday—strangers from strange places. Bigmama kept having the premonition that somebody was going to come to the church and shoot Granddaddy.

One Sunday morning, Bigmama called me at home. "Come to church today, Veda. I have a new song I want you to hear." I told Bigmama I would be there, even though I'd been staying away from church quite a bit those days.

I called and called Bob, who had taken my car the night before. I was afraid he was out drunk somewhere, and I wouldn't see the car until time for work the next morning. Jarrett and I got dressed and rode to church with Mama and Darlene.

As we pulled up in front of Ebenezer, we saw people running out, screaming, "Oh my God, he has a gun." I jumped out of the car and ran to the laundromat across the street in sheer panic. Mama stopped the car in the middle of the street. I don't know where Darlene went.

The ambulance attendants came out of the church carrying Bigmama. She'd been shot while playing the "The Lord's Prayer" on the organ. Witnesses said the mad gunman, identified as Marcus Wayne Chenault, a 21-year-old man, had been trying to get Aunt Coretta, because he asked an usher for "Mrs. King" when he was escorted to his seat. The woman thought he meant Bigmama, because she was the Mrs. King of Ebenezer. She pointed to Bigmama at the organ.

Chenault sat down, opened the case at his feet, took up his gun and started firing. After he'd cut down Bigmama, he aimed toward the door at the far left (he was on the right, just below the organ) and started firing there. Granddaddy was due to come through the door just then. Several members were shot at that doorway. One was killed. Many dived under the pews to escape the bullets.

My brother Derek was on the pulpit. He'd been toying with the idea of becoming a minister since Daddy died. Now, five years later, seated in his grandfather's pulpit, the pulpit where his dead father had preached many, many times, he watched his beloved grandmother being shot to pieces.

Derek went crazy. Chenault stopped shooting and ran for the rear door on the right. Derek took off after him. Chennault ran out behind the baptizing pool and the choir stand and tried to escape from the fire escape. (It seemed that he had planned his way out. I think he hoped everybody would be in shock, and he could get away.) But Derek caught him and beat the hell out of him. Derek later said, "I wish I had killed him."

The ambulance arrived and took Bigmama to Grady. Somehow, Mama got a chance to ride in the ambulance, since the other family members were still in the church. She said Bigmama touched her jaw (where one of the bullets had gone in) once and groaned softly. Then she was still. Mama thought Bigmama died in the ambulance.

Mama was in shock. She couldn't believe that this was happening. Surely, Bigmama would live to be the friend she had always been. The little affectionate gestures that Bigmama had always made—little shopping jaunts, surprise gifts of scarves and jewelry, shared jokes and household tips—surely not all of this could be gone. Mama could not lose her dearly beloved friend. But it seemed that God had other plans. The gentle woman, who had tried in her own way to make Mama's life a little easier over the years, was gone.

Mama had suffered her second major loss—first Daddy, now Bigmama.

Granddaddy had suffered his third, and maybe most crushing loss. In his heart, he'd known the dangers of the lives his sons had led. And he'd given his fears up to God. He'd tried to weather those storms, and Bigmama had been there to help him.

Who was going to help him now?

Aunt Christine was pretty torn up. First, the loss of her brothers, and now, the loss of her mother who was also her very best friend in life. It was her mother who had helped her through girlhood illnesses, teenage traumas, romances of young womanhood, and the trials of marriage.

Aunt Chris had worked to make her marriage happy, and it hadn't always been easy. Uncle Isaac had been brought up in a strict family. He didn't want his son, Isaac, Jr. to be pampered. One day, when I was pregnant with Jarrett, visiting Bigmama, Aunt Chris had called. "Mother, help. Isaac is beating little Isaac." Of course, I was little Isaac's protector. After all, I had been his baby sitter since he was born, and nobody was going to hurt him. Parental authority wasn't a big deal with me, and I was going to the rescue.

We rushed over, and they were in the basement. Bigmama had used her key to get in. Uncle Isaac was beating little Isaac—who couldn't have been more than seven. I'm sure Isaac had done something. Kids could be exasperating, but the punishment was very strong. Aunt Chris grabbed Uncle Isaac's arm; he shook her to the floor. Bigmama tried to pull him away—he shoved her into the wall. I started cursing—"Dammit, man, stop!" He shoved me into the floor. His eyes were flaming red with anger. Bigmama's tears finally stopped him.

Bigmama was ever the protector of her children and grandchildren. Until her death, Bigmama was a cushion, a buffer, but we had no way of knowing that she wouldn't always be around to intervene.

Now, Bigmama was gone, too. Aunt Coretta was very sympathetic, feeling the loss as well. Although seven years had passed, she still mourned Martin—and she'd lost a very good friend and supporter in her brother-in-law. Yet, she had the work at the Center to dull the pain. But that same work put a limit to the amount of time she had to give to Granddaddy. She made a special effort to let him know he was always welcome at her house, for a bowl of hot vegetable soup, and lots of love from her (when she was home) and the children.

Aunt Coretta's children were having a hard time just then. Deprived of their father, they had to give up a lot of their mother, who left the children often to nursemaids and housekeepers. They didn't doubt their mother's love; they just missed her. And they grew to understand (and later become deeply involved) in the work that she was about. And now, for them, another anchor was gone. First Daddy, then laughing Uncle A.D.(who had been their swimming coach, and champion when their Daddy died), who had tried to fill the gap that their Daddy had left, and now, Bigmama. What more could life do to them?

Angela and Isaac had their mama and daddy, but their good friend Bigmama was gone. Bigmama had lived just around the corner; they'd seen her every day. She'd loved them and hugged them and they were bewildered at this loss.

Al didn't talk about Bigmama's death too much. In fact, when Daddy died he had stopped talking unless he had to. When he did talk, it was in slow monotones. How sad he was. Another star had gone out in his sky.

Derek turned to God, announcing that he would preach, right after Bigmama's funeral. He was filling a gap for Granddaddy, I think. Derek had the sensitivity to know that Granddaddy was feeling the loss of his sons and now his wife so deeply that almost nothing could bring him up from the depth of despair. Derek tried with his announcement that he would take up the torch, the songbook, and the Bible. Tragically, during these days, Derek also sought comfort in drugs as well. The problem would escalate in the next few years.

Darlene suffered almost as much as Granddaddy. She had been so close to Bigmama, and out of all the eleven grandchildren, Darlene had more of Bigmama's looks and temperament than any of us. Although Darlene was light and Bigmama was dark, Darlene had Bigmama's hips and legs, and Bigmama's sense of humor. Darlene had inherited Bigmama's love of shopping and pretty things. It was always Darlene who bought Mama pretty dishes, pots, and pans. Darlene decorated the house for Christmas.

Darlene and Mama stayed very close to Granddaddy. I refused to admit that Granddaddy was as low as we all could see he was. I closed my eyes to Granddaddy's misery. It was easier to lose myself in my own tragedies. But I couldn't put away my fears. Bigmama was gone. Would Granddaddy be next?

Even during these trying times, Granddaddy still loved sports. I remember that one day, during the days after Bigmama's funeral, a stranger came to Granddaddy's house to pick him up. He said that the mayor had sent him to get Granddaddy for a ball game. They left the house. The mayor saw someone leading Granddaddy into the tunnels underneath the stadium. He sent his security. Whoever the man was who had Granddaddy ran away. The mayor said he had not sent anyone to get Granddaddy. We were all very watchful after that.

Bigmama was gone. The gentle anchor of our family, who fussed at us to take pictures, scolding us when we wouldn't cooperate, telling us, "pictures are history," was gone. I could still hear her saying, "You all must behave." She, along with Granddaddy, had kept us together. All my life Bigmama had been a second mother to me. When I was little, she bathed me, combed my hair. She taught me how to dress and how to be a lady (and I could be a lady when I chose to be). Bigmama taught me about sex, and talked to me about love. In the last few months she had talked to me about Bob. "Veda, he is dangerous. He pretends to be nice enough, hanging around here, doing favors. But he is dangerous. Please be careful, he might hurt you."

Three weeks after Bigmama's funeral, Bob did hurt me. We went to a party that he insisted on attending. A man flirted with me, I danced with the man. Bob jerked me away and dragged me out of the house. Two friends, Rita and Ken Chambers (who Granddaddy had married three months before), followed us to the car. Bob was standing on the side away from them, stomping on my feet and saying, "Say one word to them, and I'll kill you!"

Rita called, "Veda, are you all right?" I smiled through tears and lied, "Yes, we're going home."

Bob drove me home, breaking the windshield as he tried to reach across and slap me. The impact jarred his anger. I think the pain broke through his alcoholic haze. He started crying, "I'm okay, sweetie. Forgive me. I'm sorry."

I took advantage of Bob's maudlin tears. "Look, Bob, let me drive you home. I have to go and get Jarrett, I'll be back." Bob agreed and I took him to his apartment. I went home, and started packing clothes, preparing to leave town and Bob the next day. I had to get away!

Late that night, the doorbell rang. It was the police. Bob was out selling some of my personal things that I had brought to his house right after Bigmama's funeral. (I had argued with Aunt Chris and Aunt Woodie to get those things. Aunt Chris said that I couldn't take anything out of her mother's house. I said that I could take what I damned well please as long as it belonged to me. I took some unopened wedding presents and some other things, including a necklace Mom's Mobley had given Bigmama on a visit to Atlanta. Bigmama had promised me the necklace—so as far as I was concerned, it was mine. Aunt Woodie and Mrs. Walker had been highly offended to hear me curse Aunt Chris out. Granddaddy had come in, and our squabbling upset him so bad that I left in a huff with my things. I took them to Bob's for safekeeping.)

Bob kept the jewels all right, just long enough to sell them for money for some more whiskey. The police had seen him, wavering in the street, selling the things out of the trunk of my car. (He had gotten over to Mother's somehow, used the spare key and taken the car.)

That was the end for me. I had been publicly humiliated. Bigmama's feelings about Bob were coming true. I had to get away before he killed me.

The next day, I got my car—Bob was in jail, I think. I didn't care. I left town, for Louisville. I went back to Jerry, who didn't exactly welcome me with open arms, but it was the only place I could hide.

Back in Atlanta, Bob was hounding Mama and Granddaddy every day. I didn't stop to think one moment how much trouble this was for them—they were still bereaved—and they had to be bothered with a crazy fool.

I took a job in Louisville; Helen got me on at Dupont, where she had worked for years. Helen was a lady and a jewel. She stood by me again. She recognized me for the selfish manipulator I was, but she loved me anyway. I had ruined the life of her son, and now I was back to work on him again. Still, she tried to help us make it work this time.

Helen and Granddaddy paid cash money down for a house for Jerry and me. I went to work every day and paid for the carpeting, the washing machine, the kitchen utilities, and the furniture. Jerry seemed surprised at my attitude. Since I was so resourceful, independent, and acting like I could handle everything, he just let me.

We took turns cooking, and he kept the house clean. In fact, Jerry was a stickler for neatness. When I suggested that we get married again and make a family for Jarrett, he said no way. I was too fat, too much of a nag, and I would just try to drag him back to Atlanta into the King menagerie again.

We argued, and things got worse. One night, we actually got into a fight. Jerry threw me to the floor, and stomped my leg so hard that I limped for weeks after the incident. Jarrett was so upset that he threw up all night. The next morning, I started throwing things into my car. Jarrett and I were going home.

I went back to Granddaddy, and he welcomed me with open arms. He was heavier, and seemed to be moving slower. I guess grief was still tugging pretty hard at him, even though six months had passed. Jarrett and I were constant company for him, though. I stayed closer to home now, having been hurt so much in the last few months. I really didn't care to date much.

My friend Janice Hale was single at the time, and sometimes we went out together. Phyllis and I would go out when she was in town. In time, though, I got lonely and called my friend from my childhood days. He had gotten his divorce and was living in an apartment. He had a lady, though, and I wasn't really up to the competition. She could spend the night with him, I wouldn't. I had to get home to Jarrett and Granddaddy.

My friend didn't like children, either. He and his wife had had problems because he refused to father a child for her. That's part of the reason they broke up.

I really cared a lot for this friend, but I couldn't have a man who hated children. I had one child and wanted more.

I was sad, dejected. I dragged myself to work every day (at Gray Line of Atlanta, where I was a tour guide and secretary to the vice-president). The guys there would tease and flirt with me, but I had no heart. My boss, Bill Merritts, got so tired of seeing my moping face that he said, "I'm going to introduce you to a good man."

I smiled then and said, "My friend, there aren't any."

But there was one good man, and Bill was going to introduce us. God had taken pity on me once again, and sent a blessing. So, I would meet and marry Cliff Beal, and we would have five children. I would finally become the mother of the six children I'd always wanted.

CHAPTER SIX

Granddaddy held the undisputed title of patriarch of the family. He gloried in the role. Three successful, accomplished offspring, eleven grandchildren and three great-grandchildren—he was proud of his dynasty. For the most part, his position was uncontested.

Uncle Isaac's family lives way off in Missouri. They are a supportive family, but they aren't able to visit very often because of the distance. Aunt Coretta's parents lived in Marion, and during their lifetimes, spent holiday visits and shared letters and phone calls and the like. Aunt Coretta remains close to her siblings as well. Still, somehow, during Granddaddy's lifetime, as father and grandfather to the whole "King clan", Granddaddy commandeered the role of patriarch for us all. For the most part, the in-laws were secure in their roles, and we co-existed in peace.

Such was not the case with Bigmama Bessie. She wanted as much attention as Granddaddy received from her grandchildren. She thought and planned during her middle years—years spent away from her only child Naomi and her five grandchildren. She would leave Cleveland, Ohio, and go to live with "Neenie" when she got old.

Daddy was pretty understanding of his mother-in-law. When Mama was having her children, Bessie didn't have time to come for each laying-in. It was months, and sometimes years, before she ever laid eyes on her grandbabies. But Daddy sent Bessie money whenever Mama said she needed help.

In her younger days, Bessie was a pretty woman, with dark brown skin, whopping big legs and hips, and a very tiny waist. She could bend from waist down and touch her toes. She was vain, living to dress up and receive compliments—especially from the opposite sex.

As soon as Daddy married Mama, Bessie felt her job of raising Mama was over. She took off for Cleveland. In Cleveland, Bessie married; not once, but twice. Mother, who had never known her father (he died when she was a baby), lost the companionship of her mother and never got to know her stepfathers.

Mama took it all in stride. Left alone, a bride, expecting a baby, she clung to Daddy. He was all she had, except Granddaddy, who told Mama, "Christine doesn't approve of you, you know. But I'll always stick by you." (When Daddy married Mother, there was much discussion about a King marrying the daughter of a domestic worker. Aunt Chris, having been gently bred, would have desired someone a little different for a sister-in-law. Over the years, Aunt Chris was very generous to us, but Mother never quite forgot the initial feelings and reactions to her background. Daddy would have enjoyed a little spunk from Mama, but she withdrew into a shell, leaving Daddy to fight the battle of gaining approval for his wife, alone.)

If Mama missed Mama Bessie, she never said so. Once in a blue moon, Bessie would call for a train ticket and she'd come for a visit. During those times, we remembered her as a jolly woman full of smiles—and good cooking. We enjoyed her jokes and her food, but we never really got to know her.

Soon after my sister Darlene died, Bigmama Bessie left her young husband in Cleveland and came to live with Mother. Mama Bessie figured that since Daddy was dead, and I was married and living away from home, my brothers would soon move out of the house and she and Neenie could grow old together.

There were many surprises in store. Bigmama Bessie's dreams of being a cherished grandmother were soon shattered. My brothers didn't mean to give up Mama's attentions or the house to a lady who had been away for years. They really didn't even know Mama Bessie. Bessie couldn't stand the fact that Mama was still cooking for them, and picking up after them like they were babies.

"Neenie, these boys are too old to be living here with you. They need to get married and get their own house."

Maybe Bessie had a point, but my brothers were not going to be run out of their own house, their Daddy's house, by their once-absentee grandmother. And Mother, devoted to her children, was caught in the middle.

Bessie started listening each time the phone rang. If Granddaddy was on the other line, wanting a favor from one of my brothers, Bessie would complain, "Why you go running over there to help Reverend King? He's a rich man. He can hire people to help him. Here I am, your poor grandmother, and I can't get you to take me to town."

My brothers didn't feel a need to explain that Granddaddy had been behind them from day one, and that when Daddy died, Granddaddy stepped right into the father role for them. What had Bessie ever done to make them know her?

I felt a little different about my grandmother. After all, she was Mama's mother—and I didn't have to live with her day in and day out. So I didn't mind doing things with her once in a while. I'd take her shopping, or buy her perfume, and do other little things. It was no sweat off my back, and I liked to have people like me.

But soon, the good deeds were hard to maintain. Granddaddy got wind that I was giving Bigmama Bessie a little attention. He'd call the house, and she'd be over for a visit. Suddenly, he'd need a head of cabbage from the store.

If Bigmama Bessie needed to go to the doctor, Granddaddy would need to go, too. They didn't share space well, either.

One year, I had a birthday party for Cliff. I invited Granddaddy, and I asked Bigmama Bessie to come and make some of her famous hot rolls. Before Granddaddy arrived, Bessie was in her glory. She was pulling pans of hot bread from the oven, strolling through the house, barefoot, with pans of hot bread. "Hot bread, made in the shade, get it while it's hot!" The people loved her show as much as they loved her bread.

Then, Granddaddy came in, and the guests flocked around him, cutting down on Bessie's audience. Needless to say, the bread cooled off while Bessie steamed up. Granddaddy spoke to her, and she rolled her eyes before answering, "Why, Reverend King. I didn't know you were coming." The competition was getting stronger.

In the meantime, Bigmama Bessie was wearing Mama out. Bessie didn't want Mama to work, she didn't want Mama to date, she didn't want Mama to go out of the house.

At this time, Mama was having an occasional lunch or dinner with her friend, Reverend Fred Bennett (one of Daddy's closest friends, and Uncle M.L.'s chief field marshal during the civil rights movement). Every time mother got ready to go somewhere, Bessie would pull a tactic. She would fall into a daze, she would wander off in the streets, she would accuse everyone of trying to sabotage her. Bessie clearly didn't mean for Mother to be away from her for one minute.

It all came to a head one day when I was giving Mother a break. When Mother got home, Bessie was crying, "Veda really is crazy!" I let my eyes get wild as I said, "Listen old woman, you make people think you're crazy. I am crazy mad! If you pull this junk one more time, I'll beat the mess out of you!" Mother almost fainted, and then had to keep herself from laughing when Bessie turned to her. "Veda really is crazy, Neenie. Why didn't you tell me?" (I did feel pretty crazy and silly when I heard the story two days later that Alveda Beal was on Boulevard fighting an old woman. The story circulated for months.)

Bessie was in and out of the hospital over the next few months. She was a little senile; her potassium level was abnormally high. She would concoct a special tonic, taking unripe bananas, soaking them in some alcohol and something else until they turned black. The she would rub the tonic all over herself. And she'd eat the remaining overripe bananas from the bunch, too.

Granddaddy was especially funny during this time. When Bessie was in the hospital, Granddaddy was all sympathy. "Poor soul, she's just pitiful, isn't she?"

But when Bessie was out of the hospital, keeping Mama, my brothers, and me hopping around to keep her out of the hospital, and tying up our time so we couldn't run errands for Granddaddy, Granddaddy's tune changed. "That woman is nothing but trouble. What can poor Naomi do with her? Bessie is a mess." When Bessie and Granddaddy would run into each other during these days, they had relatively little to say to each other.

I began then to really understand Mother's personality. Her capacity to show deep care and faith for each member of her family was incredible.

All the time, Bessie was chanting, "The blood of Jesus."

When Granddaddy called, I told him what was going on. "I told you that woman ain't nothin' but trouble. Why you keep fooling with her, Veda?"

I tried to explain. "Granddaddy, she is my grandmother, just like Bigmama was." He let me know I'd make a mistake by saying, "Hell."

"Well, she's Mama's mama, and Mama loves her. I love Mama, so I have to do what I can to help."

Bessie's potassium level improved enough, and her kidneys started functioning enough for her to be transferred back to Hughes Spalding's Psychiatric Unit.

At Spalding, the staff was finally beginning to believe that something was wrong with Bessie. She was admitted to the ICU with a high potassium reading of eight. Dr. Jimmy Graham said she should be listed in the *Guinness Book of World Records*, because nobody had ever survived with such a level. Bessie had registered seven or eight each time she was in the hospital, and recovered enough to go home and raise hell.

It didn't look like Bessie was going to recover this time. Granddaddy was in the same unit, with congestive failure. When he first discovered Bessie in the unit next to him, he said, "I'll be damned." Later, when he found out she was really sick, he got up from his bed and tried to talk to her. She didn't respond.

When Bessie regained consciousness, Cliff and I went to see her. Bessie looked at Cliff. "You're looking handsome, son. You'd better put Veda down. She's going through the change of life and I'm getting my period." Cliff laughed; Bessie was sixty-two years old. But I didn't think her joke was funny.

The hospital social worker suggested that Bessie be transferred to a nursing home. Mother wouldn't hear of it. She wanted to try and have someone care for Bessie at home. When Bessie was well enough to be released, Mama took her home and hired a private duty practical nurse. Within a day, Bessie was slipping off from the nurse and into neighbors' houses. Bessie didn't want a nurse to stay with her. She wanted Mama.

Mama agreed to put Bessie in a nursing home. She and I spent several days looking for a suitable place. Mother told Bessie that she would be going to a home. "Mama, I can't take care of you. You run off, get lost. I'm afraid you'll hurt yourself. You'll have to go to a nice home where they can take care of you."

Bessie started to cry. "You don't love me. Those boys just want me out of here. They ought to move. If I was Reverend King, you wouldn't put me in a home. He is a millionaire. He can pay somebody to keep him. Why can't you stay home with me?"

I wasn't going to have Bessie lay a guilt trip on Mama and make Mama change her mind. "Bessie, Granddaddy would never pull half the junk you do. So he'd never need to go in a home. I told you that you were going to keep acting up until people got tired. Now, Mama is tired." My eyes dared Mama to open her mouth.

Granddaddy was glad to see Bessie go to a home. "I think that's the best thing, Veda. Your mama spends every penny she has trying to keep Bessie up. Then she comes to me for money to help with her bills. Maybe now, your mama can get some relief."

We took Bessie to the home. It was nice, as such places go, but Bessie had to be kept in an area where people were not ambulatory, or needed constant watching, because there was staff for those needing special attention. Bessie's roommate was an amputee. Bessie was shocked and said, "She doesn't have any legs. That woman is pitiful. Neenie, I can't stay here."

The poor amputee's feelings were hurt, and she wheeled herself out with her leg stumps sticking out. Bessie looked at me and said, "This is your fault. You want me here."

I tried to keep from smiling. I did want Bessie there for a little while. I hoped that a stay in the nursing home would teach her not to manipulate people.

Bessie worked on Mama's mind. Mama went to visit every day, and took Bessie home each weekend. Finally, Bessie talked Mama into getting her a release. I thought it was too soon.

Bessie knew that Mama had a new friend; she wanted to see if she could complicate this new relationship.

I warned my mother. "Mama, tell her she can't come home. Let her stay somewhere else, but ask the nursing home to hold a bed in case it doesn't work out. Bessie's just playing another trick."

Mama didn't reserve the bed, and Bessie was up to her old tricks. Within a few days of her stay at the nice private home Mama had found, Bessie had tried to date her landlady's boyfriend. And Bessie was sneaking back to the church that taught her the speaking in tongues routine that usually set her off on a tangent.

We readmitted Bessie to Spalding until a bed could be made available at the home. The bed was not soon available. I asked a friend, Thomas Brown, owner of Landmark West Personal Care Home, to take Bessie for a few days. Landmark is a nice, clean, facility, but it is a home for the street people who get sick and have nowhere to go. Needless to say, Landmark wasn't classy enough for Bessie. Realizing she wasn't going to get to go home, Bessie decided the other home was better than Landmark.

Bessie returned to the home and did okay for a while because Mama and her friend would pick her up every weekend and take her to dinner or somewhere nice. The last time Mama took Bigmama Bessie for an outing, Bessie announced that she wanted to leave the home again. Mama said no. Mama and her friend were going to take Bessie to dinner and to the ballgame. Bessie pulled her stubborn, comatose act.

By the time they reached the restaurant, Bessie couldn't walk. Mama and her friend went into the restaurant and got carry-out food. When they returned to the car, Bessie was limp as a dishrag, and seemed to be out cold. When they got Bessie back to the home, she woke up enough to ask if Mother had changed her mind, and decided to let Bessie out of the home. Mother said no, and Bessie decided to starve herself to death if mother wouldn't let her have her way.

I made Mama see that Bessie was set on a path of self-destruction. Bessie was admitted to Grady Hospital with kidney failure. Mother and I went to visit her. The hospital staff whispered loudly as we went by, "It's a shame the way those Kings treat that old lady."

Bessie was up to her old trick, badmouthing the King family again. She called Granddaddy a miser, Mother a slut, and me a whorish bitch. I think she was becoming delirious.

Bessie hated being hooked up to IV units and heart monitors and other machines. "You don't love me, Neenie. Just let me die—pull the plug and let me die." Mama looked like Bessie had hit her; she was so hurt. "Mama, I can't let you die. I've done everything I can for you. What more do you want?"

Bessie set her jaw like a stubborn mule, and those were the last words she ever said. Each day, Mama went to see Bessie. I went every two or three days. Bessie was drying out like a shell, but the doctors said her constitution was so strong, that her body was fighting her mind's will to die. They asked Mother if she wanted them to disconnect the life supports. Mama refused.

Finally, after several days in Grady, Bessie died—just before Granddaddy, Aunt Christine, Aunt Coretta, Angela, Yolanda,

Bernice, Dexter, Isaac, Jr., and I were to go to California for the 1984 Democratic Convention. Everybody but I was going as a Mondale delegate or supporter. I was for Jesse Jackson.

Everybody but Aunt Coretta postponed the trip until after the funeral. Mama wanted a graveside funeral. The wake was at Hanley Bell's (the funeral home the family always uses). Mama laid Bessie out in a beautiful coffin, and her hair and make-up were done beautifully. But in death, Bessie still had that stubborn mule expression that she always wore when she didn't get her way.

At the funeral, my preacher brothers, Derek and Vernon, did the eulogy. I sang "The Lord's Prayer."

A contest that had lasted more than thirty years was finally over. Bigmama Bessie had left us to Granddaddy. There was no way of knowing that he would be leaving, too, in a matter of months.

CHAPTER SEVEN

Bill Merritts and Granddaddy were great friends. Granddaddy had met Bill some time ago, and asked him to give me a job when I came back to Atlanta. Bill knew that Granddaddy would approve of the man I was about to meet.

Bill arranged the meeting at Paschal Brothers Restaurant (a favorite family restaurant, owned by a black brother). He and I were sitting at a table having coffee when in walked Eddie Clifford Beal, future M.D. He was honestly the handsomest man I had ever met. He reminded me of Granddaddy and Daddy, not in looks because he is a tall man, 6'3", and Daddy and Granddaddy were both 5'8." He carried himself with confidence and assurance. I'd been looking for both in a man.

Eddie Beal (everybody called Cliff "Eddie" in those days, before little Eddie was born) smiled, he had gold caps in front. Daddy used to wear gold caps (but I thought gold teeth belonged in the 'fifties. I wasn't stupid enough to say so then, though).

We went to the LaCarousel Lounge (part of the restaurant) for a drink. For me, it was love at first sight. I had found a new savior. I could just tell that here was a man who could deal with all of my tricks.

And Cliff did. For the next year or so, we had a turbulent romance. My friend Phyllis was ecstatic about the relationship. She, like me at the time, was into astrology. She charted my sign along with Cliff and screamed to her mother Aileen, "Mother, this is incredible! Everything matches up!"

Granddaddy was very impressed with Cliff; after all, he was in residency now and would soon be a full-fledged doctor. The fact that Cliff was specializing in psychiatry amused Granddaddy. Daddy's field was psychology in college, before he turned to theology.

Mama, Darlene, and my brothers liked him, too, although they didn't see much of him. Jarrett was a little reserved around Cliff, for some reason.

Cliff's family wasn't nearly as impressed with me. They'd heard about my wild shenanigans during the past few years, and decided that I was a "wild woman."

Cliff didn't pay much attention to their warnings. We continued to date. He had a girlfriend, but I didn't care. I was fighting for my life—I had prayed in my despair (Shirley Barnhart, a member of Ebenezer, had told me about how she'd prayed for a good man and found her husband. When I was down, just before meeting Cliff, I had prayed to God for a good man)—and God had sent me Cliff.

I pampered Cliff. I'd go over to his house (he lived with his mother) and wash his hair and manicure his nails (he would drop hints after we were married to make me remember and do the same little things). His mother thought I had no shame, the way I came to her house and acted like I was already his wife.

I wasn't so sure I wanted to be Cliff's wife; I hadn't been very good at marriage before. But I did want him. We went on a cruise to the Bahamas, and his other girlfriend found out. I think they had an argument. He started seeing more of me and less of her.

One day, Cliff and I had a date. I called Phyllis and asked her to run with me to a happy hour before time came to meet Cliff. We stayed too long. When I got to Cliff's house, he was gone. Phyllis and I went on to the LaCarousel. Cliff was there with his arms around another woman. Phyllis and I played it cool. We took a table. Cliff looked up and saw me, excused himself to go to the restroom, and came straight to our table. It was hilarious. I said, "Go back to your precious, brown-skinned honey pot!" Cliff shrugged and went to the rest room. For the rest of the evening, he kept going to the restroom, coming past our table, picking at me.

Cliff didn't go home that night. I (who refused to dial Cliff's number during the first three weeks we dated) called his house every thirty minutes all night long. His mother was furious. I was hounding her son. The next day, in the middle of the day, he came home. He said he'd been there all night and just told his mother to say he wasn't there. I didn't believe him for one minute.

I got even. I went out with Janice one evening. I thought I was looking pretty tacky, falling into my habit of just raking a comb through my hair, with no make-up and a drab brown outfit. We went out to a club in Buckhead. While Janice was on the floor dancing, a man walked up to me and said, "You must be the most beautiful woman in this room."

I looked around, thinking he had to be talking about someone else. But he was talking to me. The man was a famous recording star.

I decided to go out on a few dates with the recording star. Word got back to Cliff (as I knew it would). He was furious. We went to a party with Bill Merritts at a hotel downtown. Cliff pulled me out into the hall. "Is what I'm hearing true? Are you hooked up with that singer?" I said, "What's it to you? I don't ask you about every lady you know!"

I thought Cliff would throw me out the hallway window. Bill came out, and Cliff cooled down. But from then on, even after we'd gotten married, Cliff acted real crazy when the singer was in town performing. He'd go off somewhere and get lost, refusing to talk to me until the singer left town.

Every time Cliff had a date with someone, I found someone to date. By now, his family was really getting furious. "See, she really is a wild woman."

But Cliff didn't care what people thought. I think he was really on a mission from God, to save me from myself—and everyone else from me.

Cliff's brother Walter found a girl from Washington, D.C., and decided to get married. His family, Bill's family, and Darlene and I went up for the wedding.

At the wedding, Cliff was introduced to a young lady and he started flirting with her. I got so mad I went out on the porch and threatened to burn the house down. Bill came out and cooled me off.

I sang at the wedding the next day, and we started back to Atlanta that night. In the car, Darlene kept complaining about her heart. Cliff thought it was emotional, that she was still suffering over Bigmama's death. He patted her on the back and told her to relax.

After we were back in Atlanta a few weeks, my family had another shock. Darlene, who had eaten a big meal of country-fried steak, cabbage, rice, gravy, and cornbread, had gone out jogging and had a heart attack. She died, even as Vernon administered mouth-to-mouth resuscitation, as she lay on the track field.

Vernon called me at Granddaddy's and gave me the news. "Darlene is dead." I was alone in the house. I didn't know where Jarrett and Granddaddy were. I screamed, shouted, pulled my hair, saying, "Nononononononononono!" I pulled myself together and went to Mama's to see if it was really true. It was. She was gone, my sweet, fun-loving intelligent sister (she was in a dual-degree program at Spelman and Georgia Tech, breaking out of the traditional Spelmanite role to study electrical engineering.) Even though she'd thrown a pair of manicure scissors at me last week, stabbing me in the forefinger, I would miss her terribly. We had just started getting to really know each other, and I loved her.

Al was in the front yard, staring up at the sky when I got there. "What next?" God only knew. We had another tragedy, and another funeral.

All of Darlene's school friends came to the funeral. Her boyfriends (she had two, both of whom had been pressuring her to marry them) were saddest of all. They cried and cried.

Mama's face was heartbreaking. Her mother-in-law, her brother-in-law, her husband, and now, her baby girl—it was a nightmare. Oh, God—could she bear it?

Granddaddy, of course, was crushed. Just one more loss, one more cross to bear. Was it Darlene's heart? Her Bigmama had had heart palpitations, and he was feeling a little strange in his chest now and then, too. How much could his old body bear, now? Physically, he was getting weaker, the pain in his ankle from the pin the doctors put in after a car accident, throbbed. The prostate surgery that he'd torn open in his haste to leave the recovery bed had been mended, but it was still not healing properly. And his heart was burdened down with grief. It would never mend.

Just after Darlene's funeral, Cliff and I went to Granddaddy. I might be pregnant, and we wanted his advice. What should we do? "Do? What else is there for you to do? You'll get married."

Somehow, from my perspective, God and I had landed a lifesaver in a sea of trouble. Cliff was going to marry me. One night, at ten o'clock, we called my family, his family, and Bill Merritts, and told them to come to Granddaddy's house. It was too soon after Darlene's funeral for a wedding. Granddaddy was going to marry us then and there. We'd had the license for several days while we talked back and forth about the marriage.

I talked real big saying, "You don't have to marry me. I don't need you. I have a big family—and a Granddaddy who can take care of everything." I was falling back into the same tactics I had used when I'd wanted to test Daddy's love. I was boasting that if he wouldn't love me, Granddaddy would.

Cliff married me and we lived with Granddaddy. At least I lived with Granddaddy. Cliff slept at Granddaddy's but he kept his clothes at his mama's and went home each morning to bathe and dress for work. So, our legal address was his mother's house.

During my pregnancy, I was very insecure. If Cliff were twenty minutes later than I thought he should be, I would have a tantrum. I kept poor Granddaddy awake for hours sometimes, complaining.

One night, I got real worked up. A couple of people had called with new versions of the old rumors. I had married Cliff for his money. (His family, based in Rome, Georgia, was quite affluent.) Cliff was a doctor . . . I had some nerve thinking that I had a right to a doctor.

Here was the other side of the ugly coin. Cliff had married me for my money. It was some big joke. I had no money. And the myth of Granddaddy's millions was not to be taken seriously.

But tongues were wagging. People were saying that I got pregnant to catch Cliff. Nothing could be further from the truth.

In keeping with a life-long superstition—I felt had a special mission to replace loved ones as they were taken from our family. I believed that God had sent me the blessing of a new baby because Darlene was going to die. Babies have a way of being born when tragedies come into our family. (In fact, I was a little surprised a few years later when Granddaddy died. I got pregnant, but Janice was already pregnant—so the pattern must be changing. Then it occurred to me, Bigmama Bessie had died during that same year; we needed two babies.)

By the time Cliff came home, I was overwrought, and needed to talk. Cliff was late and I was waiting for him. When he came home, he was sleepy and tired and wouldn't talk to me. I went and got the bleach bottle and started pouring it all over him. Granddaddy heard the commotion and came to the door. Cliff was sitting there in a puddle of bleach, bleary eyed and yet, somehow amused. He is the most patient man. Granddaddy ran his hand through his hair and asked, "What did you do that for, Veda?"

From then on, anytime it looked like Cliff and I would be ready to have a difference no matter where we were, Granddaddy would say, "Go get your bleach, girl." Cliff and I would laugh and forget whatever it was we were differing about.

So once again, I was a married lady. I wasn't so sure how to be a good wife. I'd had little experience, and had sought less advice. I decided to draw from the only marriages I'd had an opportunity to observe.

Mother was always the perfect wife and mother. She kept her house (from the little apartment in the Williams home to the ranch-style home in Birmingham, and then the elegant Louisville establishment, and finally the pretty Atlanta house, nestled away in the trees by the creek) beautifully. Almost every night that I could remember (from the time I went to live with her and Daddy when I was eleven), Mama would mop the kitchen floor before going to bed. And she would never fuss when Daddy came home at eleven in the evening or two in the morning, with friends and movement people more often than not, demanding cheese and eggs, sausage, bacon, and hot bread. Mama kept herself neat and pretty all hours of the day. And she kept us on schedules, making sure that we enjoyed school, church, and social activities, while keeping a house chore routine that satisfied Daddy (he insisted that we help with the housework).

Mama and I were becoming even closer. She helped me to know how to be a wife, and a mother. She taught me how to respect my marriage. From Mama, I learned to make a man feel king of his house.

Bigmama was my other example. She had been a lady who enjoyed activities away from home, but knew the importance of keeping the home fire burning. And she would make lunches for Granddaddy to carry to work. She helped him keep his weight under control, and always tried to have things nice and pleasant when he got home. From Bigmama, I learned to cook fast, good meals and keep the house comfortable for my husband.

Aunt Christine was a career wife. She worked every day, and yet got home in time to cook pretty meals. She fixed up her house with modern appliances to help make her house tasks easier. From Aunt Chris, I learned that you don't have to sacrifice a career for a pleasant home life.

Helen Hatcher was a career wife, too. She taught me how to keep romance alive in a marriage. She would always fix intimate dinners for her husband and herself, call him honey, and keep comfortable pillows about. "Love doesn't have to die with marriage," Helen once told me.

I tied all of these memories together, and weathered the first months of my marriage. I always made sure Cliff had something to eat when he got in the door. I'd turn the television to his favorite shows. I'd give him the best spot on the couch. (As the years went by, I would tease my girlfriends, threatening to write a book entitled, *Fix Dem Plates*. I'd vow that the only reason marriages weren't working so well today was that women were too independent. I felt that we could enjoy our careers, but we shouldn't mind pampering our husbands a little, too.)

During our first months of marriage, there was never a dull moment at Granddaddy's house. When things got too quiet, Granddaddy would shake a loud bell he kept next to his bed, expecting everyone in the house to come running. When we got there he'd laugh and say, "I didn't really want anything, just to see if you all were here." Soon his sister, Woodie, came down for one of her visits. I didn't always like for Aunt Woodie to come, because if there was one person alive who had as much influence over Granddaddy as I did, it was Aunt Woodie.

Aunt Woodie would spend hours with Granddaddy, tweezing hairs from his chin, rubbing lotion on his skin, and sharing old memories that I knew nothing about. Aunt Woodie had been a hairdresser in Detroit for years. She'd left Stockbridge soon after Granddaddy, and made her way north, where she'd picked up enough Polish to make her natural aristocratic characteristics shine to their greatest advantage. Aunt Woodie was wise and worldly, and could see through most of my games.

She and I waged a few skirmishes, each of us vying for number one position in Granddaddy's esteem. Aunt Woodie (she was seventy-five then), would boast of all the projects she and her husband Jerry had going in Detroit. (If what she had going was so great, I wondered why she didn't just go back home?) She'd boast about riding her bike and playing tennis. (I could just see her gray old head bobbing around a court.)

And she would talk about her active sex life. I was really curious about that—since I've always said I mean to be sexy when I'm ninety. She'd kid Granddaddy about saying that his days with the ladies were over. She could put Granddaddy in the best moods with her stories.

And Aunt Woodie, just like Granddaddy, had the gift of sight, too. She'd hint of things to be, and make me nervous, because sometimes I could sense things, too. And I was frightened of the power. I didn't want to admit that people could be blessed with visions.

Aunt Woodie was a naturalist. She was sure that she could help Granddaddy lose weight with some of her herbs and brews. She would go out into the woods and pick roots and berries and steep them, and bring them in to Granddaddy to drink in a tea. He did look a lot better after he would drink them. I was a bit jealous. Since Bigmama died, I had been the one to help Granddaddy with his weight. I didn't want to share the honor, even if Aunt Woodie was helping him. I realized that my attitude was selfish, but I didn't stop trying to outdo Aunt Woodie.

Aunt Woodie helped keep away the boredom of the months of pregnancy. She went home a couple of months before Eddie was born.

The months flew by, the rumors died down, I became comfortable being a wife. Eddie was born, and as soon as the doctor held him up for Cliff to see, Cliff smiled, made an "okay" sign with his fingers. Little Eddie, at birth, looked just like his Daddy. I was reminded of a story from long ago, when Daddy told Mama, "Girl, you'd better be glad that baby looks like me." We had another Eddie. Granddaddy, Mother, and Sally Mae were delighted. Cliff and I were happy parents; there was just one tiny shadow—too bad granddaddies A.D. and Cliff, Sr., and Bigmama King weren't there to see their new blood.

Soon after Eddie was born, Cliff was called to the army. He wasn't particular about going because he already had a blooming medical practice, with several patients. But he had to go. He would drive to and from Augusta just about every day—going to the fort—coming back to see his patients, baby Eddie, and me.

During Cliff's military days, Celeste was born. So, we had Jarrett, Eddie, and now Celeste. Our family was increasing, and Cliff wanted to be out of the army, to be with his family and his rapidly growing medical practice.

Jimmy Carter was president now, and he and Granddaddy were great friends (thanks to Granddaddy's prayer and hug with President Carter at the Democratic Convention that won the hearts of the millions of television viewers). Granddaddy appealed to President Carter to help get Cliff out of the army. Carter was such a stickler for regulations that he investigated every channel available for getting Cliff released. Finally (I don't know if it was an act of Carter, God, or Cliff) Cliff got out, with an agreement to repay for the military dollars he'd used to get through medical school.

Soon after Cliff was out of the army, we decided to move into our own home. Cliff and I both preferred inner-city living to the quieter pace of suburban life. We bought an old home downtown, near the place where he was born, and where his mother still lived. The house was renovated within a few months, and we moved in.

Marissa Neal, our governess, helped us move into the new house. She kept us amused with stories of the days when she'd been governess to Aunt Coretta's children, to Harry Belefonte's children, and years before, to actor Phil Silvers' children. "Nursie" was a jewel, and after she left us (when Celeste started nursery school), she would go over and help with Granddaddy when he became ill.

After Nursie left us, life became hectic in the new house. I had a husband, three children, and a new political career (another story completely—see chapter nine). I was torn between house chores and (legislative) House (of Georgia) chores.

My cousin Clara (who had divorced Bennett years before) had left her government job in Las Vegas, Nevada, and had come to Atlanta. She was going to stay with Granddaddy, but I invited her to stay with us. I needed the help, and Clara, coming from a big family (she was "Baby Hill" of Cleo's family), would enjoy the company.

Our days with Clara were a time of excitement. Clara found a job as a medical assistant. She would dress up every day and go to work, then come home with funny stories. When she was home, she spent time dodging Bennett, who would follow her around in his car. Clara was aristocratic, too, in her own way. She had such a classy way of dressing and speaking. And she was a Catholic. The children and I would go to mass with her sometimes.

Granddaddy was a bit jealous of the attention we were giving Clara. Clara had lived with him and Bigmama when she was a young girl. She had worshipped him, wanting to be like a daughter. When Granddaddy sent her back home, she felt rejected. Over the years, an antagonistic relationship developed. And now, Clara was back. Granddaddy felt like Cliff and I were taking sides. We were really just helping out a kin in need.

Finally, Clara wanted me to choose between her and Granddaddy. Who did I love most? Of course, nobody could ever come before Granddaddy in my eyes (except maybe Cliff and the children). Clara got mad and moved out. She called me on the phone one day saying, "I have a gun. I have one for you, too. Meet me at Five Points, and we can play Russian roulette."

I didn't know whether Clara was kidding or not. I called the police. She was really hurt; I had had my own flesh and blood arrested. Granddaddy wanted to hear none of it. "I told you to leave Baby Hill alone, Veda. Call her mother. Cleo'll know what to do."

Aunt Cleo talked to Clara, and Clara went back to Las Vegas. She would call us from time to time to let us know she was okay.

For the next few years, life went on pretty well. Then the Atlanta Child Murders started happening. We were living in our new home by then. We'd had an alarm system put in (just as we had in our other home, since we were living downtown). Granddaddy didn't feel comfortable with us being downtown, alarm system or no alarm system. He'd call every day, three or four times (as opposed to his usual one or two). "Are the children okay?"

The city was in turmoil. Mayor Maynard Jackson and Commissioner Lee Brown couldn't make heads or tails of the murders. Little boys (and finally girls) were being snatched and found dead days later. The city was looking real bad. The National Medical Association and the Auxiliary to the National Medical

Association were to meet in Atlanta in 1980. (I was an officer in the Auxiliary that year.) The mothers refused to bring their children to Atlanta.

Granddaddy panicked. "You see, they have sense. You'd better keep those children inside, Veda. You're too careless." His routine daily calls that I expected at about 6:00 A.M. and 7:00 P.M. increased from 2 per day to at least 5. He was constantly checking on the kids.

He survived the panic, and a man (Wayne Williams) was jailed. Police said the murders stopped, although nobody believed the crimes had been solved. Granddaddy didn't relax. "It's not all over yet, Veda. Watch those children."

I reprimanded the children for laughing, but he said, "That's okay, Veda, they're just children."

That was Granddaddy, all right. Always concerned for the children, and all of his children. He nourished the family as no one else ever would. Granddaddy helped my marriage to work. He helped me raise my children. He helped Aunt Christine, Uncle Isaac, Mama, and Aunt Coretta raise their children. He helped them with their projects, their causes, and their personal lives. What would life be without him?

CHAPTER EIGHT

Granddaddy spent the last fifteen years of his life reshaping his plans. He was not the kind of man to accept defeat. His attitude and philosophy of going on with God sprang from a deep and abiding faith, and a streak of stubborn determination that he got from his mother and his father.

Many times, Granddaddy told the story of how his mother sent him on an errand, and a white man stopped him on the way. The white man told Granddaddy to do something for him. Granddaddy said no, and the white man whipped him brutally. Granddaddy ran home, crying to his mother. His mother went right back dragging Granddaddy with her, and took to beating the man about the head and arms, telling him that he'd better not ever lay a hand on her child again. Granddaddy's mother was not one to be cowed by the experiences of life.

Granddaddy once told me how his Daddy had told him, "I don't care how long I have to live in this system. I'll never accept it."

Granddaddy had to live in the system. The society had killed his sons, and finally his wife. His dreams of building a religious dynasty had gone up in smoke—but Granddaddy didn't quit. And he never stopped changing the system.

"I don't care how far I have to go. What I have to take. I will never stoop so low as to hate anybody." These famous words of Granddaddy's carried our family through the many turbulent years that followed each tragedy.

Just after Daddy died, Aunt Coretta intensified the drive to complete the Martin Luther King, Jr. Center for Social Change. The center would be a place where people could come to learn about the teachings of Dr. King. The Center would be a source of programs reaching out to help the world community in peaceful, non-violent ways to solve the ills of our society.

The road to completion of the project was not easy. Aunt Coretta was forced to travel around the country and the world, speaking to raise money for the Center. SCLC, under the influence of Hosea Williams, civil rights veteran, now Georgia state legislator, accused Aunt Coretta of stealing money from the mouths of poor people for personal gain. Hosea once told me, "I have never felt comfortable in Coretta's home." I couldn't see why he hadn't felt comfortable. Aunt Coretta was a movement wife, and accepted troops day and night, when her husband brought them in for food and strategy.

The truth was that no one knew how much Aunt Coretta and her children had really sacrificed for the movement. They had given up husband and father to the world—never knowing the normal joys and sorrows of family life. Uncle M.L. spent precious little time with his family, being a man who gave himself to the world, rather than to family. And Yolanda, Martin, Dexter, and Bernice were just small children when they heard the news that the father they had never known had been shot in the head.

And while people learned to criticize Coretta for her regal carriage (calling her "Queen-King," when she would float into events late—seeming to onlookers to be oblivious to time schedules—appearing to feel that the world would adjust its schedule to hers), they never took into account the fact that she had to hold her head high, to keep from collapsing under the heavy burden that had fallen into her lap.

Daddy King's sons were dead. Daddy King was growing old and tired. Coretta's sons, and Naomi's sons (now that A.D. was dead, too), were too young to pick up the torch. She accepted a grueling schedule. Appointments and telephone calls were backed up so close together that she was often late from one appointment to another, trying to squeeze a lifetime of Martin's dreams into the short hours of each of her days. Coretta was not about to see years of struggle, strife, and near victory blow away in the turbulent wind now sweeping the scene in the aftermath of her husband's death.

After Uncle M.L.'s death, Aunt Coretta and her children could have lived quite comfortably on the proceeds of Uncle M.L.'s publishing contracts. Financial gain did not motivate Coretta King to take up the banner of her late husband. In fact, by continuing with Martin's work, Coretta put herself and her children in a situation similar to that which existed during Martin's lifetime. Coretta found herself giving every available cent back to the movement—a deed for which she had often criticized her late husband.

The sacrifice was worth it, though. The King Center, with the objectives of keeping Martin's philosophy and teachings of non-violence, grew each year. The offices moved from Coretta's basement to the Inter-Denominational Theological Center. From there, the Center moved to a renovated house redesigned for office use, next to the birth home on Auburn. Soon after, the King Center Complex was founded, with administration-program-archives buildings. Freedom Hall-Conference/Cultural Arts facility, Dr. King's Crypt, Freedom Walkway, Eternal Flame, and the Chapel of All Faiths were completed.

Now people can visit the center complex and study Dr. King's teachings. The birth home, screening room, library and archives exhibition hall and gift shop all give tangible evidence of the hard work and sacrifice of family, friends, and supporters of Dr. King's legacy. As the official national memorial, the King Center now provided programs for the people: Institute on Nonviolence, Institute on Cultural Affairs, the Labor Institute, Scholar Internship Program, the Early Learning Center, Voter Education, Basic Skills Academy and the King Week Program. Over the years, most of the family have taken active roles in various programs.

My mother went to work at the King Center, just after Daddy died. This was the first real job Mama had had in several years. She had chaired church committees, and was involved in some community activities. She often enjoyed singing in concerts for the church. But while during Daddy's lifetime Mama had worked at the bank and had dabbled in catering and interior design courses,

Daddy never wanted Mama to work. He preferred a wife who would run his house and greet him at the door with a smile and a kiss as he went out and came in.

Mama, too, had given her life to the civil rights movement. The long days and nights, when her house was overflowing with troops from the movement who often camped out on her floors and turned her kitchen into a restaurant, were part of her history. And the death of her husband, at a time when two of her young sons were just approaching manhood, would never be forgotten. And now, Mama was forced out from her life as a mother and wife. She had to fend for her family. Mama turned to the only life away from home that she knew—the civil rights movement. Only the movement had changed. Gone were the singing, marching men and women, the bomb threats, and the scare tactics. Now, Mother's days were filled with record keeping and telephone calls for the new Center. Soon, she started working in the gift shop.

While developing the programs for the early learning center and the basic skills academy, Aunt Christine soon found that she was needed in the area of books and accounting for the Center. When she first became treasurer for the Center, Granddaddy laughed. "Your brothers used to joke about how you would lock the refrigerator when we would leave you in charge of them and the house, when you were young. What would they do if they knew their sister was in charge of the records for the whole Center?"

For many years, Uncle Isaac took over the souvenir-concession department for the King Center. The watches, calendars, napkin holders, books, and other items that people were selling for profit all over the country (often without sending a dime to the Center), were now being sold at the Center.

During his lifetime, Granddaddy took an active role in the Center. He attended board meetings, made suggestions, and gave his support wherever it was needed. He wanted to see his son's work continue. The Center was the rebuilding of his dreams.

During her lifetime, Bigmama was very supportive while the Center was being built. She had her suggestions; her support was freely given. But the area that appealed most to her was the restoration of her old family home. Bigmama donated the Williams family home to the Center, and it became the "Historic Martin Luther King, Jr. Birth Home." Later, the Center turned over the rights of the home to the National Park Service.

I was not happy with the changes that were going on with the Center and the National Park Service. I felt that outside forces and King Center Board members had questionable motives about the Center, and that Aunt Coretta and the rest of us would suffer as a result. This would turn out to be true. In his book, *Growing Up King*, my cousin Dexter elaborates on this tragedy.

Even though I was concerned about the changing tide, my activities with the Center increased each year. I created the logo for and edited the King Center newsletter. I helped Yolanda (who was now director of the cultural program) and her mother's sister, Edith Bagley, with the Cultural Program, which boasted such talents as the Alvin Ailey Dancers, Stephanie Mills, and Leontine Price from year to year. (We even saw an end to the age-old feud between Granddaddy and Dr. William Holmes Borders, pastor of Wheat Street Baptist Church. For years, the two men competed to have the largest church on Auburn Avenue, if not in Atlanta. When Granddaddy's name gained national and then international attention, Borders' crusade grew stronger. His congregation grew larger. Granddaddy and Borders came close to stopping to speak with each other. Then in 1975, Yolanda needed a place to hold the cultural night for the King birthday celebration. Borders' church, which could easily hold 1,500, seemed the logical choice. She negotiated for the space, got it, and held the activity there. Granddaddy attended, complimented Borders, and the feud seemed to be over.)

But for many years, I felt that I was not really a part of the Center. The celebration was all about Uncle M.L. What about my Daddy? He'd been bombed, beaten, jailed, and probably killed as a result of the movement. And yet, not one little room that would be built in the multi-million dollar building would even have his name. They were naming the whole project after Uncle M.L.

I knew Uncle M.L. was the real hero, had the worldwide visibility. But I wanted people to know my Daddy, too.

The final insult came when the King Center helped Abby Mann to make the "King" television movie. It was okay, as movies go. There was a lot of action. Much of the family, including myself, had cameo spots throughout the film. But the characters were not true-to-life.

Paul Winfield (excellent, talented actor as he was) was too tall, too quiet, and too serious to portray Martin Luther King, Jr. Throughout the movie, Paul kept bending his shoulders, making people wonder why he was slumping or slouching. I think he was trying to identify with the physical statue of the man as King was several inches shorter than Winfield. And the wardrobe people had done no research. They had Winfield wearing loose collars, poorly knotted ties, and crumpled suits. Anybody who knew my uncle knew that he was an immaculate dresser who often changed shirts several times a day. And there were too few moments of camaraderie with his men. The true essence of King was lost in the movie.

Cicely Tyson (marvelous actress) struggled very hard with what she had to work with. Cicely met and talked with Aunt Coretta, and she saw the regal carriage, the underlying love and compassion, and the natural sensitivity of the woman. But in the film, the director often squashed every nice moment that Miss Tyson strove to create.

Howard Rollins (brilliant in *Ragtime*) just could not create a believable Andy Young. He looks nothing like the man and lacks the natural sense of joviality and humor. Rollins was intense throughout the whole picture. Life in the movement was fast-paced, with many intense moments. But there was a lot of love and laughter that the unconvincing pillow fight scene near the end of the movie just didn't get across to the audience.

The greatest insult from the film was the portrayal of my Daddy (admittedly, it was hard for me to be objective, but so many people agreed). The actor who played Daddy was also a very excellent actor, but he knew nothing about the man my Daddy was. Nobody seemed to feel that much creative consultation was needed for this character, so the actor had to go on what little he could find. As a result, Daddy was portrayed as a weak, shallow, high-strung man, emotionally attached to his brother to such a degree that he fell totally apart at the time of the shooting. They made Daddy seem much shorter and fatter than Uncle M.L. In fact, Daddy was taller. They dressed him like a slob and Daddy was always a sophisticated dresser.

After the movie, I felt betrayed. Nobody understood my father. Nobody recognized my mother as the widow of a man who had contributed so much to the civil rights movement.

The family had been so excited about a movie that gave, at best, only a general portrayal of the events of the movement. The human drama was misinterpreted.

A few years later, another project came into being. A director/playwright wanted to do a play about the "Boy King." Rand Hopkins contacted me and asked how to go about getting consultation from the family on the project.

I gave Rand Christine's and Yolanda's phone numbers at the Center, and suggested that he talk to them about the play project. Rand tried to contact them, but after a couple of attempts, he gave up and went on with the project on his own. Aunt Chris and Yolanda were rather busy during this time, and the play was not a priority for them. It was for Rand.

Rand put the play together and asked Jarrett to take the title role. I was honored with Rand's choice. Jarrett is a good actor, and had performed with Rand's company, "Stage Directions," before. I was a member of the board. I knew that Rand's choice of Jarrett for the role was due to Jarrett's ability, rather than his family connections.

The family suspected otherwise. They felt that Rand wanted to exploit the King name. They were totally unsupportive. Granddaddy, trying to go along with the family consensus, grudgingly agreed to give an interview with the cast at my insistence.

On opening night of the play, Andrew Young attended, and was very moved by the performance. He said that it was a good thing for children of today to see how young Martin Luther King, Jr. grew to be the man they read about in history books.

Since there wasn't another work of this type available for public viewing (so little had been done about young Martin), people were excited about the piece.

The characters were not quite authentic because the actors were not able to interview family members in order to develop the characters. But the portrayals were moving and totally inoffensive. There were smiles and tears throughout the play, from Mayor Young and many others as well.

On the last night of the play, Granddaddy, who had not been able to attend due to illness, got up from his sickbed to come and see Jarrett perform. He had seen every piece that Jarrett had ever done. He was not about to let his great-grandson down now.

Granddaddy was wheeled into the theatre, too weak to walk (this was two weeks before he died). As he came through the stage entrance, and was wheeled into the auditorium, the audience roared and cheered with approval. They were so glad to see the real-life "daddy" of the "Boy King."

As Granddaddy watched the play, he became very involved. He chuckled at the humorous moments, wiped his eyes at the emotional moments, and smiled a special smile at the romantic moments between the characters King, Sr. and his wife Alberta. I asked him, "Was it really like that, Granddaddy?" He nodded his head in agreement, "yes".

A beautiful award was given—a sculpture depicting King at various stages of his life. The artist, Hopkins, was the brother of Rand Hopkins. Granddaddy was unable to leave his wheelchair so Aunt Christine, Mother, and I accepted the award on behalf of the Center. Aunt Chris took the award home, and Aunt Coretta and the Center staff didn't see it.

Several months later, I insisted that Aunt Chris take the sculpture from her house and send it to the Center so that a proper thank-you note was sent. A beautiful letter was sent then, and I felt better still. I couldn't understand why, when the family had supported the King movie—with all its problems, they couldn't have been a little nicer about the play *The Boy King*.

I became embarrassed about other things, too. I was beginning to realize that people were beginning to resent and ridicule my family. When we would ask Granddaddy to call and request complimentary tickets for ball games and rock shows, they would give him the tickets, but we'd hear rumors that "those Kings are begging again. You'd think with all the money they have to build that Center, they could buy tickets to a show."

We didn't take notice of what this asking and begging was doing to Granddaddy. He was a proud man, who had worked his way from a country town to the top of a family. He, who was known by the world, reduced to begging for favors that the world would have been happy to give. After all, hadn't he and his family given their very lives so that men and women could be free?

For this reason, the King family, immersed in our own pain and sorrow, was taking human kindness for granted. We were forgetting human nature. People were quickly forgetting that we had given up our normal, natural order of our lives so that they could sleep downtown in once-segregated hotels and that they could eat in once "white-only" restaurants. People were forgetting that their $25,000 jobs, their multi-thousand-dollar businesses, and their political seats were bought with the blood of our fathers, with the tears of our families. Why should we Kings feel like we deserve special privileges? We could buy our tickets, pay for our parking, like anyone else.

The spotlight at the top is bright, but fleeting. People were turning on us. Aunt Coretta was being accused of hoarding power, and Granddaddy was accused of trying to run the city. I wondered if my family wasn't getting too far away from the people. Was that why people were forgetting how much we loved humanity? Daddy, Granddaddy, and Uncle M.L. used to walk the streets, shake hands with the people, play pool, eat a rib sandwich, and drink a beer (except for Granddaddy, who didn't drink).

Granddaddy was still pretty much loved by the masses because he, like his sons, enjoyed getting out among the people, rubbing shoulders, talking, sharing life's experiences. He hadn't lost that fascination for learning new things. But he was getting old, and didn't get out as much as he used to. And Bigmama, bless her heart, up until the day she died, didn't feel safe with Granddaddy walking the same streets he'd been walking for more than half a century.

I didn't like the way that people were feeling about us. I was resentful, but felt on the other hand that we as a family were somewhat responsible. To all the world, thanks to the snakes and wolves around us, it appeared that we held out our hands for favors, but did nothing to let the people know what we were doing to help the community today. A lot of people were getting rich on our efforts, and stabbing us in the back at the same time. It was a lack of communication, a lack of marketing, I guess. We were living on past laurels. It was time to wake up—get back in touch with the people we were still dedicated to serving.

CHAPTER NINE

Granddaddy had always been one for remembering funny stories. We'd have family dinners, with close friends as guests sometimes, and people would ask Granddaddy how some things came to be in his family.

At our last family dinner with Granddaddy, I called everybody together to announce that I was going to run for a seat in the United States Congress. The family gathered, and before we got into what would become a major debate, someone asked the question, "Veda, how did you ever become interested in politics anyway?"

I pointed to Andrew Young, who was at the table with his wife Jean. Then, I pointed to Cliff, and I pointed to Granddaddy. "There are the three men who are responsible for my interest in the world of politics."

I explained how I'd first taken an interest in politics during my days in Louisville when the governor appointed me on a youth task force. I met a black state legislator then, Georgia Davis, who impressed me greatly. Then, a few years later, I became a very active volunteer in Andy Young's campaign for congress. But I had never seriously entertained the idea of running for office myself until Granddaddy invited me to accompany him to a Democratic Party dinner one evening. I asked Granddaddy to tell the story.

Granddaddy reared back in his seat, full of crispy duck that I'd fixed especially for him. He pulled at his suspenders and smiled.

"I had tickets to the Jefferson-Jackson dinner, and I needed somebody to go with me. Veda and Eddie (Cliff) were with me at the time, but Eddie had just come in from Augusta. He said he was tired and would stay home with baby Eddie. Veda had just had the baby a few weeks back, and hadn't done much to fix herself up yet. But she seemed excited about getting out. She rushed to take a bath and came to my room in a little while, looking like a fat doll, dressed up in something pink. Cliff was sitting on my bed reading the paper. He looked up at his wife and asked, 'What you put that on for, Veda?' Suddenly, Eddie jumped up and headed across the hall. When I asked him where he was going, he stuck his chest out saying, 'With you! I got to protect my interests!'"

When everybody finished laughing, Granddaddy looked at me and smiled. "Veda did look pretty good that night."

I took up the story from there, telling how I sat between Granddaddy and Cliff as the local politicians were introduced. Suddenly, Cliff leaned across me, looked at Granddaddy and winked. "Why don't you run for city council, Veda?" I was astonished. Granddaddy was, too, for a minute, then a gleam came to his eyes. "Sounds like a good idea to me." Between the two of them, they decided that it was time to have a politician in the family. I ran for city council, and I lost—because no one knew me—and I got into the race at the last minute. But I got name recognition. People found out, from my day-to-day knocking on doors and visiting small business establishments. They believed that I knew the issues, and that I cared about the people.

Losing the race was like falling off a horse for me. The best cure was to try again. But I was pregnant with Celeste by now, and could only lay the preliminary groundwork for a campaign. But, as soon as Celeste was born, I put her on a pallet next to baby Eddie and my sister-in-law Pat's baby Mi-Mi (over at Sally Mae's house) and Pat and I would take off on the campaign trail.

Granddaddy and Cliff were fully behind me in this race, as were Cliff's family, and Mother, and my brother Al. Granddaddy and Cliff raised funds (Cliff was my major financial supporter). Sally Mae and Mother were lifesavers with the children. Al roused himself and put out brochures (he's usually hermit-like, shy, reserved, keeping to himself). Vernon and Derek thought I was grandiose and crazy. Aunt Christine wasn't so sure that the life of politics (with its intrigues, schemes, and strange bedfellows) was the kind of life for a member of the King family. I insisted that I could keep my nose and my mind clean, and be an effective political activist.

Aunt Coretta was supportive but busy. I think she would have welcomed an opportunity to share advice with me, but I didn't bother to ask. I was out to give the King family a new image, to try for territory where no King family had gone before. And I wanted to do it on my own, without too much support from the King name.

Andy Young introduced me to my campaign consultant, Helen Bullard (now deceased). Helen was well-known in the Atlanta community. She took a liking to me. "Don't overexpose the King name, dear. Let Beal be the name people recognize." So, I became Alveda King BEAL, with the Beal in big, bold letters. My brochures were printed in "Helen blue," guaranteed to be a winning color.

My campaign advisor, former legislator E.J. "Big Daddy" Shepherd, was very enthusiastic about the campaign. "Let them know that the Kings aren't stuffed shirts. Get out there and meet the people!"

And we did meet the people. I, with my crew of faithful friends, Pat Beal and Joyce Dobbs, knocked on over 700 doors that summer. This didn't seem like such a big number, but a candidate can win a seat with less votes. When the votes for the 28th district legislator came in, Alveda King Beal, campaign underdog, was the winner in a race of three candidates. We had won without a run-off!

My family was really surprised. They'd never expected me to go so far. I'd earned my college degree, a paralegal certificate, snared a good husband, had two babies, and now, I was a bona-fide politician. It only goes to show what a fighting spirit and good DNA can do for a person. The deed was done; now, to win the populace.

What would people think? People thought many things: "Another King trying to take over," "Those Kings think they have everything now," or, "Alveda is really a nice person, not like the rest of those uppity Kings." Reverend Bennett, a very reliable source of grapevine information, got the news to me. I didn't really care what people thought. They knew that there was a King out on the streets, among the people again.

I became known as a flamboyant character. I upgraded my wardrobe, went on a diet, and changed my hair color and style. I took on major issues, became very outspoken. During the tragedy of the child murders, I suggested (tongue-in-cheek) that if we would have public flogging and amputations, people would think twice about committing crimes. The newspapers named me: "Alveda the Hun."

As a mother and homemaker, I took a serious interest in the prevention of fetal alcohol syndrome and prevention of family violence. A law permitting the judge to require appropriate counseling in cases of family violence was added to Georgia's laws because of a bill that I passed.

Somehow, the real problem came from the black power structure. Like Jimmy Carter, who turned America upside down with his election, I hadn't been in the cards. A member of the King family had entered their ranks. What were they going to do with me? I couldn't be bought or controlled. As far as the locals were concerned, Daddy King was bad enough. The old man had a hand in just about every aspect of the black community (he was on the board of the CTB Bank, Morehouse College, and he'd cosigned notes for half the black preachers and businessman who were successful today). He was the unofficial lawyer, financial advisor, social worker, and politician for much of Atlanta's black community—and his fingers extended into the white world as well. And now, this—he'd put his darling granddaughter in office. What next? Did "Daddy King" want to run the whole town?

Granddaddy didn't want to run the town—and he didn't really put me in office. He was just the catalyst. He'd always say he wanted a "businesswoman, a lawyer, and a politician in the family." Well, Aunt Christine, Uncle Isaac, and Dexter were proving to have the keen business minds; Derek, Vernon, and possibly Martin and maybe Jarrett and little Eddie would be preachers; Isaac Jr. and Bernice (who later actually finished law school and theology school at the same time) had been slated to be our lawyers. What else was there for me but politics? I had to shine in Granddaddy's eyes.

My natural inclination was for the arts and show business. I loved to sing, act, and dance. I had appeared in a few movies and stage plays even. On stage, in a leading role in *Tambourines to Glory* (a rousing gospel musical), I played a preacher. I used Granddaddy's white robe, and borrowed his preaching style, to bring the audience to shouts of joy and laughter.

But Yolanda and Jarrett had already cornered the actors' market, and most successfully. I wanted something that would make people proud of A.D. King's daughter and Daddy King's granddaughter—something all my own. And I was a winner at politics.

I called on some of the natural charisma and honesty I'd hope I'd gotten from Granddaddy; some of the gentle persuasion I'd learned from Bigmama; the roguishness, zest, and fearlessness from Daddy; the gentile feminine charm from Mama; the gutsy manipulative skills of Bessie; and the oratory power of Uncle M.L. I rolled all of these traits together. They were there in my blood. And I used them to become a successful politician.

I made friends in the legislature; I learned fast—kept my eyes and ears open and my mouth shut. I became "Miss Alveda," to House Speaker Tom Murphy. I learned that men (and women) could be fair, no matter what their color or labels.

I passed more bills in four years than some legislators had passed in ten. I was enjoying my success. I ran my second term uncontested. But the wolves were after me. At the peak of my legislative career, three things happened to change the course of my political career.

First, U.S. Senator Herman Talmadge, known by the public as a hard-nosed, powerful, yet racist and alcoholic politician, was having trouble being re-elected to congress. By this time, Atlanta, with a 60+ percent black population, decided that there would be no more "good old boys" elected to office with their votes.

Talmadge's father, Eugene, had been such a racist governor that when a group of little black school children went to the governor's mansion to sing Christmas carols during his term, he left them outside in the cold, while inviting the groups of little white children in for hot chocolate. This was just a mild example of his racist tactics.

Herman Talmadge followed in the footsteps of his father during his early political days. But as the black voters' population increased, Senator Talmadge's office became known for its constituent services—for blacks as well as whites. Many blacks, when stopped on the streets of Atlanta, could recall when Talmadge did something to save their lives or their careers.

But the black Atlanta power structure, led by Mayor Maynard Jackson, was out to get Talmadge. Their chosen candidate was a man I admired, Lt. Governor Zell Miller. While Zell, too, in his younger days has a record that wasn't a whole lot better than Talmadge's early record, Zell had proven himself to be a fair-minded man during his term as lieutenant governor. He was admired and respected by many, including me.

For a long time, there were no questions in my mind as to who I would support. As a state legislator, I knew and trusted Zell Miller. I had no problems with seeing Talmadge go.

Then, one day, I was sitting on Granddaddy's bed listening to the news. There was a story about how black Atlanta was bringing Talmadge's record to the public eye.

Granddaddy sat in his rocking chair and squinted up his face (a habit that he had acquired recently, during his heart episodes—we never knew if he was in pain or if this was just a new habit). He grunted a little. I asked what was wrong.

"They just aren't treating Talmadge right. He came by to see me today, and I remembered so many times that I had to call that man to help some of my members. He never refused us, and he always did something to help."

Cliff was sitting there, too. "Are you going to help him, Dad?" Granddaddy sighed and shook his head. "I wish I could, and I would if I were younger. But I'm old and tired now."

Cliff looked at me and said, "Maybe there's something you can do for Talmadge, Veda."

The next day I called the senator's campaign office and offered my services. They were surprised and delighted. Curtis Atkinson, the senator's black staff assistant, got in touch with me immediately. Soon, I was busy, going around the district, making speeches for the senator. "I know the man was a racist. And he used to drink. But Martin Luther King, Jr. said we have to love those that have done us wrong. Herman Talmadge has changed. We must forgive, even as Christ forgives. Talmadge has done a lot to help this district—he has helped black and white alike."

The black power structure was furious. A decision had been made. Talmadge was going. Who did I think I was—new to the world of politics, yet jumping into the enemy camp? Talmadge was not to be forgiven. Neither was I.

I was involved in a business venture at the time—a group of women was negotiating for a concession at the new Atlanta airport. They told me that I needed to pull out of the venture. They could not support Talmadge, and they were afraid my support of the senator, in direct opposition of Mayor Jackson and so many other members of the black community, would hurt their chances of getting the contracts.

I pulled out of the venture, but continued to support Talmadge. The pressure for me to denounce my support became almost unbearable. My hair turned gray. I gained weight. But I kept working for Talmadge. I believed the principles, for which my father and uncle had died for—which my grandfather still lived by—hatred is destructive. Only by forgiving and working together could we solve the problems confronting us.

Things got so bad, finally the newspapers were tearing away at me. Cliff was helping out with the calls at home, since people were calling and criticizing my support every day. Cliff was so supportive, but I was still feeling pressure. I went to Granddaddy, climbed onto his lap and put my head on his shoulder. He was surprised. "Get off my lap, girl. You're not a baby anymore."

I wasn't a baby but I needed his support and reassurance. "Granddaddy, the public is tearing me apart."

Granddaddy shook his head and put his big hand on my head. "Veda, why do you always get so deep into things? I thought when you said you were going to help Talmadge, you meant a little something. You're way into this mess, now."

I asked him, "But you don't think I'm wrong, do you?"

Granddaddy pushed me off his lap, and looked up at me as I stood there, hoping that he was still with me.

"No, Veda. Talmadge was in trouble, and he needed help."

Talmadge won the Democratic primary, but he didn't win the general election. He lost to Republican Matt Mattingly, who rode in on Ronald Reagan's coattails in that landslide election that sent Carter back to Plains.

Talmadge lost the race, and I won some political enemies—people who had never really supported me were totally against me now.

I had set a pattern by now. Self-respect was outweighing political popularity more and more in my decision-making process.

I had another major decision to make. I was lobbying heavily for my prevention of family violence bill. I went to Speaker Tom Murphy and asked for his help in getting my bill to the floor. He spoke to the rules committee and the bill was voted out of committee to the floor.

The very next day, a bill regarding the Board of Regents (who govern our university's system) was to be voted on. Early that morning, Speaker Murphy called me aside. "Miss Alveda, this bill is probably going to pass, but some of us are going to have to vote against it. Can you vote against the Regents bill? Have you made any commitments?"

No one had approached me about the bill as yet, so I told the speaker that I would be voting "no."

Right after lunch, the bill came to the floor for debate. Soon, my black colleagues started receiving notes from Jesse Hill, president of Atlanta Life Insurance Company, president of the Atlanta

Chamber of Commerce, and member of the Board of Regents. He wanted the caucus to vote yes, for the bill.

I waited for about twenty minutes. I received no note from Mr. Hill. I went out into the hall. I felt that I owed Mr. Hill the courtesy of explaining how I'd committed my vote to the speaker.

Mr. Hill was a close friend of the family. Granddaddy had asked Mr. Hill to help me get my apartment a few years back, and he did. Mr. Hill had assisted me in an important business venture, helping my associates to raise capital—which they never repaid to him. Mr. Hill was very supportive of the King Center.

I approached Mr. Hill as he sat in the hallway, talking to male colleagues. "Mr. Hill, may I speak with you?" Mr. Hill was talking rapidly to several people at once. He was known for his hard-nosed, rapid, business tactics. He moved and talked so fast that people often agreed with him before they really had time to absorb what he was saying. Mr. Hill, talking for one split second, glancing at me, said, "Wait a minute, Alveda. I'm talking to these people."

I waited five minutes, and tried again. "Mr. Hill."

Mr. Hill became aggravated. "Alveda, I'm talking about something important. I'll see you later."

I waited for twenty more minutes, talking to my colleagues as each walked away from his hallway conference. I tried one more time. "Mr. Hill, I must speak to you!"

Mr. Hill simply waved me away and started talking to another group of legislators.

I waited in the hallway, trying to speak to Mr. Hill until the buzzer rang for us to go back in to vote.

All of us legislators returned to our seats. Mr. Hill went upstairs to the gallery to watch his votes come in. We voted. I pressed "no." The red light came up on my panel. My name was recorded on the large board with "no" clearly visible.

Jesse Hill counted those votes that should have been his. Mine was not there. He looked at me. I shrugged. I tried to call him to explain, but he refused my calls. I had Granddaddy call, but Mr. Hill's fast-working mind was locked fast on hostility. I, the girl he had helped so many times, had turned on him. I had embarrassed him publicly. He had never met such an ungrateful person. What could Tom Murphy and the House leadership have possibly offered me that could compare with the friendship and support that he had given my family over the years?

Tom Murphy and the Georgia Legislature had given me respect as a legislator. They heard my bills as they came to the floor. They included me in on committees and even made me a chairman of a subcommittee on education. They had sent me away to a conference on education. They had not taken my support for granted. They had sought me out.

The Regents saw their bill passed. Jesse Hill was commended for his lobbying efforts. I lost Mr. Hill's support. I don't think I lost his respect, though. I don't think I'd ever had it. But I won support for my bill, and it passed. And I kept my self-respect.

My legislative career was growing, but I was making political enemies every day. I was not to keep that seat of which I and Granddaddy were so proud, much longer.

Reapportionment came. A federal mandate came down, requiring the state of Georgia to redesign legislative districts so that a more proportional number of blacks could have a chance to be elected to public office. The leadership of the house was against plans submitted by the legislative black caucus. I was in full support of the caucus. Ironically enough, though it was not the leadership of the house that sought to do me in. It was a black woman, senior legislator Grace Hamilton, who had promised to deliver the black support to the leadership plan.

When I refused to support Grace's efforts, she told me, "You can kiss your seat good-bye." She couldn't wait to cut away at my voter population, decreasing my support. She did. Most of my voters were now in a new district. I would have to scramble for votes, start anew. Grace wanted to see me sweat. But I knocked her off her vengeful horse of power. I didn't even run.

Cliff and I had been talking for a while about a new political pursuit. Reapportionment was giving more votes to our congressional district. Some people were saying that the seat (held by white incumbent Wyche Fowler ever since Andrew Young gave it up to join Jimmy Carter's administration), should go to a black. I felt the seat should be held by a woman, and that as a black woman, I might have a chance for the next seat. If not, then, I could take a break, get my master's degree, teach for a while, spend a little time with the kids, and run again next time.

The game plan was set. I was going to announce on the night Joe Frank Harris (friend and fellow legislator) won the primary race for governor. Granddaddy and I had endorsed Joe Frank in his bid. Granddaddy liked to back winners, and I convinced Granddaddy that Joe Frank was going to win. I brought Joe Frank over to the house to meet Granddaddy prior to the endorsement. Granddaddy looked at Joe Frank and said, "You're a fine figure of a man. You stand up tall. I like you." Joe Frank and Granddaddy became friends.

The very night I was going to announce my bid for congress, Ben Brown, a former legislator, came up to me at Joe Frank's victory party. "I hear you're going to run for congress. Please don't. Julian (Julian Bond, state senator, civil rights activist, and once named as a possible presidential candidate) is going to run. The black power structure is with him." I gave over, and took a break from the political arena to get my master's in business. I later took a position as instructor in business at Atlanta Junior College.

Julian Bond shocked some and disappointed many by backing out of the race at the last minute. Nobody ran as a Democrat. State legislator Billy McKinney ran for Congress as an independent, but lost in a city of Democrats who were fully supportive of Wyche Fowler.

Two years later, it was time for me to run again. I called my family together. I wanted to announce my bid early so that there would be no doubt on my intentions. As I watched the faces around my dinner table, Andy Young, Jean Young, Aunt Coretta, Aunt

Chris, Mother, and Granddaddy, I was looking for clues. What were my chances?

Suddenly, Granddaddy blurted out, "You can't win, Veda. Ain't nobody got no money to throw away. Nobody can beat Wyche. You'll win next time."

There, I had it. The rumors were true. For once, the black power structure was united, behind Wyche Fowler. Reportedly Wyche had promised several people that if they'd support him this time, he wouldn't run again. He'd let somebody else have it, "next time." Granddaddy had echoed the rumor.

It was too late for me to back out. The announcement for the race was in the mail to the press. I went ahead, with little support from my family. I was nervous now. It was hard for me to keep battling; I'd been away from the political battleground for a while now. Cliff wouldn't let me feel sorry for myself. "Keep your head up, and keep going. You've done it before." Cliff was my sole source of financial support. People took my race as a joke at first. Then, Hosea Williams entered the race. I couldn't believe that Hosea thought he could win.

I remembered my first serious conversation with Hosea—when I'd first entered the legislature years ago. "Hosea, I'm tired of you attacking my family. If you keep it up, you'll have to deal with me. And remember, I'm A.D.'s daughter." He wasn't as non-violent as his brother. "I mean it. No more dirty remarks about Coretta, Granddaddy, or the King Center."

Hosea had given me some excuse about not being able to relate to Coretta, not being made welcome in her house. I didn't care. He wasn't going to slander my family and get away with it.

Somehow, Hosea and I formed a truce. We even co-authored the King holiday bill a couple of times. And when I left the legislature, I didn't give him a second thought until he appeared in the newspaper, accused of driving under the influence.

Now, I was forced to take notice of Hosea again, as a serious contender for the same seat I was seeking. Hosea was a wonder. He attacked Wyche Fowler with vigor. I liked Wyche, considered him a friend (in fact I'd called him before announcing my candidacy). I had no intention of joining Hosea and the two other black candidates—Henrietta Canty and Bob Waymer—in their attacks on the man's political agenda. Besides, it was sheer folly. Wyche's record was damned good. I was in the race to win or to show. I quickly realized that a good showing was all I could really hope for.

Granddaddy finally came out of the corner for me when Andy Young signed an endorsement letter for Hosea. People were shocked. Why hadn't Andy remained neutral? Granddaddy shocked the hell out of everybody by signing an endorsement letter for me.

Andy, Hosea, and I had a major confrontation. They took for granted the fact that I had been a child during the early days of the movement when they were lieutenants in Uncle M.L.'s movement; they assumed that I was still a child playing games. They suggested, in separate telephone conversations, that I should "forget Washington and stay at home and mind my children." I could be Hosea's office manager.

As far as I was concerned, they were condescending chauvinists. I didn't realize that I was ahead of my time. My job was to forge the way for the future black female mayors and congresswomen. I didn't understand. I was a winner, and I wanted to win!

I was furious, and I mounted a counterattack. I called Hosea an old warhorse, a ravager, and raider of poor people. I called him and Andy chauvinists. I told them they were living in the 'sixties, and that if my father and uncle were here today, they would be in full support of women running for office, rather than staying home running somebody else's offices. My press secretary got carried away and suggested that the press look into the F.B.I. files and investigate Hosea's past record. I was accused of walking over my uncle's and father's graves. I was reminded that they had been chauvinists, too. I refused to be put down for being a woman, and a few years younger than they were. I gave my story to *USA Today* and it went over the world. Hosea denied the story and Andy apologized to me for his statements.

Aunt Coretta was furious. I had publicly embarrassed Andy Young—family friend, Uncle Andy. What could I be thinking of? Had I forgotten the love, support, and encouragement given to our family over the years since Daddy and Uncle M.L. had died? No, I hadn't forgotten how Andy took the responsibility for helping the children and family of his dear friend, Martin. That's why it was so hard for me to take Andy's reactions to my candidacy. Did he really mean that because I was a woman, and a few years younger than he and Hosea, that I had no right to run for congress? Should my age and gender cause me to take a backseat to Hosea, even though I had been the first to enter the race? Would my father and uncle have suggested the same thing? Probably not. Daddy had encouraged me to be whatever I wanted to be. And yet, Aunt Coretta said I was not thinking of the damage I had done to Andy. Okay, so I was taking it too far, but couldn't she see my point?

What was she thinking of? I had been insulted. Hosea was being duped—and didn't have enough sense to know it. Aunt Coretta admitted to me, "Andy knows Hosea can't win." If Andy knew Hosea couldn't win, were the rumors true? Was the support from the black power structure a ploy, to frighten people into thinking that the old warhorse, might win if they didn't run out and vote for Wyche? If only the many civil rights organizations existing today could pull together with a common cause. What power, what power.

The strategy worked. The press went along with the game and printed stories of a two-candidate race. I was rarely mentioned. And when I did get a chance to make a good showing in a live television debate, there was little mention of that in the papers the next day.

Wyche won the race, by a landslide. I called to congratulate him. He said, "I'm not surprised, Alveda. You were the only one to call me to announce and you're the only one to call now."

I shared a story with Wyche, about how Granddaddy had made fund-raising calls for me. "I know she can't beat Wyche, but please send her some money anyway." Wyche had big laugh over that. I did, too. I understood the position Granddaddy was in, committed to Wyche politically for years, but committed to me for a lifetime of love.

So, the congressional seat was to remain with Fowler for a while. I could live with it. There would be other races for me.

But there wouldn't be many other political experiences that Granddaddy and I could share, though. I was so glad that I'd had a chance to spend one last grand time with him in the political arena.

Right after Bigmama Bessie's funeral in 1984, we went to the Democratic Convention. On the flight, with Granddaddy, Angela, Aunt Chris, and Isaac, Jr., there was little talk about politics. I kept Granddaddy distracted with small talk. I had an attack of motion sickness (as I always do when traveling) and begged Granddaddy to watch *Romancing the Stone* with me to keep our minds off the flight and the battle to come when we landed.

Granddaddy was a staunch Walter Mondale supporter. I had started out with John Glenn, leaned toward Mondale, but joined Jesse Jackson when he came to Atlanta on a tour after freeing a POW named Goodman.

My family (except Mama, who was also quietly supporting Jackson) was furious. Jesse, in their opinion, had committed the greatest of sins. He'd argued with Uncle M.L. just before he was shot. The story has it that Jackson followed Uncle M.L. to the terrace at the Lorraine Hotel in Memphis, and was arguing with him, when he was shot down. Then, Jesse was supposed to have pulled off his shirt and dipped it in Uncle M.L.'s blood. My question was, if Jesse had been at odds with my uncle, if there had been a power struggle, what set him apart from the many others who lusted for the seat of power? Many thought that they could do a better job than Uncle M.L. Jesse was a young hothead back then, and had done much to redeem himself in the eyes of the world. And if Jesus could forgive murderers and thieves, if Uncle M.L. could forgive white racists, and if Granddaddy could preach about not hating anybody, why were we holding a grudge against Jesse Jackson?

I was tired of holding old grudges. The country had something to be proud of, our black children had a positive role model—something now other than Mr. T. and the Jeffersons. I gave up the ghost and announced my support of Jackson to *JET Magazine*. My family came to a meeting at my house, accusing me of a publicity stunt. I told them that my support was sincere.

I'm afraid that Aunt Coretta took my support of Jackson as a personal attack against her and Andy, especially when the Jackson delegates booed her and Andy Young at the convention in San Francisco. Aunt Coretta accused me of being "just like Jesse. You're power hungry. I feel sorry for you."

I felt sorry for her then. She and Andy had gotten away from the pulse of the people. Andy and Coretta were convinced that black support belonged fully behind Mondale. They were forgetting the democratic process—that people (black voters included) had a right to support the candidates of their choice. No one, not even a major black leader, could dictate how blacks would be voting.

Andy, Coretta, and a host of other black national leaders promised to deliver the black vote for Mondale. Jesse Jackson promised to deliver a new vision of hope and pride for the black race. Black people responded overwhelmingly to Jackson.

It was very hard for Andy and Coretta to accept the mood of the masses. Andy fought to maintain his position, and even went so far as to speak against Jackson's platform planks in favor of Mondale's before the delegates of the convention. Jackson's delegates (anxious for an opportunity to strike out at Andy to vent their frustrations over his lack of support of Jackson) started to boo. Interestingly enough, many, many others joined in the booing and within moments, the auditorium was filled with loud protests. Andy was forced to leave the platform. His press secretary fainted from the shock of seeing his hero and leader of so many years—who had escaped relatively unscathed from many experiences where his outspokenness was against popular opinion—booed from the hall of delegates.

Aunt Coretta attempted to reprimand the black leadership for their blatant display of dissatisfaction at a meeting the following the evening. The people at the meeting tried to afford her the dignity and respect that they felt she deserved as the widow of Dr. King. They listened to her opening remarks without comment. But when Aunt Coretta started calling the roll, reminding them of how Andy had paid his dues, she was booed off the floor.

Jesse Jackson stood and called for order, appealing to the audience for a spirit of love and respect. He reminded them that they had all traveled the same road, and should not be trying to tear away at teach other. His was a call for unity.

Some of the people from Andy's staff told Aunt Coretta that Jesse went into another room as soon as he made his speech and started laughing. She took his action as an insult.

I tried to look at the matter objectively. Jesse was bitter, after having had to fight the so-called leadership for respect and support that never came. That same leadership was resentful of the fact that Jackson had come so far without their support. There was bitterness on all sides. If Jesse did laugh, he did it privately, and refused to attack or ridicule publicly. Keeping his feelings away from public attention could not have been easy. But he knew that the public wouldn't respect an attack on the personalities that they had looked to as leaders for so many years. If Jesse was to be a new hero, he had to stay with the pulse of the people.

Granddaddy didn't fall away from that pulse. He recognized the power behind Jackson. Right after Jackson made his moving speech to the delegates at the convention (which Granddaddy listened to from his hotel suite), there were tears in his eyes. Aunt Chris saw them and said, "Dad, if you feel that way, you need to call Jesse."

Granddaddy called Jesse and Jesse came to see him. They buried the hatchet. Two days later, near the end of the convention, we were backstage of the platform. Jesse came up to Granddaddy, who was sitting in a wheelchair. Big, tall Jesse Jackson, sat in Granddaddy's lap, and they hugged each other. Granddaddy said, "Son, if there's ever anything I can do, you can call me."

Angela was so glad to see them make up. She'd been in tears over the split in camps throughout the whole convention. I'd taken her to a private meeting where black leaders appealed to each other to join ranks, whether they were in the Jackson or Mondale camp. I said, "God and the people have given Jesse Jackson this time in history. We have but to acknowledge and accept him."

Angela and I saw Granddaddy accept Jesse. We saw him let go of a grudge he'd been carrying for years. God allowed Granddaddy to free his heart of all anger. We had seen another miracle.

Still, it's funny how things turn out. During the next two decades, I would find myself on the opposite side of the fence from Jesse. It turns out that he, who had been a staunch pro-life advocate, would become pro-choice. I, who had been pro-choice, would become one of America's strongest African-American voices for the Pro-Life movement. I would also embrace the school choice movement, and end up in a national television debate with Jesse, who was opposed at the time. I, the ultra-liberal, would become a "compassionate conservative." Much of my philosophical change had to do with my "born-again" experience in 1983. Always a maverick among a whole family of mavericks, I would leave Ebenezer and the traditional religious house, to seek the Holy Spirit and answers to spiritual questions that were increasing in my life. Meanwhile, our family was undergoing another transition as well.

CHAPTER TEN

What happens to dynasties when their patriarchs die? Do they fall apart, like huge cakes of clay, cracking and breaking when their life juices cease to flow in the veins of their departed leaders? Do they dry up and blow away like drifts of dust and sand, no longer united by the life forces that once held them so closely together? Or do they rip and tear away at each other, violently and viciously fighting over the spoils left behind by those that once held the family together for generations after generations?

Thank God that our family didn't crack, or dry up, or break, or drift, or rip away all of the love and strength that we'd gathered to ourselves with Granddaddy's guidance for all the years that all of us have lived.

At Granddaddy's funeral, Reverend Otis Moss talked about how we must now live in a world without Daddy King. Granddaddy was born in 1899 and he died in 1984. "The twentieth century has never known a day without Daddy King. All of us in this church were born into a world that had Daddy King," Moss said. The statement was profound at the funeral, and now, almost twenty years later, and into the new twenty-first century, we still remember and feel the effects of a world with Granddaddy.

Back then, it seemed that the world (and the wolves) were just waiting to see the "King Mystique," or the "King Dynasty" fade and crumble. Even before the funeral, people would call various members of the family and try to pit one of us against the other. But the family was and remains united—out of love—and I guess out of habit. Granddaddy was always such a stickler for family unity. With his regular family meetings, and Sunday family dinners, he pulled and kept us together.

Just after the funeral, I started raising hell. We called a meeting, just as Granddaddy would have done if he'd been alive. I shocked and hurt everybody with my reactions to his going. Just prior to the meeting, I called my brother, Derek (who along with Aunt Christine had been named co-executor of Granddaddy's will), and said that I was ready to hear the will.

Derek, with trembling voice, said, "Veda, how can you even think about Granddaddy's will? He's not even cold yet."

I, having accepted the fact that my Granddaddy's body was dead and soon to be gone (we'd dressed him at the funeral home just a few days earlier. His skin was cold. His spirit was flown), answered in what must have seemed to Derek, cold and unfeeling tones. "He was cold the day he died. People usually read wills right after somebody dies. We never read Bigmama's, remember? It's been ten years, and you all still don't know what she left you. I do, because I read letters from her lawyers. And I don't intend to wait ten years to see what my Granddaddy left me."

Bigmama had died ten years before. In her will, she left provisions for the education and support of the "the children of Alfred Daniel Williams King." Granddaddy was executor and Aunt Christine was administrator. Due to shock and grief, somehow, they could never bring themselves to disclose the terms of the will to the family. We didn't even know the will had been probated until two days after Granddaddy's funeral, when I started making investigations. On top of that, Aunt Christine had come to Mother, Al, Derek, Darlene, Vernon, and me on the day of Bigmama's funeral to have us sign a waiver. We, in our trust and grief, signed away our rights to be notified as to how the affairs of the estate were to be handled. I never got over my hurt at not having the privilege of reading what she left for me in her will. I had no intention of waiting ten years to see what Granddaddy had to say.

Derek communicated my feelings to Aunt Christine, and needless to say, she was even more upset than Derek was. I also called the lawyers and shook them up, saying that I was within my rights to have both wills read, and I intended to do so. A family meeting was called.

At the meeting, I was vehement in expressing my feelings. Isaac, Jr. called me a grave-digging carpet bagger, accusing me of caring so little about Granddaddy that I couldn't wait to get my hands on whatever I thought he'd left me.

Derek chimed in with what I'd said about Granddaddy being dead and cold.

My brother Vernon, who'd climbed out of his car to go into the meeting with some remark about, "Let's go in and get screwed again," shook his fist and turned on me. "I just don't understand you. You have no respect for the man (Granddaddy)."

Aunt Christine started in with her reminders about how "I toilet-trained you, Veda. I helped to bring you up. And now, you accuse me of keeping something from you."

By now, I was pretty close to tears of frustration. Nobody really understood what I was trying to say. Cliff, moved from his position of quiet observation, held up his hands. "Wait a minute. I think we need to know just what it is that Veda wants."

I took a few deep breaths and tried again to explain. "When Bigmama died, she left a message of love and support in her will. Nobody ever bothered to read it to any of us. And now, Granddaddy's dead and we have a right to know what he left us. Not just the money, you can have the money. Everybody here knows that I don't care a hill of beans about money, you can have the money. Money is just money to me. It's a tool. I don't love it. Granddaddy used to say so himself. I just want to know what he had to say, and I don't mean to wait ten years to find out."

I think they were finally beginning to understand. Aunt Coretta helped to smooth things over with a remark about how everybody must be upset about me saying that Granddaddy was cold the day he died. "They can't accept it the way you do, Veda. They remember Granddaddy as warm and loving. For you to call him cold is too much for them to accept."

I apologized and gave some remark about Granddaddy's spirit being warm and alive forever, and how he'd never die for me, and heads began to nod in understanding and agreement.

Then, Uncle Isaac asked if they would promise that I wouldn't have to wait ten years, could I just wait a few weeks so that the press and the public could back off. "People are just waiting for something like this to happen. Let's wait until things calm down. I promise that we won't have to wait ten years."

I agreed to wait, and we held hands and prayed. About six weeks later, Aunt Christine called another meeting. There was another air-clearing session where one family member confessed to having taken money from Granddaddy and couldn't understand why several of us had taken the offense personally. "I mean, it wasn't like I was taking money from you, unless you were mad that he (Granddaddy) didn't have so much to give you since I was getting so much."

I was remembering all the nights Granddaddy had called me, almost crying about not being able to sleep for fear that someone would come and steal his money. I explained bitterly. "Let me tell you what you took from me. Not the money, I didn't need Granddaddy's money. He'd given me so much over the years—not just money. He gave his love. He gave himself. You took from me when you hurt Granddaddy. When he lost his peace of mind, you broke my heart. You didn't have to steal from him. Everybody knows that any of us only had to ask Granddaddy, and he'd give us whatever he wanted. I saw him in pain, and was powerless to help him, powerless to stop you. I hated you so much I wanted to tear you apart with my bare hands."

Aunt Christine, seeking her usual role as peacemaker, said, "We can't judge you. We can't say whether you were right or wrong. You were just going through a stage. We'll just have to pray and get through this together, as a family."

I was totally amazed. All the time this person was stealing from Granddaddy, little was done about it. The stealing continued until Granddaddy died. Now, when all excuses of sparing Granddaddy more pain were invalid—he was dead now and beyond caring—we were still setting the problem aside. Treating it as if it was no more than "growing pains." How often had we failed to come to task with our young? How many problems had been set aside rather than straightened out?

And yet, was I any better? I was moving Jarrett from household to household—unable to help him find a happy balance in life. After ten years, he'd still not accepted my remarriage. So he was to end up living with Aunt Christine, spending some nights with Mother or Bernice because I couldn't find answers to our problems.

And here we were, at a meeting, to hear Granddaddy's will, wondering how to go on, without Granddaddy. The will was read. I was satisfied, not too surprised. Granddaddy did not leave the millions the public had often accused him of hoarding. He could have been a millionaire, but his soul never dwelt on miserly thoughts. Granddaddy bought what he wanted for himself during his lifetime, and he lived well. He accumulated some property, but he spent more than he saved. He'd loaned more money than he ever collected. He started more churches and businesses than some small banks could boast. Granddaddy virtually financed Ebenezer's building projects, and supported the church until he died. His salary was always modest, as was his estate when he died. For a man of his statue and prominence, Granddaddy had accumulated surprisingly little wealth. His was a wealth of spirit.

Granddaddy had given his house to Aunt Christine, and had divided everything else among Aunt Chris, his ten grandchildren, and his three great-grandchildren. I didn't care that it would be months before things could be dealt with. I just wanted to know that he'd cared enough to provide for us all.

In a way, some things changed and some things remained the same after Granddaddy left us. Aunt Christine was pretty quiet for a long time, and I realized how she must feel. She'd make remarks about being alone, and we'd all remind her that she still had all of us. Still, everyone from her generation and immediate family was gone.

I told Jarrett, who was pretty depressed with the loss of Granddaddy, and the separation from Derek and Janice who'd moved to Florida, "I know you're sad. But don't think you're the only one who's lost something. Just the other day, Cliff was telling someone to call Granddaddy for advice. I had to remind him that Granddaddy is gone. How do you think Aunt Christine feels? She has no mother, both of her brothers are dead, and now her Daddy is gone. But she keeps going on. And Nonnie (Mother), how do you think she feels? No father. No husband. Her baby daughter's dead. Then Bigmama and Mama Bessie died, and now, Granddaddy." For the longest time, she would go to the cemetery all the time just to be close to them.

I missed him, too. Granddaddy was my best friend. But I had to keep telling myself, "We can make it. You can make it. We have God, and each other."

In the next few days, I communicated this same conversation to Mama and Aunt Christine. We were all sharing in the same loss, and we were still a family.

In the weeks and months that followed, we continued to pull together as a family. When Derek was installed at his new church, Tabernacle in West Palm Beach, Florida, we all went down (except Cliff, who was a little ill). Even Mama Lillian, who had helped Mama and Daddy with every move to a new church, was there to help Derek.

In his installation sermon, Dr. Roberts said, "No matter what happens to this family, God always has a ram in the bush." Derek had been looking for a church, and as Granddaddy foretold, Derek got a wonderful church. The King family, with all of its losses, now had a new baby, Derek II. The King Center, with all of its struggles to grow, would be spearheading the celebration for the upcoming national holiday.

I must confess that I remained somewhat the fly in the ointment. Since Granddaddy's death, I had become somewhat quiet, not having the strength to fight and provoke as I had in years past. And I missed Granddaddy's buffering effects. While he was here, somehow no matter what I said, or what I did, he would be there to smooth things out, and to rescue me from harsh repercussions. Then, too, it was easy to be a steamroller, when I had his clout to back me up.

Without Granddaddy, I wasn't so sure that I could stand alone; part of the family and yet somehow different. There were still opinions that I clung to that were not in agreement with the family's. I was offended that no member of the King Holiday Commission nor the King Center acknowledged Daddy's contributions to his brother's life and cause. I felt hurt that Daddy was generally forgotten about in the scheme of things. More often than not, no member of our immediate family would be included in any of the main King holiday programs.

I tried to insist that my song, "Let Freedom Ring," be included as part of the public programs. Of course, everybody thought that I was once again seeking attention. And in a way, I was. I have always wanted and needed attention and approval. But that's not the only reason that I wanted them to use the song. "Let Freedom Ring" had been published, recorded, and nationally recognized by a famous disc jockey, "Jack the Rapper," who sent copies of the record to disc jockeys all over the country.

The lyrics:

1. We can celebrate life, but not our freedom
   We can celebrate living but we ought to try giving.
2. We can celebrate and learn to love one another.
   We can celebrate and try to call each other brother.
3. We can celebrate the things that the freedom seeker preached
   We can celebrate the things that he did his best to teach

REFRAIN: We can celebrate the life of Martin Luther King.
We can celebrate and shout, LET FREEDOM RING!

CHORUS: Let freedom ring, let freedom ring, and thank GOD
That King had a dream!

The lyrics and melody came to me in 1974, as I was driving down the expressway, thinking about the Center, Daddy, Uncle M.L., and Granddaddy's saying, "Thank God for what we have left." I was thanking God, and the song came into my head. I felt that I had a right to express my feelings about what Uncle M.L.'s life meant to me as well as to others.

But the family never really helped me do anything with the song. I felt neglected and rejected again. I tried to insist that the song be used as part of the program making King's birthday a national holiday. I was called anxious, pushy, and aggravating. I backed off, wishing Granddaddy were there to help me get my way. I just didn't feel like fighting anymore. But I was hurt. I felt that I had a right to make a major contribution. I felt that as Daddy's daughter I had a responsibility to represent him at the programs.

It became a real problem to go out among the public. Though I'd lived with it for years, that old problem that all of my family members have lived with from birth, was becoming unbearable. Like most famous families, we have no privacy. We can't go out and fade into a crowd and know the peace of anonymity.

After Granddaddy's death, I wanted privacy. I wanted peace. I wanted to just be myself. But when I went out, whether it was to a grocery store, to a movie, for a walk, or anywhere, I would find people staring at me. They'd come up to me and say, "I know you, I've seen you somewhere." Insisting on holding on to my own identity, I'd usually say, "I'm in politics, and I've done some acting locally." But people are so persistent. "No, it's your face. You're one of those Kings!"

Then, I'd feel as though I were in a glass jar, isolated and alone. I felt alone because for me, the last real King was dead. Then, I'd remember some of the good things I'd gotten from Granddaddy, Daddy, and Uncle M.L. And my head would come up, I'd toss back my hair, and answer with renewed assurance, "Yes, I am one of those Kings."

People were calling on me to become politically active again. I didn't feel that I had a reason to seek office again. Most of my political activities had included Granddaddy and Cliff. I still had Cliff, but not Granddaddy. I was tired and sad, and feeling that I couldn't do it without Granddaddy. But people were still calling me "giant killer." Some of them even wanted me to run for mayor against Andy Young. Cliff even got a call from one of Andy's people, thanking him for getting me pregnant so that I couldn't run that year.

I wouldn't have run anyway, because the family was totally behind Andy Young. I wasn't so sure. Andy had been mayor for four years, and during that time, he'd performed wonderfully as a diplomat, negotiator, and ambassador for the city, but his administrative talents weren't nearly as sharp. I wanted to see a mayor who could pull the city back together. But I wasn't up to fighting the family and all of Andy's supporters, too. I had it in mind to run for Fulton County Commissioner the following year, and know that I'd need my energies later.

I really started to really miss Granddaddy. I'd find myself eating fried chicken, and wishing Granddaddy was there to chew the bones and then spit them into his hand and hold them out to me to throw away. I used to do that particular job with my nose turned up, but I wished for the chance again. I would work in my garden, turning up worms and an occasional garden snake, and remember how Granddaddy couldn't abide the thought of snakes. Tears would mix with the dirt on my face. I would pass his picture on my mantle, smiling at the thought that while I was growing up, I thought he was six-feet-tall, and seeing in the picture that I was almost as tall as he was. And my eyes and heart would burn with tears. I would even dream of going to his house and not finding him, and wake up with tears streaming from my eyes, missing him. I was still feeling lost, and somehow alone. I missed Daddy, too, and Bigmama, and Al. It seemed as if those closest to me were so far away. I had yet to experience a full and lasting relationship with God, so I felt so all alone.

Yet, as I spent time reflecting, I saw members of my family emerging. Mama was becoming assertive, making it known that she intended to be included in upcoming activities. Derek was established in a big church. Things were working out.

I was learning to sit back and give God a chance to work things out. I was learning not to fight my family so much. My family, Granddaddy's family—somehow, we'd survive.

And that is the miracle of the "King Mystique." We're just a family, with real human problems and joys, just like any other family. We're not plastic people, picture-perfect heroes and heroines.

We are flesh and blood people, who laugh and cry, and live and die. But we love, with the tenacity of that old man who left Stockbridge, Georgia, on foot nearly a century ago, with the smell of the mule clinging to his clothes and the fear and love of God in his heart. Granddaddy's love and God's love are a real and permanent part of our family. That's why we love each other. That's why our family is strong.

EPILOGUE

A smart person once told me, "Never forget the law of unexpected outcomes." We all make decisions that seem right at the time. Years later, we find ourselves looking back and wondering whether we made the right choices and how things would have been if we'd done it all differently. The song says: "Regrets I have a few, but still too few to mention." I can't speak for my family. I'm sure they have a mixture of blessings and sorrows like I do. If I could do it all over, I'd be a better mother, never weigh over two hundred pounds, and learn to fly airplanes. Still, I've been true to my childhood dreams. I always said I didn't want to grow old and wish I had done anything that I didn't try at least once. I've enjoyed my life, and still do.

It's safe to say that the King Family has had its share of the unexpected. My life is no exception. Today, I find myself divorced for the third time, having been remarried and divorced once again. I did cause quite a stir when I formed a new friendship with a gentleman, Stanley Johnson. You can imagine what people were saying, especially since I have dared to welcome yet another opportunity for possibilities with Stanley Johnson, who shares my same birthday. Stanley is tall, dark and handsome, witty, fun, generous and gentlemanly. Yet, many question the wisdom and maturity of embracing life to its fullest, especially when one is past the half-century mark.

Truly, I have been called everything including, thank God, a child of God. There is great speculation on whether I'll marry again. Dear reader, I can truly tell you today that only God knows, and may His perfect will be accomplished in my life. I honestly feel a bit like the woman at the well in the Bible when Jesus said to her:

John 4: *7 There cometh a woman of Samaria to draw water: Jesus saith unto her, give me to drink.* ***8*** *(For his disciples were gone away unto the city to buy meat.)* ***9*** *Then saith the woman of Samaria unto him, How is it that thou, being a Jew, askest drink of me, which am a woman of Samaria? for the Jews have no dealings with the Samaritans.* ***10*** *Jesus answered and said unto her, If thou knewest the gift of God, and who it is that saith to thee, Give me to drink; thou wouldest have asked of him, and he would have given thee living water.* ***11*** *The woman saith unto him, Sir, thou hast nothing to draw with, and the well is deep: from whence then hast thou that living water?* ***12*** *Art thou greater than our father Jacob, which gave us the well, and drank thereof himself, and his children, and his cattle? 13 Jesus answered and said unto her, Whosoever drinketh of this water shall thirst again:* ***14*** *But whosoever drinketh of the water that I shall give him shall never thirst; but the water that I shall give him shall be in him a well of water springing up into everlasting life.* ***15*** *The woman saith unto him, Sir, give me this water, that I thirst not, neither come hither to draw.* ***16*** *Jesus saith unto her, Go, call thy husband, and come hither.* ***17*** *The woman answered and said, I have no husband. Jesus said unto her, Thou hast well said, I have no husband:* ***18*** *For thou hast had five husbands; and he whom thou now hast is not thy husband: in that saidst thou truly.* ***19*** *The woman saith unto him, Sir, I perceive that thou art a prophet.* ***20*** *Our fathers worshipped in this mountain; and ye say, that in Jerusalem is the place where men ought to worship.* ***21*** *Jesus saith unto her, Woman, believe me, the hour cometh, when ye shall neither in this mountain, nor yet at Jerusalem, worship the Father.* ***22*** *Ye worship ye know not what: we know what we worship: for salvation is of the Jews.* ***23*** *But the hour cometh, and now is, when the true worshippers shall worship the Father in spirit and in truth: for the Father seeketh such to worship him.* ***24*** *God is a Spirit: and they that worship him must worship him in spirit and in truth.* ***25*** *The woman saith unto him, I know that Messiah cometh, which is called Christ: when he is come, he will tell us all things.* ***26*** *Jesus saith unto her, I that speak unto thee am he.*

Truly, three failed marriages and no husband today—goodness knows it tries this heart and soul. When I think back over all of the mistakes I've made, and the grace of God that continues to carry me through, I stand amazed. I think about the two abortions I had before I was born again in 1983. Public testimony of these losses has often been painful, and more often embarrassing to my family. Yet, many times, other wounded mothers and fathers who are victims of the deed of aborting their children have come to me to find out how they can have peace. The peace and forgiveness is in God, through the shed blood of His Son Jesus, who shed His blood for us.

> Romans 3:1 says: *There is therefore now no condemnation to them which are in Christ Jesus, who walk not after the flesh, but after the Spirit.*
>
> Don't get me wrong. People will condemn you. They will stand in your face, doing the same thing, or worse, and accuse you. Don't let it bother you. *Have faith in God!* (Mark 11:22) Do not judge others. Leave vengeance to God, He is an able Judge, Defender, Deliverer, and Protector. Forgive quickly, love always, even as Christ loves us, and walk in the confidence that God loves you. Jesus died for you, and rose again and is with God, praying for you right now! Seek to know Christ, to know the Father and the Holy Spirit, to be one with them, and to worship God in spirit and in truth.
>
> John 3:16 says: *"For God so loved the world, that He gave His only begotten Son, that whosoever believes in Him, shall not perish, but shall have everlasting life."* I invite you to believe right now and receive Jesus as your Lord and Savior, if you have not yet done so.
>
> Let's pray together: Heavenly Father, in the name of Your Son, the Lord Jesus Christ, I come. I do believe Your Holy Word. I do believe that Jesus is Your Son, born of the Virgin Mary, died on the cross at Calvary, shed His blood for my redemption, rose again, defeating Satan and the forces of hell, and is now in Heaven, with You at Your right hand, praying for me. I thank you Father God, Lord Jesus, and

> Your Holy Spirit. Right now, I repent of all my sins. Please forgive me, and receive me into your family, into your kingdom, into your marvelous light. Baptize me with your Holy Spirit, fill me to overflowing with the evidence of the fruit of the Holy Spirit and a new prayer language. I receive it now, Father, and will serve you all of my days. In the name of my Lord and Savior, Jesus Christ, I pray. Amen.
>
> If you prayed that prayer, and believed it in your heart (Romans 10:9), we are now related. We are members of the household of God! Welcome!

Today, I am an evangelist and lay minister, having been led to the Lord in 1983 by Carolyn Conley. I began my new Christian experience at Fellowship of Faith International Church with Pastor Wayne and Gerri Thompson. I am especially grateful to them and to Pastor Woodrow and Francine Walker, who were such wonderful teachers in my early walk.

Having known the Lord since 1956, when my friend Phyllis Norwood Fisher and I were baptized by Granddaddy at Ebenezer, I had lived life with only a marginal relationship with God for many years. There's an old saying: "Make new friends, but keep the old. One is silver, the other gold." It is very risky to name names and to try to acknowledge friends and people who impact upon our lives, for indeed everyone we meet and touch makes a difference in our existence. Yet, I want to acknowledge that our family, like any family, could not have made it to where we are without God and our friends. I have named some friends throughout this book. I'd like to say thanks to a few more, and ask forgiveness for those I do not name. All of you are in my heart always.

For all of my childhood friends, I say God bless you. For my bridesmaids at my weddings, thank you. For my massage therapists and chiropractor, hairdressers, body therapists, for my colleagues at the college and in all professional walks, thank you. Thanks to all of you who voted for me, believed in me. To my friends and fellow brother and sister Civil Rights Veterans, especially Rita and

Princella, may God bless you. My brothers and sisters in Christ, we'll be together forever! To the lady who became my sister after Darlene was gone, you're one of a kind. To all of my compatriots on the Sons of Thunder Project, especially to the lady who worked closely with me for three years, and sat up for hours listening to the vision for "Sons of Thunder," God bless you. To my children and grandchildren, you are my joy and my greatest blessings. To Mom, thank you for your beauty, your strength and your love. To my brothers, aunts, uncles, cousins, family, spiritual mentors, my life couldn't have been as full of joy without knowing and belonging to you! Jesus calls all who accept Him as Lord, his own. I pray that we will all be together forever.

For fifteen years, I have been a member of Believers' Bible Christian Church in Atlanta, Georgia, where Alan McNair is pastor. Studying with Pastor and Sister McNair has saved my life and strengthened my walk with God over the years.

I'm still doing a little acting, writing, and publishing books and songs. It is my sincere desire to serve God with all that he has given me in this life. I encourage you to grow in God's Word, His faith and love, and pursue those gifts He has in store for you.

After serving the community as a college professor for nineteen years, I revisited politics at yet another level. Prior to changing political parties, I decided to seek the office of the president of the Atlanta City Council. After that unsuccessful and controversial race, I left the Democratic Party for the Republican Party, where I was to serve the children and families of America as a political appointee. Political differences forced me out of that position, and once again, I found myself wondering why I ever entered into the political arena. I am content now as an independent voter, without a party, yet in true service to the only True, Wise, and Living God!

I am the blessed grandmother of five. Jarrett and wife Annetta have Uriah, Daniel, Gabriel, Aaron, and their new baby brother, Jaden.

Derek and Janice are divorced, also. God is good to them, though. They have two handsome, wonderful, brilliant sons, Derek II and Kyle.

Vernon is married to Robin Scott King, formerly of Washington, D.C. After two blows from Satan, they lost their first two sons who were born prematurely and taken just as swiftly. Vernon and Robin survived the losses. They are the blessed parents of Victoria Chelsey King and little Venus.

Isaac, Jr. was married to Jackie White Farris. They are divorced. Isaac was vice president of the King Center, and is now director of the King Day Care Center. He is also a political strategist.

Isaac's sister Angela is married to Willie Watkins, an Atlanta entrepreneur, and they have a delightful daughter, Farris Christine. Angela, in the tradition of her mother and grandmother, is an educator. She and Bernice have accomplished what our women before have not been able to accomplish. They are both authors, Bernice having the best-seller *Hard Questions and Heart Answers* and her famous sermon, "A Prophet Without Honor." Both women have earned doctorate degrees. While I have received an honorary doctorate, I am still matriculating to complete my earned doctorate.

Dexter, in the spirit of his father, has taken on the responsibility of leadership. As a visionary, he, as president of the King Center, is taking the organization in a direction that is not always popular, or even understood for that matter. Martin Luther King, Jr. once said that in order for the civil rights movement to be a success, it would have to gain the attention of the media. King realized that without the media, without public notice, thousands would be slaughtered. People of goodwill had to know what was going on before they could be moved to act or assist. Dexter has a new approach to dealing with the media.

Today, Dexter King is moving the vision of the King Dream through the information superhighway. Fiber optics, the Internet, and the cutting-edge technology that is available are Dexter's tools. His new book, *GROWING UP KING*, is a poignant, candid literary tribute to the trials and tribulations of growing up in the legacy of his father, Dr. Martin Luther King, Jr. Many people can't and won't understand why Dexter is doing what he's doing. Yet, has the world ever understood visionaries?

Yolanda continues to carry the dream and the legacy to the world through her gifts in the arts. She is an accomplished actress. Her brother Martin has taken on the mantle as president of the Southern Christian Leadership Conference, and is also a motivational speaker and conducts leadership workshops across the country and throughout the world. He is a goodwill ambassador as well.

Brother Alfred has gone on. Like Darlene, Al dropped dead while jogging. Satan is wicked.

Derek, Vernon, Bernice, Jarrett, and I continue in the heritage of our forefathers. We are all ministers of the gospel of Jesus Christ. They are ordained preachers. I am a member of Believers' Bible Christian Church, where I am a graduate of their school of ministry. As usual, I took the less trod road, and ventured away from our traditional Baptist heritage to find the "fire of the Holy Ghost."

After leaving Ebenezer, I was the first of family to become part of a non-denominational church. I became "filled with the Holy Ghost." At first, the family had a hard time with the doctrine of "other tongues" and "laying on of hands." Of course, times are changing and we are all becoming more and more on "one accord."

We are all very blessed to have such a wide five-tiered generational span, where two of our mothers are grandmothers and in my case, my mother is a great-grandmother. Their matriarchal wisdom is invaluable. We continue to be a blessed family. In their golden years, Mother Naomi, Uncle Isaac and Aunt Christine, and Aunt Coretta are still a source of strength and wisdom. We, the next generations, are growing and knowing the reality of the legacy each and every day that passes.

Yet, not many days pass that we don't remember where we came from. I can remember Daddy and Uncle M. L. together, laughing and playing with us when we were little children. I can imagine them in that car ride on a long dark night so many years ago, with Daddy vowing to pay back rude drivers by shining bright headlights in their eyes, and Uncle M. L. gently reminding Daddy that love is the more excellent way. I can remember Granddaddy and Bigmama, and their dreams for our family.

Yes, we are the Kings of Georgia, and our "Sons of Thunder" may be gone on to glory, but they are not forgotten. Our legacy is filled with passion and power, sorrows and joy, struggles and victories. Those who are gone on before us remain very close in our hearts. As I bring this memoir to a close, I can almost hear Granddaddy, forever near, saying, "Thank God for what we have left."

THE AUTHORS

Alveda C. King is a minister of the Gospel of Jesus Christ, college professor, songwriter, political and civil rights activist, and author of several books, including *I Don't Want Your Man, I Want My Own.* She is mother of six, a grandmother, and lives in Atlanta, Georgia.

Jeff Prugh reported for the *Los Angeles Times* for 21 years, including six years as Atlanta bureau chief. He is author or co-author of three books, has been a consultant to ABC News and *Dateline NBC*, and served as executive editor of his hometown daily, the *Glendale News-Press,* in suburban Los Angeles.

About *Sons of Thunder*

This story of the King family—their stormy, God-inspired, romantic, and often adventurous lives—adapts its title from Mark 3:17 of the Bible, because A.D. and Martin King were fiery preachers.

It explores provocative episodes of the civil rights movement, in large part through the remembrances that A.D. King shared with his daughter, Alveda.

Sons of Thunder examines the civil rights movement's triumphs against extraordinary odds and the human flaws and frailties that give texture to this explosive chapter of our history, recasting the story in a fresh, compelling light.